THE BOOK OF SANSEVERO
The Dice *of* War

✦　✦　✦

THE BOOK OF SANSEVERO

✦ ✦ ✦

ANDREA GIOVENE

The Dice *of* War

Translated by Bernard Wall

Houghton Mifflin Company Boston

1974

FIRST PRINTING   C

FIRST AMERICAN EDITION

Library of Congress Cataloging in Publication Data

Giovene, Andrea, 1904–
The dice of war.

(His The book of Sansevero, [3])
1. World War, 1939–1945 — Fiction. I. Title.
PZ4. G515Dg3   [PQ4817. I814]   853′ .9′14   74-5060
ISBN 0-395-19432-6

Originally published in Italy under the title
L'Autobiografia di Giuliano Sansevero
© 1967 Rizzoli Editore, Milano
Printed in the United States of America

CONTENTS

TRANSLATOR'S NOTE

Readers may be helped if one or two points of background are filled in for the period when the events told by Andrea Giovene took place. The Allied Forces landed in Sicily and threatened the Italian mainland while Sansevero was in Greece. In July 1943 King Victor Emmanuel called in Field-Marshal Badoglio to take the place of Mussolini who was arrested. More than a month later the King signed the Armistice with the Allies (September 8). Mussolini was liberated from imprisonment by German parachutists and founded the 'Republic of Salò' in North Italy under German control. Meanwhile South Italy was being conquered by the Allies and remained nominally under the control of the King and his government.

In Greece as elsewhere there were partisan movements, and the Greeks knew their left-wing group as the 'Andartes'.

THE DICE

To Denise Digne, of course, I am an enemy. Before the war I would have been a welcome and favoured guest in this small hotel in the Upper Durance. On rainy evenings I would have drunk muscatel wine with her and the others – the muscatel fragrant with spices and spirituous to the nostrils – that she makes from a secret recipe. In the afternoons I would have played bowls outside here on the rectangle of flat earth greened by the damp; I would have played with the other guests – a family, an uncle, the daughters. But though the war weighs down on me and crushes such memories like footsteps on grass, they always spring up again, which is all the more surprising as these quiet homely activities never really happened.

An abstract but impenetrable curtain has been erected up here, just where another equally immaterial barrier – the frontier – has collapsed. And because of these unrealities, my life and that of Denise Digne have become crystallised into hard and fast systems, rather like substances that are transmuted at a temperature below freezing-point: I on my side am an officer of the occupying army billeted by a requisition order; she on her side is a member of the oppressed people. And above us towers the castle of the situation, as high and confused as the scaffolding of a building whose form and purpose are unknown.

Denise is large and silent with white skin and black hair and eyes. Her choice of clothes up here in the mountains is surprising. Her voice is soft, perhaps because of her reserve. I know nothing about her except that in those first weeks her husband was reported missing on the Maginot line. It is said that misfortune draws people together. But I think that Madame Digne – who detests me for wearing the uniform of a despised enemy – is drawing hermit-like isolation from her misfortune and making this its first direct consequence. Pain has closed up her spirit as cold closes the pores. Given such conditions, she does her very best not to see me at all, which does not worry me and also lets me out of a difficult confrontation. The wall of irreconcilability erected between us also protects us by dis-

pensing us from explanations. As for formal relations, she manages
the little hotel with exemplary efficiency, and apart from the
orderlies and the telephone personnel I am in any case the only
occupant. In the evenings, though not till then, they all gather
together round the kitchen fire downstairs, dark shapes, smoking
and drinking; but they all immediately stop talking if for any
reason I have to put my head round the door.

I carry out my military duties with the scrupulousness of one
who knows that in certain circumstances routine is the best pain-
killer. On June 22 a fragment of stone left a romantic scar on my
face from my chin up to my forehead – very noticeable though
superficial. This happened in Mentone. So for more than four
months I have benefited by exemption from taking a similar risk.
Ever since that first huge flare-up, hardly thinkable in the austere
folds of these mountains, the sector up here has been not merely
quiet, but dead. The whirlwind then moved off elsewhere and we
hear pale echoes of it only in those uninformative news bulletins
that hardly hold the attention. My unit is divided into several small
groups and is guarding the bridges, tunnels and passes over a span
of five miles as the crow flies. It is exhausting work and might even
seem superfluous, but I carry out my inspections all the same, not
only by day, but getting up at dead of night and in all weathers.
The men receive me as if surprised that anyone should bother about
them, even to inspect them; they stand to attention in the silence of
their thankless task. I do not raise their morale, but neither do I
take any action against them even if I find one of them asleep at
his post; I just shake my head. 'Then why on earth does he come
at this hour of the night and in such foul weather?' Of course they
say this sort of thing to each other – in undertones. And it is good
that Madame Digne, too, talks as softly as she does. Perhaps we all
need silence, like a weary herd when evening comes.

I usually get back to the little hotel at nightfall, when all is quiet.
The few men attached to the Command are out, except for the one
sitting resignedly at the field telephones which at that hour are
silent too. Now and again shadows pass beyond the kitchen window –
men who whisper a few words to Madame Digne and then move off.
But a few days ago I found a man sitting in the vestibule at the small
round desk that must once have been used for checking in visitors;
he was holding a cup between his hands and playing a solitary game
of dice. He seemed utterly engrossed, as if wanting to read in the

little black and white cabala something he already half knew. And when I drew near I saw with surprise that his dice were not the usual sort but the tarot dice of the ancient Greeks, the sort I had seen and examined in my days at Licudi – the knuckle bones extracted from a lamb's heel that the boys used to play with.

'Does fate exist?' he asked me with such ease of manner that he might have known me already and was going on with a conversation we had already begun. 'If I could put these little bones in exactly the same position in my hand, throw them from the same height, at the same angle and with the same force, then they'd hit the surface of the desk in exactly the same way as before and give me the same score. Dice don't escape the laws of physics even for an imponderable, and a mathematician could give you a precise calculation of the result if you provided him with the data. But the data aren't known, or rather we're not in a position to ordain them in advance. Would you call that fate?'

This man was lean, unkempt and very poorly dressed, with a rough but melodious voice and dark eyes embedded in deep sockets. He wore a small ring in his ear like a gypsy. As I looked at him without answering he came round to the front of the desk and introduced himself.

'Demetrio, the Seer,' he said. 'I'm here with my medium Priscilla to give a show to the Armed Forces. I'm honoured to make your acquaintance.'

Then his eyes went back to his dice lying brightly and enigmatically on the desk, the symbols showing a pair of fives.

'No!' he went on, giving me a long purposeful look. 'There's no such thing as fate, so there's no such thing as chance. It's just our incapacity to foresee circumstances. It isn't by chance that you came into collision with that fragment of stone in the Mentone cemetery. It's that you didn't know on what day and at what point that bit of stone was going to fly.'

That the incident had happened at Mentone he could have learnt from one of the soldiers, but I felt sure I had said nothing to anyone at Bay about it having taken place in the cemetery. He foresaw that I would hesitate before replying, and with perfect timing shouted loudly towards the kitchen as if someone had called him:

'I'm coming!' And off he went.

If one of the shadowy figures beyond the kitchen window was

his mysterious Priscilla, then it was possible that through her he exercised some faculty or other to transmit or penetrate thought. But what surprised me was not so much that he had identified a place – the cemetery – lodged in my memory, but that he had entered into my secret yet vivid sense of being guided not quite by the fortuitous nor yet perhaps by my own will, but by a power always intent on putting me to an ever more difficult test and obliging me to accept it.

And, indeed, what but this power could have made me flee from the deep South, and from an adventure as intense as life itself? What had wrested me from my melancholy picking and choosing among Uncle Gian Michele's bookshelves, and brought me up to this exact spot, to lie with my face against a tombstone in the Mentone cemetery, while shells from the French Lebels were smashing those sacred marbles to pieces?

It was from the cemetery that the attack on the town began; so there was nothing illogical about Demetrio's words. I had arrived at the Naples District Command, my trusty assignment card in my hand, at a moment of violent upheaval. The Office for Directives needed a liaison officer as requested by the Cosseria division, and they found just what they wanted and from the right corps (not to go into subtler points). Liaison officers nowadays have nothing in common with Risorgimento messengers galloping through gunfire. And it was certainly not on horseback that General Gambara would dispatch me into the babel of the advance line, nor on horseback that I would have to remain in the thick of the attack. It seemed an ordinary affair of chance. But between the Gothic-style reading desk used by my uncle to pore over his infoglios, and that tombstone momentarily preserving my life, there lay a link so strange that it called for interpretation. I looked for one: and I read – with some difficulty, for my cheek was pressed against the stone – I read out of the corner of my eye: 'Marianne . . . 191 . . . Pari . . .'

Where were you, O gay Paris, raised like the pennant of a medieval knight on tourney day? I no longer wanted to stay with my face pressed against that stone; I wanted to get up and run towards France, not to conquer her, but to become part of her. But that loose fragment of stone (which, this time, even I could have foreseen), kindly joker that it was, had torn my 'buccinator' and 'masseter' muscles (as I learnt later at the Base hospital), and I could feel blood running down inside my collar. What had ordained that my spirit would find solace in all this as if I had paid my debt to that piece of earth? I would never tell anyone, not even Uncle Gedeone, that I had tried (though without success!) to lift myself up a little, so that a drop of my blood would fall on the tombstone of 'Marianne . . . Pari . . .' An offering rendered all the more absurd by D'Annunzio's harangues, and one which would horrify our rulers today, and embarrass their descendants, who by then would have other names. So I willingly followed the stretcher-bearer who took me behind the lines; the advancing troops saw me, and perhaps my spectacular appearance both disturbed and elated them. 'The others were coming back all covered with blood,' they would say on a latter day, 'but we swept on regardless!' No, Demetrio is right. It is rhythm, not chance, that governs all this. I let myself be put on a stretcher and no longer felt remorse for my participation in the capture of Mentone – unseemly as it was so to disturb its cemetery . . .

As I write, following the vagaries of my thoughts and memories, a strong consoling aroma wafts in from the kitchen. Though rare in Italy, coffee can easily be found here at Bay – they say it is contraband from Switzerland. The same applies to the aquavit, very strong; and to the tobacco, which is excellent – that, too, comes down from the mountains. At fixed hours Madame Digne sets the table for the non-commissioned officers of our Command; and for me in a little separate room. During the day she also serves tea or muscatel wine, and puts them on the mantelpiece without either of us uttering a syllable. But the other day I was not alone. The military police commissioner from another little village higher up had come down here, and a second lieutenant from the Alpine regiment had come up from the valley to join us. It appeared that one of our planes was missing above the slopes of the Assiette.

'It's a single-seater reconnaissance plane,' said the commissioner with his bureaucratic attitude to daily horrors, 'and we don't know whether the pilot was able to use his parachute at the last minute or not. He's a sergeant, married three weeks ago in Savona.'

Madame Digne, coming in at this point with the tray, must have heard. I made a sign to the other two that the news was for our ears alone. But to start a search for the plane now, and in that area, would be a desperate undertaking. It was nearly eleven, and only four or five hours of daylight remained. Yet were the pilot alive, and no help brought to him before nightfall, he would have to bivouac up there at fifteen degrees below zero.

From the field telephone we put out monotonous calls to all guard posts, getting benumbed replies from them all. We began again with the same words, while the Tyrolese clock beat out the minutes during which, it could be, that young man's life was draining away – the young man who had left his wife of three weeks' standing and gone and crashed on the 'sacred mountain-tops' to kill himself, as some would think, 'nearer to God!'

Having received some rather vague information, we set out leaving the doors open to the cold (as I now remember), though the house at two in the afternoon was empty and the telephone silent among the coffee cups. But our help was no longer needed. The boy must have spun down and fallen like a stone, and it was tough work disentangling him from the wreckage by torchlight, wrapping him up in the tent canvas and dragging him down the steep slope. At one point the bundle slipped and broke open. No one dared to look.

Then we went to the little church at Bay, and stayed there till the approach of dawn with the second lieutenant and the chaplain. A part of the boy's face, and the chin, were almost intact. The chaplain had left the young lips uncovered and pure between the bandages. We knew that his wife would have a safe-conduct from Savona the following day. I returned in the icy dawn with the cold biting into my bones. I found Madame Digne in the kitchen in the half-darkness.

Before going to work, when it is still night, the labourers come in here for their drop of absinthe; that is why she always gets up so early, and I realised that my return had coincided with this habit of hers. Coffee had been prepared in a large pot for a lot of people. The gesture with which she gave me mine was, as usual, dictated by duty. I was drenched in snow and mud and had not had a clean-up for fifteen hours now – the hours spent searching on that moun-tain and then the rest of the night in church. I had an indefinable smell sticking to me which I myself noticed. I knew that my recent scars had reddened under the lash of the icy cold; and that she was covertly looking at them.

'Yes,' said my conscience with irony, 'we played you a dirty trick pouncing on you just at that moment and gutting with cannon-fire the little tourist shops at Mentone, complete with their beauty products. And you certainly didn't run out to welcome us! Mussolini "needed" I don't know how many dead; but from his own people, to make them pay his debt! Not from your people. Yet it was you who gave them to him.'

The silence between us was as smooth and cold as a sheet of glass. Her duty as a woman was to show care and solicitude, as it had been with my Aunt Francesca when I went to stay with her, and as it had been with Incoronata when I returned from the sea. But with Denise everything that she ought to have done and did not do became an act of hostility. Oh, no doubt, if one of those two dictators had made an offering in Rheims Cathedral, and the other had been present at the elevation of the Blessed Sacrament in St Stephen's in Vienna, they would have understood that the nations that venerate similar monuments can perhaps submit to occupation but certainly not to subjugation. What is happening at this moment is an outrageous mistake; but have those suffering under it thereby earned the right to throw in yet a further portion of pain and evil? Why do I leave my soldiers alone, when I should really send them before a court-martial? But I look at their peasants' faces, sweet and serious in sleep, and I see the thoughts passing through the dark chamber of their minds, a woman, a field, a village. And this is also why I consent to withdraw from the pleasant drowsiness of that corner by the oven – so that those others can come in: the French workmen whom I know to be outside the door waiting for me to go.

I woke up late and saw snow outside the window, bluish in the mist. Yesterday I was thinking about Rheims, so I fleetingly dreamt about it last night, and now it is in my mind. I remember that when I was there in my Latin-America travel agency period I also saw snow from my inn window. 'Rheims is the pride of France' was inscribed on the walls of the communal room, and round the ornamental scroll was a gay composition of ribbons and rosettes in blue and vermilion. That inn was a rustic affair with large wood-burning stoves smoking day and night as in a woodman's hut. But soon after waking I would be brought a goblet of that famous champagne, the flower of the region and of the best vintage, sparkling and limpid like an enchantress's eye. And as I looked at the snow and thought about Catherine I savoured that exquisite essence that shakes off indifference, opens out your spirit to the day, seduces you and beckons you on.

It was in this mood that, shortly after, I stood looking at the fantastic mass of the cathedral, magnified and deepened by the thick surrounding mist. A most heroic structure, protected against the breath of evil by holy dragons, gentle monsters, and mighty devoted claws. These heavenly legions welded into the stone not only acted as a barrier but sprang forward to threaten and disperse. Wings, symbols and saints proclaimed that this was an impregnable bastion, the Word in stone, consecrated in virtue and by the power of God.

Yet Rheims cathedral was empty that morning, and very cold. Far above me I could hear the fluttering of the pigeons living in the vaults. I saw more leaves than flowers in front of Our Lady on the second altar to the left.

'In winter, in weather like this,' explained the pious old woman, keeping her distance, 'we can't get the money to buy flowers . . .'

If Rheims was the pride of France, why should it have been granted to me on that morning – just to me, a mere travel agency employee – to provide for the dignity of worship in her cathedral, the most famous cathedral in the world? Certainly not as a result of chance. The Seer is always on the right track. No, it was so that at some future date I should be able to be tolerant towards other men – men of that very same country – when, without even wanting to get to know me, they refused to enter the room where I had paused for a while in a state of total exhaustion. And so that I should then be able to go to sleep with no bitter thoughts.

I stayed in my room when the airman's young wife arrived, but far away as I was I heard her cries: 'Dino, my Dino!' They must have been trying to hold her back so that she would not touch that shattered body. 'How many others must weep,' I asked myself almost angrily, 'because people have paid with their lives even before they have loved?' Shaken and stricken by those cries, I felt that the whole war should serve only to atone for Nerina's death so many years ago, for the perversion of Licudi, for the rough red hands of Arrichetta who had become a scullery-maid in Milan. Then I felt ashamed and would almost have liked to take the dead airman's place if only that girl would stop crying.

I have spent the whole day on tours of inspection and got home late to find Bay silent again. The little church was closed as I came up. And as soon as I entered the hotel's communal room everyone stopped talking; but this time I sat down, with the result that the others got up one by one and made off. I was left alone with Denise Digne.

To my amazement she said something. 'Surely in the course of the war,' she said, 'you must have seen others . . .'

I noted her emphasis. By 'others' she implied only those who had fallen on her side and at our hands.

'Yes,' I answered, 'but I didn't hear the weeping.'

Why did she not weep now? Openly, without hiding her face? Perhaps I have not said that I feel pity even for Denise. Was she so frozen in her grief for her own dead man that she had no thought to spare for that other man smashed up at the age of twenty? Does she want to reserve all compassion for herself? How did such hatred come into the world – a hatred that refuses to recognise even someone who is absolutely equal to ourselves?

Now the days are slipping by, for I shall be leaving here shortly. For some time my left eye has been giving me trouble, the one that only just escaped the stone. There has been a burning sensation ever since that night on the mountain. The military doctor has been up to examine me and has ordered that I should return to Italy for a while . . .

Going down towards the valley I saw the little hotel high up above getting smaller and smaller and then fading away among the brown and white streaks of trees and snow. But I shall remember it as an agreeable place. In my imagination I have played bowls on its small rectangle of beaten earth, played bowls with a charming family that came up on a Sunday trip. One of the girls (or so I fancied) was called Nicole. And she gave me a mischievous smile when she left.

*

To tell this part of my story I have used a fragment of a diary that I kept at that time, a habit I had started in my youth. The flames of war were spreading over everyone now, just as the unknown sea of life used to flood in over the young boarders at my school. Things were assuming such gigantic proportions that the only safeguard against them was the quiet work of the individual mind within its own chapel, somehow filtering into its own small world the complexities of the great world. Most of that diary was lost as a result of subsequent events, but the fragments that remain bear witness to thoughts and feelings I would otherwise be incapable of recapturing. Both logic and theory have established that our past is irrecoverable. But my mind grieved for reasons other than these buried ones.

Standing in front of my makeshift easel – a board propped up against the back of a chair – I looked out from the long window of my Uncle Gedeone's house (where I had gone for my convalescence) and watched the evening dissolve in a haze of light over the Riviera di Chiaia, beyond the tall hotels of the Villa. Painting was all very well; but where did one start? How did one circumscribe those throbbing depths within the space of a piece of paper and on only one plane? How include the Lerici palace in that filmy trail of houses, given that it too must only be a tone of colour? Certainly that low glint of the sea against the light, and the rapidity with which it changes and darkens, do not exactly lend themselves to prolonged contemplation or searching meditation. But it's the intention that counts. And a man who has made so many attempts to shape his life, and has found himself each time left with something stunted or incomplete, will be able – by questioning every line of a stretch of landscape – to draw close to the discipline that will encourage him to try again.

'Don't strain that eye,' advised my uncle.

At first, and after such a long lapse of time since those ears and noses done with charcoal at school, my unpractised hand floundered in the void. In seeking the initial line on to which to hinge all the rest, my unruly pencil traced on the white sheet of paper not what I saw externally but a tentative inner vision, one that brought the line back on itself, crossing it with strange arabesques from which hung drops, festoons, lanterns, sinuosities of all kinds: a strange harlequinade of shapes springing out from its own self: arrows, plaster mouldings of roses adorned with pistils or little wings – all exploding round a composition which, though at first out of perspective, seemed finally to converge on an invisible point in space round which balance was finally achieved.

'Marinetti isn't in it!' was my uncle's comment. He had regarded Futurism as a mere joke and was incapable of even conceiving what had subsequently taken place in the figurative arts.

Yes, painting! Even before song, even before the spoken word, the drawing on the wall with flint was surely man's first means of self-expression. Nature had already endowed each animal with its own mark, so the cave-man traced his sign on the walls of his cave, the product of some dim aspiration that already harboured his creative urge. It was from that moment of absorption, dedicated to the sketching of that shape, that man's duality had sprung and art was born.

My uncle did not contradict my theories. He was too sensitive to look on these interests of mine as anachronistic, though as soon as a gust of wind arose his nostrils caught the faint odour of the dust-cloud hanging motionless over the bombed-out quarters of Naples – almost half of the city. But it was perhaps better to pretend to forget the war rather than live it in terms of vengeance and remorse; like an insect that seeks protection under a leaf in a storm and takes no notice of anything else.

I had left Naples tumultuous and excited under the June sun, and I had hardly recognised it on arriving at nightfall at the station square nine months later. There had been talk of a ship loaded with munitions that had exploded in the bay in the San Giovanni area; but even worse was a blast that had flattened more than a mile of the Rettifilo and hollowed out all the surrounding hills. The huge thrust had gone right up the Corso and towards the centre, ripping thousands of fixtures from the façades of those two hundred five-storey buildings; and the fixtures, held up by the framework of the balconies, had stayed dangling over the void like faces without limbs; sinister witnesses to a tragedy that had already been played out. An indefinable smell permeated that yellowish gloom and an acrid dust-cloud hung motionless like a chunk of impenetrable air.

As I walked towards the distant Riviera di Chiaia along the almost unnegotiable road, I could not help thinking of my father Gian Luigi as he was fifty years ago – the passionate young man who used to walk along this very road every day so as to save his tram-fare and build a city that others were to enjoy and yet others destroy; while he dreamed of the young Annina, my mother. (It was so long since I had seen my mother and my brother Ferrante and Checchina! They were safe in a country villa between Sulmona and Aquila in the Abruzzi. Only the common people had remained in Naples to be pounded by the war, the people who had never believed even half the ideas of the Fascist regime, and whose small portion of well-being ever since 1860 had perhaps only come to them from foreigners!)

Here was the piazza Nicola Amore. And only a mayor bearing that name of Love could have ridden the tempest of Naples between the filth of the poor quarters and the dreaded spectre of cholera. Yet from that mezzanine floor over there, I had heard the crowd in a frenzy of excitement watching the young Belgian princess passing by – the new bride of Umberto of Savoy. It was a national holiday and the window where I was standing belonged to a representative of a cloth firm. Ten or twelve tired and badly-dressed employees were crammed round it in a circle, so that I could see nothing. But I heard the thunder of applause swelling and then fading. At one point all those poor people shouted in one voice as if to split their throats – especially the poorest of all: 'Maria José! Maria José!' Should the stupidities of the well-to-do rebound on such poverty as this, capable as it is of such an ecstasy of imagination?

My uncle and I exchanged very few words that evening. He drew me to the light of the long window to examine my wound, and for the first time I saw a dark flame flashing in his mild eyes.

'When you think of all that goes to make and produce a man!' he said. 'Nights of suffering because the baby has coughed, is feverish, has come out in spots, or anything else. Years to send him to school, negotiate with his masters, supervise his lessons, preach at him, take him a hundred times to be examined: his eyes, his stomach, his glands, his tonsils. Then with a hail of scrap-iron without anyone knowing who is firing or at whom, the work of half a life is ruined for the next half – that is, if all goes well.' He stopped to take a better look at me. 'With time it won't show so much,' he went on. 'Good God, they might have killed you!'

Might they? No, I think not; at least, not yet; not if the Seer had correctly intuited what I myself already knew: that the flow of my life would not come to an end until I had discovered its meaning. And this was why, in those tired days that passed idly by, after disturbed nights when enemy planes loomed from the darkness and explosions blindly tore at the womb of the city – this was why, as I stood before the new canvas propped against the back of the chair, I tried to find some basic line in the vast landscape, some point that would then carry the whole thing after it.

Tucked away in our graceful churches, defenceless against this insane persecution, the dark canvases by such painters as Stanzione, Cavallino or Preti were surely intimations of life, hints, guide-lines. . . . In the orchestration of their composition I saw research and wisdom together with marvellous results and solutions! Each mass, or plane, or shape, and the tones, and the various shades of light were interlinked with all the others down to the tiniest detail. They were the fugues and accompaniments of innumerable fanciful perspectives: each one resting in its own harmonious place, yet reaching out towards imaginary spaces. Though drawn from truth, this fantastic vision was capable of creating a different and even more extraordinary truth – one that came to rest in a sweet modulation of colour and a motionless lake of light, presented with a serene certainty dazzling to the mind. Was it not perhaps in this way that we ought to understand and shape our lives?

I noticed the noise coming from the anxious and tormented city – like a wave that breaks on the shore then draws back and spreads out, seeking its new form; then breaks again, and so on *da capo*, following the invincible rule forced upon it in perpetuity; yet ever-changing. And beyond stretched the whole country with its undulating coastline, exposed now, like bared breasts, together with the fabulous heritage of its way of life and its monuments – but putting a brave face on the assault and chaos. It was this smiling spirit that had inspired so many great paintings, measured the beat of so many poems, erected so many miracles of architecture, and it was this spirit that would in time restore rules and measure. But a spark of that spirit could meanwhile measure things within myself; putting them in place, separating this from that, making distinctions – in the linear clarity of judgement managing to redeem disintegrated and sorrowful material.

Gradually, I regained my serenity. Mentone and Bay had both helped me in their different ways. I would never have thought along these lines at first, when, after my uncle's telegram, I had stayed with him for about a week before leaving for the French front – in that little sun-drenched villa of his where he spent the summer. He had seemed rather distracted at that time. The huge calamity engulfing his people was too much for him; his modest life based on the canons of goodness and dedication was being turned upside-down; and his resignation, as a believer, to the unknowable Will, did not spare the suffering of his human heart. My neglect of him during those years and then his realising – as a result of my silence – that Licudi was lost to me and that that sacrifice had been in vain, meant that I had added to his other sorrows; but he felt he could not reproach me now that our lives, like everyone else's, were lying heavy on our hands, darkened and stripped of all meaning.

Now and again he would refer to the war, but I think only to test me; and his traditional ideals, which had also been those of many of our ancestors, suffered humiliation at the silence that immediately crept between us. He knew that in one way or another I would become involved in the war; but he did not like to think that I would involve myself for the danger rather than for the glory; not so as to bring about the triumph of an idea but so as to annihilate my thoughts and submerge myself in union with them.

It was my uncle's very affection and uneasiness on my behalf that made him so excessively agitated. But my confession would perhaps have upset him still more; because when I had heard those irretrievable words bawled over the radio in that little station at Celle, and when I realised that they put an end not only to my time at Licudi, but swept away everyone's time in one huge hurricane, something resembling a cruel joy had slid into my heart. Many many years before, when Nerina had died, I had found refuge in renunciation and uncertainty – the very opposite, in fact, of the affliction and fear which it had seemed to the others. I knew that almost nothing remained of the tension by which the First World War had been sustained; and that this time the army would not be only disunited but reluctant, embarking in its turn on dark currents that could only lead to danger and pain. Nevertheless, as I had fallen from my Paradise, I felt these two to be necessary to me.

The ambiguous atmosphere that was to surround the whole of our intervention freed me from even my last scruples – not so as to exempt myself, which I would not have done, but for reasons I would have carried within me even when wearing my uniform again. It was no longer a question of a few poor Licudi fishermen being indifferent to the Abyssinian enterprise; this time it was the vast majority of the Italians who felt the war to be extraneous to their genuine feelings and impulses; they did not want it; they had not even believed that it would happen. Their shouts in the piazza had been theatrical lapses, flashes in the pan, decorative formalities for downing tools in the lunch hour; and the country, tormented by doubt and chastened within this ambiguity, resigned itself with difficulty to living the most open lie of its history.

As for me, I had been estranged for so long from a society I could not feel to be mine that just as I had not shared its enthusiasm – whether true or false – so now I did not share its arguments and fears. I did not see the war as a fact involving this people or that, but as a crisis investing as protagonist simply and solely mankind; and, with mankind, myself. If my first challenge had taken place in the tiny world of my school, and later of my family; then in the Milan pensione, at the Palazzo Grilli and in the regiment, and recently in Licudi where a whole village was involved, this time the context was excessive, and I had to prove myself in a river swollen to overflowing. But just as I had never feared living, I knew now that I had no fear of dying. If there were danger, then I was ready, the more so because I was alone; and the unexpected reversal of situations and values and of what has so often been a very heavy burden, was now my best protection. For years everyone's life had gone on calmly and serenely in its customary comforts, but now it was struck at its very foundations. Huge sacrifices and huge sorrows were indiscriminately awaiting those who possessed the most, those who were bound by the deepest affections: the underground revenge of the unattached who, if even against their will, had stored up their strength for a greater ordeal. These were stern and somewhat ruthless thoughts, and I did not impart a word of them to my uncle for fear of hurting him. But my mind was confused: I believed that I had wrongfully tried to make an Eden on this earth and for that reason had lost it; I believed I was old and weighed down by the sorrows of many years; and I had only presented myself so as to have a look.

When I got back from the District Command with orders to join the Cosseria Command within twenty-four hours, my uncle looked down and said nothing; then gently made a sign with his head as if consenting to a grief but also to a duty and accepting both. With his characteristic industry and forbearance he helped me with my preparations. But at a certain moment, and as if lightly telling an anecdote:

'There's a cripple in one of the little streets behind here,' he said, 'a cobbler. Yesterday I heard him laughing and singing for the first time. I asked him why. "It's the sound people who are going off to the war this time," he said. "When my turn comes, I'm stopping here." '

He did not take his eyes off me. If he had read my thoughts he was telling me that they were unjust; that I would not affirm my valour merely because others were weak. After the Mentone episode which passed like the wind, that is to say during the boredom at Bay and then two stupid months wasted in infirmaries and hospitals, I had written little to my uncle. But when I saw him again, though only two or three seasons had passed, he seemed to me much changed. Thinner, and hence taller. As he sat with his absorbed look and his now quite-white hair, he reminded me of

Gian Michele and perhaps of my father too. Without wanting to
admit it to myself, I found him rather frightening. Once again, and
even in those terrible days, his Christian stoicism did not desert him.
I went down to Paola and asked the old solicitor, who had handed
Gian Michele's estate over to me, to administer it for me for the
duration of the war. When I got home my uncle was out. My ill-
starred sister Cristina, who had been in a state of mental breakdown
for sixteen years, was on her deathbed. He had deliberately gone off
alone, wanting to spare me those dreadful hours. 'If we'd had to
suffer together,' he had written in a note, 'we'd have suffered more.'

Alone for the first time in my Uncle Gedeone's house (as I had
been in the past in Uncle Gian Michele's), I was uneasily aware of
a ghost that seemed to weigh on me more heavily than the man
himself; for in the style of each object, and its placing (however
subtle this was), and in the habits and niceties of taste to which
each bore witness, I found all the virtues whole and intact that lay
beneath his kindly air and gentle reticence; his loyalty, his respect,
his constancy. Indeed, even at this moment he was fulfilling his
heroic duties. Where were all the others? Why, from all the branches
of the family tree, was it always he who was called upon? – always
he who was ready to get up and go?

Oh, Cristina, who will ever again give me such anxiety as you
gave me when you went away, or such joy as when I found you in
that smart little tea-room, wearing your prettiest clothes, your
small jewels neatly stowed in your bag?

Yes, the magic of painting! That slow rethinking in which
memory flows without jolts, as smooth as the oil on the brush,
stripped of everything that has tainted it with bitterness and dross,
made bright and clean even where things were dark and hostile
before. And the whole blended and harmonised like the colours on
the canvas: half-tones, fleeting fusions from which yet further
images and thoughts (whether very old or new) spring forth from
all the depths. Yes, memory! But not as it is shown in Joyce's
chaotic deformations; nor yet as presented by the debilitated and
debilitating Proust, a series of flashes, now frequent and vivid, now
slow and blurred, within an endless night. And still less Freud's
kind of memory, heavily marked with his race, a doughy mess of
sex. But memory as explored by the Saint. The memory by which
Saint Augustine came to know God.

My uncle returned well after nightfall, and in the darkness of the balcony gave me the simple yet bitter details of Cristina's end.

'But it wasn't the day before yesterday that she died,' he said. 'She died many years ago. She didn't notice anything. There was nothing left of her.'

After I had finally given up my impression of the Riviera di Chiaia landscape, a complicated network of forms came to life on my new canvas, shaping itself by spontaneous germination. On a crystalline background fringed with white like a fresh September sea, there sailed two erect and fantastic apparitions: sailing ships or gigantic swans, as white as mountain peaks. On one side there appeared a veiled face going downwards and enveloped in a sort of fire; and this in its turn became concretised in a massive dark object, almost like a boulder which at the same time suggested the form of a heart. On the other side there was a wing with a mighty bunch of feathers over muscles as strong as limbs. The whole blended within a tone of hard enamel: the perfection and flawlessness of crystal or marble.

When my leave was over I left this masterpiece with my uncle who examined it through half-closed eyes, moving his head and his hand this way and that as if he wanted to follow its movements.

'The strip of blue,' I suggested to myself, 'is the sea at Licudi. That veiled face up there is Nerina. The sightless chimeras are Cristina who has passed all unseeing into the beyond. And that cold grey surrounding the base of the wing is for Denise Digne. And that fine touch of scarlet is for Catherine: today I have finally forgiven her just as France and Paris must forgive us and me.'

'What'll you do now, Uncle, alone in Naples?'

'I was alone at first, when no one needed me. Now I have people to look after, as many as I want, so they will keep me company. With these air-raids, we have to evacuate the homes and hospitals and hostels run by charitable organisations. Do you know how many there are? A hundred and six. The Prefecture has made me responsible for this.'

By now our last evening together was drawing in over the Riviera di Chiaia. The already-pale shadows had quietly disappeared as if absorbed into the earth. Soon it would be night; but the mighty landscape would not sleep; it would await the howling of the sirens heralding the air-raid. The homely lamps would suddenly be extinguished. My uncle would light his candle. He had not ended that day's work. He would not go down to the shelter.

That bridge over the Crostolo! A majestic edifice made entirely from river flint like a fort in the days of the Gauls, with huge pillars shaped like castle-keeps or keels, and bizarrely adorned with cast-iron balustrades of an exorbitant weight and posts made in a single piece with initials and crests. And needless to say it was not done by public, but private, enterprise and merely provided access to a vast villa – the property, so it seemed, of a single eccentric individual. What that bridge was doing in that desolate place where the Crostolo loses its shape and sprawls between a wilderness of crumbling banks and impassable bramblewoods, and what we were doing there, only God and Major Nappa (my new commanding officer) knew. The lancers, trained for quite different type of work, endured with humiliation the imposition of this incomprehensible service (as those others had done at Bay); but they too must have understood that the war, though in the early enthusiastic days proclaimed as being short and victorious, was in fact only just beginning. I myself had had no more than a glimpse of its endless and murky theatre, like a peeping-Tom at a chink in a wall; and this new pause could neither displease nor deceive me. Others, meanwhile, were playing their parts, and owing to the distance we carelessly followed their mime though their voices never really reached us. But the stage would soon open up for us all.

I liked Reggio Emilia very much, judging by the short period I was able to stay there at first, and then the times I had to go there to report to the Command. Today it is almost impossible to re-discover the texture of our lesser cities before they were turned upside-down by the whirlwind of urbanisation, the consumer-goods civilisation, and the grotesque proliferation of the motor car. A strong and independent race, the people of Reggio are by nature frank but cautious. There were so many gratings in the city, gardens closed by high walls, and an infinitude of silent courtyards behind barred gates. The architecture was modest for the most part, with plain shutters flush with the walls, simple roofs, belvederes, dormer windows. However, the shades of colour, quickly weathered to perfection by wind and rain, provided delightful backgrounds and romantic flights interspersed with little porticoes or trees. The last mists of March increased the unobtrusive sweetness of the place. At certain hours of the evening when the weather was fine, the brick churches of Reggio took on the colour of flesh: they came alive.

'Not suited for foreign service.' It was with this viaticum that I resumed my posting in the homeland. The oculist-captain had urgently prescribed that I should avoid damp, sun and dust. He evidently believed that such things existed only beyond the frontier, and that our national territory was immune from them. Reggio Emilia? A city as comfortable as any other, so they assured me in a fatherly way. But the group of dismounted cavalry which, on the map, was stationed there, in fact only maintained its Command there; the rest were dispersed on the usual sentry service as far as the Cerreto Pass on the heights of the Apeninnes. Almost immediately I found myself surrounded by snow again, under Mount Valestra. A couple of weeks later I was at Albinea in connection with that already-mentioned bridge over the Crostolo in the foggiest, muddiest, least sheltered place in the whole valley, rich in such places though this network of rivers is. 'A bad throw of the dice,' I said to myself.

In those months the war was fluctuating uncertainly but virulently, like a disease spreading through the deepest and most hidden of ramifications. The Germans were holding down half Europe, but the destruction of the Alpine Julia division in the Greek mountains, grievous naval losses and an element of insecurity and ambiguity in our military and political conduct, and, above all, the nation's silence and those closed faces down to the poorest man in the street – all this said only too much. Yet, so unlike Naples, the country from Modena to Piacenza still seemed to be calm. Germans were seen very little and they kept themselves to themselves. Food rationing was more formal than real. My new commander and his underling – a priest-like type very old for the rank of Second Lieutenant – both lived in the age-old Albergo della Posta in the centre of the city and kept a good table at the Cannon d'Oro – where they only came under the fire of highly spiced sausages, chicken soup with the best possible parmesan cheese, and all served under the patronage of Lambrusco wine. For form's sake it sufficed for the cutlet to be hidden under the spinach and, halfway through lunch, for them to stand to attention with an aggrieved look while the radio poured out a bulletin so watered-down as to make one reel.

Age apart, this Major Nappa was an officer of the Reserve like ourselves; but it was said that he owed his rank to service done the cavalry squadron of Nitti's Royal Guard in 1921. He was a small *rentier* from Caserta, the kind who possesses a strip of land for growing hemp and an agency for agricultural machinery or fertilisers. He knew nothing about drilling, book-keeping or arms; but his stupidity could become dangerous because it went with an irritable and distrustful character. In that first week, because he was unable to read maps, he had sent my detachment from Carpineti to a place he judged to be three kilometres away. But that was as the crow flies, because in fact the men had a seven-hour march so as to get round a tall cliff that reared up in mid-course. At dawn next day the major ordered them to return at once, hoping thus to make good his mistake. Owing to my opposition to this order he conceived an aversion to me from the start, and my posting to the Crostolo bridge was the immediate outcome of it.

It is only a few kilometres from Albinea to Reggio and they can be quickly covered even by bicycle. Disguised in civilian clothes against the regulations, I went to Reggio as often as I could. Not that I knew anyone there, but I felt the same secret life vibrating behind those great walls as I had found in Ferrara. I discovered certain accents, certain faces, familiar in that earlier world of the De Michelis and Mavì; and for reasons difficult to explain, it delighted me to brush up against those secrets – which I had violated once but were now closed to me.

Accustomed as I was to large cities, in Reggio I had the feeling of being in a house, but a huge and fantastic one – a Renaissance residence, say, where everything belonged to one lord and master against whom some conspiracy was always afoot. Those big archways giving on to the central square, and the way this square led into that other smaller one, secret and austere and dedicated to San Prospero, suggested forums or theatres where the stage is set for different events; and those Emilian arcades like military communication trenches, and those churches square like citadels . . . But it was kind of the churches to keep their doors open, so that the street reached right up to the altar and the altar right down to the street.

Partly with a view to avoiding undesirable encounters, I would go in the evenings and dine in little working-class taverns, elbow to elbow with people of every kind. They were always courteous to me yet always kept to themselves; an amiability towards the foreigner that in fact serves to set him apart and hold him at a distance in some indefinable way, precisely through singling him out for polite attentions. Most of these people were workers and all were avowed socialists – despite the efforts of the Duce and Balbo (whose Fascist squads had failed to force the 'Perma Voladora' torrent in Parma, a little to the north, in 1921). Perhaps these people sensed in me the officer, the foreigner, the master, and that was why they kept to themselves.

The majestic medieval aspect of the city's bonework, which becomes poorer and peters out in the jerry-building at the tail end, showed how wrong the Fascist regime was in wanting always to rebuild in the style of the ancient Romans, and skipping the Communes (the real roots of our times), the Renaissance and all the rest. It might just be possible to imagine the solid full-blooded people of Reggio with Roman swords and tunics – perhaps because of the Roman via Emilia; but in reality they come from the age in between, from the six lines of castles rising around the Po at Bismantova. Their mythical heroine was Matilde of Canossa; their biggest hate was for tyrants who had lasted seven hundred years. And like those tyrants, and with them, Fascism was obliged to pull in the reins with the same ends in view. At the time of the Ethiopian enterprise I had grasped the extent of the opposition of the 'deep South' to the Duce and the other Fascist leaders; I had seen it in Uncle Gedeone's silent but implacable protest, and there lay the voice of Naples. Here, in Piazza Grande, there were a few sacks of earth to protect the cathedral statues; a sort of trench beneath the San Prospero tower to catch the pieces that might fall; otherwise, to all appearances, nothing; except those reminders and reproaches. For the hour of reckoning was not to come until later.

So we all waited . . . my only occupation being the inspection of my guard posts – of which the most outstanding was the one on the Crostolo bridge. And on Major Nappa's orders I gave uplifting little talks to the lancers to keep up their morale, and meanwhile did my best with my paints. For which diversion I was reproved by the Major: 'In the middle of war . . . to pursue such schoolboy occupations!' But Major Nappa had nothing to say about the long hours his subalterns spent in certain houses on via Cavour and via Cravezzerie. Perhaps he didn't like me keeping to myself.

'Look, Sansevero,' he said, addressing me in the second person singular and thus showing off an ancient habit of our regiment to which, incidentally, he did not belong, 'Look, we've got difficulties in the administration of the group and in the collective expenses to which you, like the commanders of the other squadrons, ought to be contributing with your funds made on the "black".'

He had already sounded me on the matter before. The 'black' fund was made up of those sums earned by every commander by irregular if tolerated methods, and were then used for indispensable disbursements, in their turn not recognised by the administration. It could seem strange, for instance, that the shoes issued by our stores were always in natural-coloured leather, whereas according to regulations they should be black. Whenever a recruit arrived he had to be forbidden to go out in pale shoes though there was no way of providing him with dye: result, no exit permit. So after three or four days most of them got busy solving the problem in their own way: soot, black polish, even ink – which produced deplorable gradations of purple and red. These and many similar amenities were acquired by selling or exchanging surplus foodstuffs, or by promissory notes on long-term understanding with quartermasters, master-shoemakers, saddlers and so on. In the golden age when colonels were of the type of that good soul Count Dati, no officer would have dreamed of taking advantage of the black market for his own benefit. But from indiscretions on the part of the orderlies I knew that at Group Command things were done differently; and that Nappa had received from a sympathetic colleague of the same rank, attached to the accounts department, a friendly tip-off that there was to be an inspection of the books. This was why he was trying to get in money and recalling me to the solidarity I had neglected.

'In my squadron,' I replied, 'the fund isn't administered by me but from the orderly-room direct. Everyone knows what there is and what it's used for down to the smallest detail. How can it be transferred?'

Nappa seemed annoyed. 'I don't see,' he said, 'why you have to inform the lancers about what is a commander's duty. It's against the regulations.'

He had been scrutinising a map when I went in, but he quickly whisked it away because he found it painful to remember that time when he had made the men march for seven hours owing to misreading it. I felt that my antipathy to him, coupled with his initial ill-humour, was again shaking the dice-cup. But how could I be reconciled with him? There was yet another aspect of the situation, that of bringing together and mixing very diverse kinds of men, so as to make them live and perhaps die together, without their having a single thought or affection in common. That very large section of current opinion which had first applauded and then profited by Fascism was now shown up as disunited, cowardly, and untrustworthy. It was always this section that held the reins of command, and used them to evade its own responsibilities while at the same time procuring further privileges and profits. The call-up was governed by a system, as it were, of 'draft sections' – that is to say, not according to age but to the heterogeneous needs of the armed formations in the water-tight compartments of the administrative areas; and this favoured endless abuses, substitutions and evasions. But at that precise moment the system was operating in the opposite direction. Once a man like Nappa, who was a real non-entity in civil life, was assured of a lucrative and risk-free assignment, the call-up brought him respect, means, and power. From nagging quarrels with his wife about who had had the last word, he rose to the intoxication of command and to the possibility of absolute power over many lives.

The same thing happened with the rest of his officers. War, like all upheavals, throws up what lies underneath, and buries what is on the surface. The selection board in the cavalry courses in which I had participated in my days in Rome and then in Ferrara was extremely severe. Out of nine hundred applicants who each year aspired to rank, only about thirty were accepted. Thus in fifteen years the courses had selected five hundred officers. Subsequent regulations readmitted an indiscriminate number of those excluded and they constituted the regimental lists of the corps at home. In Nappa's entire group, hardly anyone had attained regular promotion; a further motive for keeping me on the Crostolo bridge.

So my so-called comrades in Reggio and, I suppose, in all the rest of the peninsula, endured military service as one endures flies in summer, and the countless Nappas who afflicted them as logical counterpart of the situation enjoyed things to the maximum: they had the soldiers serve them as though they were patricians while they were always deep in debauchery or sleep. A spectacle all the more depressing for the troops in that they, for their part, had sacrificed a lot and had not the faintest idea of the super-strategy of the Rome-Berlin axis. So what could the lancers think, lying in their tents in the deep mists of the river, and born, like the people of Licudi, in some village bounded by its own Calitri? Their only real enemy (like mine) was the inflamed Nappa who was drunk

with the undreamed-of possibilities of being able to command
nearly a thousand men, and having the right to be swiftly obeyed
by them. Intoxicated at being taken a drive in a truck among
everyone's smart salutes, Nappa enjoyed now and again playing
'the martinet' and holding those poor devils at attention for half an
hour at a time.

I was pondering over these things towards the end of May
while swarms of new-hatched mosquitoes were buzzing over the
green puddles scattered on the gravel. Other news echoed on the
quiet from the Olympus at Reggio. It was certain that the major
had decided to entrust my squadron to one of the officers loyal to
him (they were said to serve him as pimps) and had in mind the
twofold intention of getting his hands on that 'black' fund and of
undoing me; but he was frustrated by that 'unsuitability for extraterritorial service'. A couple of requests – one for assignment to a
camel-transported squadron in Africa, the other for a liaison
officer in the Genoa cavalry taking part in the expedition to the
Russian front (where did the dice intend to fall?) – had passed
within range and he was unable to profit by them. Indeed once,
having missed his blow against me, he had risked losing one of his
most cherished underlings. But he, too, like nearly all the others,
turned out to be 'unavailable' outside the country. This was not the
same as 'unsuited'; but it formed part of the interminable casuistry
which put nearly everyone under a different rule and a different
obligation. And now the phonogram summoning me to the Command at eight o'clock was the prelude to some other trap. But
what?

As I free-wheeled down from the smiling hills of Albinea, radiant
in the Sunday light, I was thinking about Uncle Gedeone. He had
not needed call-up papers, a uniform and still less any pay to stay
in his city and do the work of a General as well as his own cooking
and housework, whereas Nappa had assigned himself three batmen.
The bombardment of Naples was getting worse, as reply to our
vain hammering of Malta. My uncle wrote that the requisitioning
of iron gateways for armaments had caused incredible damage to
very little constructive effect. Disembowelled by attack from the
sky, ungated and unguarded, with insufficient and inadequate air-
raid shelters, with surpluses and shortages, Naples had heavy
crosses to bear. Whereas here, where I was, such thoughts were
overlaid, blurred, put out of focus by the sight of two-wheeled

carts coming down to market; by bold women on bicycles generously displaying their legs for the joy of eyes and thoughts; and finally by the low line of the Reggio landscape suddenly coming into view, with its houses and little suburbs and steeples spread merrily out, and so rosy and young-looking – even after so many years – that the war seemed like a fairy-tale; and Nappa, and all the others, non-existent.

'The major isn't in,' the adjutant informed me in his priest-type way. 'But in view of the fact that he's twice reported you to Area Command as not indispensable to the group, they've now given orders to second you to the local Propaganda Service. Here's the order paper: a real stroke of luck!'

And indeed, once I had handed over the squadron (and the 'black' fund) to the lieutenant who came to replace me (a thoroughly debauched man who immediately started looking around), I found myself transferred from the little inn at Albinea to within the comfortable walls of Reggio itself, and for a much lighter service. This time the markings on the dice were in my favour.

Propaganda: that 'sale of words instead of things', the monstrous development of which Balzac had foreseen a century before! In our time its law-maker and prophet was Goebbels, a character darker than any Shakespearean Iago, a sort of malevolent spirit, Hitler's other half, to whom Hitler had entrusted the forked tongue of the serpent while reserving to himself the deliberate cruelty of one of La Fontaine's carnivores, but in a professor's clothing. After the dress-rehearsal of the Berlin Olympic Games and the colossal Nazi parades, Goebbels had invaded half the world with his diabolical creed. Though the Allies did their best, they were a far cry indeed from the satanic inventions of this resuscitated Dantean 'fraud'. It was incredible – what he managed to make people believe, and not only in Germany; above all, what he managed to conceal. Events involving millions of men and extinguishing millions of lives slipped by almost unnoticed, and many never really came to light even later. Following in the footsteps of this example, and in chameleon-like imitation of such a powerful ally, the Fascist regime gesticulated as best it could; but it was uphill work, given the ill-will of the Italians; and the avalanche of satirical stories that circulated at that time, even if they were the unwarlike reaction of a country that did not know how to offer opposition by deeds, coupled with the passivity and ill-will of a vast number of individuals, provided excellent ballast to the high kicks of the famous 'Roman goose-step'. It was in this climate that I was called upon to expend those gifts of oratory I was said to possess (heaven knows why) in favour of the war and in stimulating the frozen spirits of some of those whose duty it was to wage it.

The General in command of the military area was a regular officer but on the administrative side, and he received me in his requisitioned villa – with small cement columns and floral stuccos. He indicated certain themes I should develop in addressing the troops, the first of which had as title 'The Justice of our War'. He told me that I would be able to work on them under the direct supervision of the commanding officer of the Propaganda Office. Should there be serious grounds, he authorised me to come and report to him.

Leaning against the marble lions of Verona that keep guard over San Prospero, I turned over in my mind the subjects the General had proposed – interspersed, I may say, with not a few contrapuntal notes of irony. It had not entered that good man's head that when a country resolves to go to war it no longer asks itself if it is right to do so; just as when one is at a dance it is better not to cast doubt on the expediency of the merry-making. And supposing I failed to convince someone – had he therefore the right to take off his knapsack and go back home? Those were the days when Aimone of Aosta was nominated King of Croatia, no less. Showing the rightness of such an investiture was no joke.

From the deep shadow of the main nave, I was looking at the colours of the little market in the smaller piazza, chock-full of fruit and vegetables under the bright summer sun, and the people going about their harmless pursuits. That square, dedicated to the good saint of Aquitaine, protector of Reggio, itself seemed like the fresh clean heart of a lettuce or a cabbage; something healthy and fragrant in the plexus of the town: to be looked at, smelt, lived. Who could have elaborated the themes provided by the General out here? Who could have summarised the reasons why there was sadness on the kindly faces of these people who till now had been happy with their vines and their way of life? And who was going to disseminate so much evil in that mild provincial water-colour as to produce first a drop and then a torrent of blood?

So it was under such auspices – while General Geloso's army was installing itself in Athens which had really been conquered by the Germans in that headlong march on the Vardar; and while Ethiopia was returning to the velvet paw of the Lion of Judah – that I prepared myself to play my third hand in a game that was to produce so many others. But this time, who was it against?

The Propaganda Office of the area (or the P. Office, as it was called) was at that time in charge of a certain Captain Toia, a man from Bergamo, who lost no time in letting me know that he had been called up by mistake and from one moment to the next was expecting the phonogram order that would restore him to freedom. For Toia was, in fact, a functionary of the Department of Finance, and out of due respect for the higher bureaucracy was exempt from the call-up. Perhaps there had been manœuvres against him on the part of his colleagues, in that network of intrigues on which careers thrive; but Toia's counter-attack was now in full swing and its result was certain. The captain was a big man with a barbarian's loud voice and shining eyes – an exemplar of what in common parlance is described as 'coarse blooded'. But he had no idea he was one of those figures that people make fun of when having a jolly evening together, for his self-assurance was the outcome of his rapid advancement. Already in the fifth grade of the civil service, though still in the springtime of life, he was about to be promoted to the fourth: which, in military life, corresponded in rank to a Divisional Commander. Hence, as a mere officer, Toia had reverted to the tenth grade, so it followed that he was supremely uninterested in the Services and passed his time in his comfortable billet in via Ariosto – with a lovely view over the churches of Cristo and San Giorgio – consuming a notable quantity of the famous local cheese washed down by the best Trebbiano wine.

With those bottles around him he was always telling me stories about his splendid position in Rome, and about the Department of Finance, one of the three omnipotent departments of the Administration, the other two being the Exchequer and the Council of State. Hitler, Mussolini, the war, Italy's feared disasters – all seemed of scant interest to him, irrelevant facts, compared with the continuity and stability of the Department of Finance; and his promotion to the fourth grade seemed to represent the only important and certain event in the years to come. Toia's hidden enemies – but he must have known them well – were putting up a certain resistance to his counter-offensive, perhaps so as to achieve some sought-after aim

during his absence, or to combat things that he had planned or
intended. So they managed to keep him in Reggio for a few months,
and thus I had to enter into some measure of familiarity with him.

Luckily, the General made his voice heard too; and as the area
was enormous and the detachments numerous I was out of town
for a week at a time. I became accustomed to being received surlily
by individual commanding officers, and had to study a type of
attitude that would mollify them. I was dealing with officers of the
Reserve, not unlike Nappa, and to many of them it did not seem
right to rattle off endless tirades to troops obliged to listen against
their will. Pretensions to oratory are a national characteristic with
the average Italian, like vanity; and whoever manages to obtain
any kind of audience tyrannises over it as much as he can. Many of
the officers were petty Fascist officials who had attracted attention
by following the great example of Ciano and Starace and, accustomed to the 'plenary meeting', felt cut to the quick.

'You,' they said to me with some ill-humour, 'you've been sent
here to tell our soldiers what evidently we are not thought capable
of telling them ourselves!'

And on the whole they were right, because in fact I had not
devoted myself to the study and exercises of Demosthenes. However,
after much reflection, I carefully set aside the subjects proposed by
the General, and tried to find something convincing in all that moral
morass. Our reverses in Africa and, towards the end of 1941, the
threat of German reverses in Russia, allowed me to draw certain
conclusions. If the Licudi fishermen had taught me about their way
of conceiving the motherland and the magnetic force that always
kept them turned towards home, Nappa and Toia had clarified the
rest. So it seemed to me that to speak of 'crowning glories' or
'incontrovertible victories' was to put water instead of wood on the
fire. Better confine ourselves within our human condition and the
pains and obligations this involves us in. So, basing myself on
Plato's *Laws*, I encouraged those poor devils to obey and, given that
they had been sustained by the law in civilian society, have patience
now that the law was against them. I explained that the policeman
who now accompanied the deserter to the military court was the
same man who had defended the boundaries of their fields; and if
they had been called up because their names were on the register,
this was because their names had been recorded there as citizens on
the day of their birth, thus entitling them to civil rights, a lawful

wife, recognised children. Truth to tell, the peasants from poor villages had never had much else; but my fifteen-minute talks seemed to be acceptable and did not appear to disturb even the commanding officers predisposed to be hostile. As for the General, he was a thousand miles from imagining what rather unorthodox conclusions were passing in the name of Socrates – who had talked in this way precisely while one of the many inexplicable crimes of history was being committed against him, as now against us. On the reports he received, the General congratulated Nappa on an 'outstandingly good man', thereby giving Nappa both pleasure and discomfort. Toia, on the other hand, laughed loudly, and made round jokes about me as he did about the General; and so openly as to make me suspect that he perhaps wanted to try me out.

My buried but deep aversion for Toia which I had observed from the start (much greater than for Nappa who was too miserable a creature to be considered for a moment on the moral plane) helped me to detect in his apparent sociability and ease of manner some sort of intention concerning me, and one which must have come into his mind when I first presented myself to him, as if at that moment he had found what he had long been looking for. Little by little my conviction about his dark purpose grew, and I felt it probing me, pressing on me, though I had no idea what it was. But when Toia sent for his wife to join him during his banishment in Reggio and introduced me to her, and for no good reason showered rather outspoken remarks on both of us, I began to get an inkling.

I had imagined the wife of that tedious individual would be one of those provincial women of little beauty or wealth who marry their husbands in the days of their obscurity and hence remain well below the career-grades subsequently attained. I found myself confronting a strikingly beautiful woman, still very young, and with manners so polite as to seem almost brittle. And when I noticed the exquisiteness of her dress revealing the minutest attention to detail, it was no surprise to learn that she was born in Parma, for that seems to have been the hallmark of the court of Maria Luisa as though in reaction to the glorious but murderous imperial display of Napoleon. At that first moment I was unable to get any further, but I felt that Toia's dark intention involved his wife, me, and above all himself.

As I needed a billet not far from the railway station – my daily starting-point – I had found one in the neighbourhood of the church

of San Pietro, on the edge of a quarter of ill-repute but teeming
with eager life. Reggio comes to a rather unexpected end in that
direction with those aulic palaces in via Toschi and via Fontanelli;
and having put up a final resistance with the majestic walled garden
of the Levi Villa, it suffers sudden shipwreck in a maze of little
streets and houses that are highly questionable where customs and
hygiene are concerned but incomparably touching in other respects
– such as the colours of those dead leaves, the yellows, the purples,
the russets, all steeped in a sense of time and irremediable decay. I
occupied a ground floor, very large and high, with the possibility
of access on to a great walled garden full of age-old trees – ilexes,
planes, cedars, and even eucalyptuses, as in our old home at Monte
di Dio. There the long dark cry of the turtle-dove could always be
heard, so unlike the graceful bird that emits it. I could almost
imagine the reappearance of the tortoises of time gone by, after an
absence of twenty years, and the very same ones at that.

For the sake of convenience, and without paying much attention
to the other customers who were mostly from the locality, I sometimes made use of an old tavern opposite my billet in the via San
Gerolamo. On the evening that I had been introduced to Signora
Toia (Albertina, as her Christian name was), I arrived rather late
at my tavern, so that it was almost empty, and the first person I
saw on entering was the Seer of Bay, the dice-man, Demetrio,
sitting next to a sleepy-eyed girl.

He showed no more surprise at seeing me on this occasion than
he had shown on the last. He rose, shook hands, and having introduced the woman with the single word, 'Priscilla,' he said with his
usual gravity and ease of manner:

'We're wandering around more or less like you, and today we've
come from Gualtieri. By now, again more or less like you, we're
militarised and dependent on the Propaganda Office. We're giving
two shows here at the Rossini theatre. Will you join us for supper?'

But here the innkeeper intervened and said he had got to close.
'But if you'd be satisfied with a cold supper I'll leave it here and go
on upstairs. Please shut the door behind you when you go. That's
all. You don't need to lock it. There are no treasures here.'

I scrutinised the Seer more closely: he was very thin; dark eyes,
ill-shaven, dirty threadbare clothes. Priscilla was a listless girl with
vacant eyes and a spotty skin. She was weirdly dressed – something
between Levantine costume and bits and pieces picked up at village

markets. She was wearing a long necklace made of shells. Despite his gold ear-ring, Demetrio was not a gypsy. For a while he had been bandmaster in his native Verona; and God alone knows what a neurasthenic from that city can be like.

We said little during supper, Priscilla not even a syllable, as though she saw nothing and no one. That day they had given a show in a barracks on the Po: straightforward conjuring tricks. But now Demetrio was in deep meditation. Then, like an artist who is forced by circumstances to live a life alien to himself but at certain moments recognises that the time is at hand for genuine creation, he seemed to come to a decision. He looked up at me as if for a final reassurance and appraisal, then, without further ado, said:

'This time let's try an experiment in levitation. The disposition of the forces is favourable.'

Without adding a word, Priscilla stood up with her sleep-walking look, removed every single object from the table and carefully wiped its surface. She then removed the chairs around it and placed them against the wall. We were all standing, Priscilla and the Seer opposite each other, I on the third side of the table, which was square, solid, and very heavy.

Demetrio concentrated for a fairly long time, then almost unexpectedly, and as if he wanted to hold on to something, he rested his wide-open hands on the table in the attitude of a master pianist about to take possession of the keyboard. Priscilla did the same, synchronising her movements with his down to a split second, as if the impetus of Demetrio's brain were operating on her nerve centres too. They remained motionless, but the gradually-increased tension made their bodies tremble owing to the impossible effort to which they were being subjected. Priscilla's eyes opened and radiated a sort of light; the spots had disappeared from her highly coloured face and she looked strange and beautiful. Drops of sweat beaded the Seer's forehead; for a moment I thought he was going to collapse; but he gritted his teeth and held out. Slowly under their naked palms, the arms of each taut and apart, the table rose.

This unreal scene in semi-darkness lasted a few seconds; then those two strange creatures gently relaxed their arms and delicately lowered the table on to the floor. They removed their hands by sliding them along the surface as if they had difficulty in disengaging them from an adhesive substance. Priscilla's eyes went out and now the repulsive spots reappeared on her face. The Seer drank a big gulp of grappa straight from the carafe and withdrew into the darkest corner where he collapsed into a chair and fell silent.

I have no idea how long things stayed like that; but I was brought to my senses with a jolt by that funereal yet slightly sardonic voice saying:

'You mustn't despair, Signor Sansevero!'

I thrust myself forward in an effort to see his face; but he held it completely hidden in his hands. I was disconcerted and would have liked to regain my grip on reality by looking under that table, now returned to such normality.

'No,' he went on in his melodious uncouth voice, 'Madame Digne up at Bay knew nothing about you, and couldn't have given me any information; in fact, it was I who explained you to her. And if you want to look under the table, or make sure we haven't any resin on our hands, then do so. But why don't you want to believe in the Powers? I did that experiment for myself alone, certainly not to take you in. I know you don't believe in the brute domination of matter; I know how often you've expended yourself' (those were his very words) 'and that you are going to be warned again, and that shortly heavy demands are going to be made on you. If you've an energy swelling within you, it's because you must give it. That's much more than lifting a table.'

We went out into the darkness of the alley. Air-raids throughout the country were multiplying. My uncle had written me desolate letters from Naples about the nightly hammering. The blackout was humiliating to a country renowned for its lights and sounds.

'I don't know how you intuit these things,' I said after a moment of self-questioning, 'but a difficult interlude has indeed come to an end. It's true that things will now change. And it's also true that I can make a fresh start.'

And without another word we parted.

The winter came early that year. It found the Germans deeply entrenched in Russian territory, but at a standstill, and the English once more pressing on Libya. The P. Office was under pressure too. My trips became *tournées*, so much so that I found I was indeed in the same boat as Demetrio. The General ordered me (even though with Socratic words) to go for two weeks to infuse fresh zeal into the troops stationed from Santa Lucia di Tolmino to Lublin, from Montenero to the Bainsizza and even to the Carso, those mountains that had been the theatre of blood-soaked trench-warfare back in 1915–1918.

Toia was extremely annoyed by all this and regarded it as an unseemly interference in his own invested command. However, he calmed down after a few angry vocal outbursts. Perhaps the plot he was weaving in his mind needed time for development; but however that may have been, he inflicted an interminable evening on me just when I had to be off again at three o'clock in the morning – an evening in which he zealously divided himself between his wife (towards whom he feigned great solicitude despite her air of indifference) and me, whom he bombarded with satirical praise. Albertina was amiable but strictly formal; yet at times I thought I intercepted certain quick glances from her at him. In my private opinion she was thinking of facts and feelings far away; and Toia's attention was concealed yet tense precisely so as to spy out her secret together with my capacity to penetrate it. He was forcing her openly to observe me, hoping to see from her reaction those hints that he felt to be perhaps essential.

I left the city in darkness, with the train coasting along beside the black castles and flashing fires of the Reggio factories, then still intact, and almost in a dream I heard the hammers of the factories over and above the clang of the train. The ground was an undefended land, oppressed by the sword. And Albertina's delicate face came back to me like something that had been stricken but was now static.

In the low kitchen nearby the women were chattering in a language to me incomprehensible. Stretched out on the warm Jugoslav *pec*, in that household in the rainy valley of the Idria, I felt the cold and exhaustion gradually melting from my limbs; and smooth soundless thoughts and images floated in the deep waters of my memory.

When morning came over the high desolate plain, the commanding officer named in my service orders – a lieutenant of the Alpine regiment, athletic but with a child-like face – took me to visit one of the ancient redoubts of the first war: a little cavern not much taller than a man, dug into the rock from which mountain water dripped. Through the slit you could see a small valley; and to capture that post guarded by a few machine-guns, two thousand soldiers had fallen. Was it the image of the motherland that pushed these ignorant infantrymen to the assault – men who had grown up with their herds on the remote slopes of the Apennines? Or were they subject to some spectre, much vaster and at the same time much less identifiable? The obligation proper to combatants, not only in a war, but in reality as a whole; a debt taken over within themselves, and paid to the whole of life?

That was a strange luncheon with the lieutenant. He had ordered two large hares to be prepared in two monumental pans, with nothing to follow but coffee in milk bowls and murderous slivovitz in coffee cups. The feast went on till darkness fell; and the lieutenant, in his fortress of alcohol and melancholy, talked endlessly of the odyssey of the Julia division and the march on Mekowo; of the famous retreat and the sinking of the ship bringing home the only survivors, those of the Gemona battalion. And he told of the high seas in which the dead were floating held up by their lifebelts, and how it was impossible for the rescuers to tell whether there was anyone still alive among those hundreds of bobbing heads.

'I was the only one alive,' the lieutenant went on, 'and for nine hours I fought against the sea and the current that prevented me from reaching the shore. Towards the end I saw a torpedo boat pass by, but they didn't see me. I had to come to a decision: either a huge effort to reach it or, failing that, surrender to the waves. But at last they saw me and came to my rescue. I was caught beneath the hull so they threw me a cable to haul me up, but by mistake I grabbed at a rope fixed to the side of the boat and hoisted myself up with my own two arms – to their astonishment. After that I went down with pneumonia for ten days, and that was another brush with death . . .'

To die for one's country: an ambiguous concept today. In the First World War the men of Cadorna had fought with their families and possessions just behind them. After Caporetto, beyond the Piave, the land that the men had fought for and lost was their own church tower. There still persisted the memory of that almost legendary past among the little detachments I sought out in the folds of the mountains – a past that seemed a remote nostalgic paradise of honour as seen from the ambiguous present. The rains, beating down on the bleak mountain-sides which twenty-five years earlier had been contested foot by foot with a mighty enemy, were constantly uncovering hidden traces of that long-ago battle waged for four years and at infinite cost in blood – the blood of poor ignorant people and all mixed up with that mud from which, after all, man was made: a dark and doleful amalgam whence neverthe-less voices were reborn.

'The other day,' so the lieutenant told me, 'the rains washed away a pile of stones and brought to light the bodies of a whole squadron – they must have been buried by a landslide after an explosion. You could even see the postures of the soldiers, and one of them still had his ninety-one in his hand.'

Their identity discs, numbers and names would be unearthed; the long-ago procedures of presumed death would be ratified; the tears of widows – now grandmothers – would be renewed. While down below Nappa was working out his petty ways and means and Toia was conspiring even within his own household. Between these two extremes lay human life: between the absurdity of self-sacrifice and the absurdity of self-aggrandisement, both equally inexplicable. Italy's lucky star would rise when she had found the balance be-tween these two: the conscience of the more generous part paying the price for the meanness and indifference of the other.

'Up there, above the Goliko,' the lieutenant went on in his hollow voice, 'that's where our hero, Dolfo, met his death. There was only a small clearing between *us* and *them* and there had been so many skirmishes that some detachments knew one another. And when Dolfo emerged from his position one of *them* shouted in Italian: "If you've got the guts, come out!" And he . . .'

That was the way it was. I felt I'd have preferred the story not to go on, I'd have preferred what I was going to hear never to have happened. The rattling of plates in the kitchen had stopped; a young man must have come in and every now and then I heard his grave voice mixed with the cheerful interjections of the women.

'So Dolfo advanced in full daylight,' the lieutenant went on, his face raised and his eyes tight shut, immersed in memory, 'he advanced with a grenade in each hand, followed by his orderly, machine-gun at the ready. It was pure suicide. Even the Greeks just stared at him without shooting. Then he cried out: "We've got guts and to spare!" and he threw the first grenade. There followed a scuffle over his bullet-ridden body.'

Few things have persisted in men's minds like the idea of a hero, from Hector to Henry IV of France and our own first-war air-ace, Baracca. But has a hero ever been defined? Has he needed to be?

I had gone to the war willingly because I had lost everything, but I would never deliberately seek death because deep within me

I felt my life to be bound up with Uncle Gedeone. Yet Dolfo was young and loved life. Perhaps he thought he wouldn't die? Perhaps he was thinking of the glorious honours he would receive if he survived? Or was he being downright vainglorious, wanting to show the others what, in his view, a man was; wanting to prove that a man is only worth something in life if he is ready to give his life away – like a coin which only counts when it is spent? Or was he thinking of Italy at that moment, and placing himself through his action among the names that in due course she would venerate, inscribed on marble tablets or encased in little bronze wreaths?

No, no, nothing of the kind. As Demetrio had said: 'I did the experiment for myself alone.' And why after all should he have wanted to take me in? He had never met me before the war and would probably never meet me again after it; I had given him neither applause nor money. He and his dreamy Priscilla had left at dawn on the morning after making the table rise. So his motive was very like the one that drove Dolfo to throw his life away on the Goliko. For no one: not to convince or deceive anyone; not to obtain anything; and in return for that nothingness, to give everything. It was the height of arrogance, a defiance of the geometrical mechanism of the Universe, where everything is linked by cause and effect, so that whatever contrives to set itself up outside the chain, whatever turns out to be without motives or aims, partakes of the Divine. Producing water from rock, suspending weight in air, dying while loving life. The new epoch was trying to vilify heroism; but this had to do with the heroism propagated by the newspapers or prompted by the P. Office. It was not that other heroism of the soldiers who, without knowing anything about claims or aims, stuck darkly to their posts through their sheer quality as men (which is precisely what distinguished them from the beasts of the forests); and still less that of the lieutenant of the Alpine regiment (now fallen asleep with his baby face on his chest) who, when exhausted with the cold and his battle against the waves, had gambled his life on the efficacy of his spirit. In last analysis, the final trappings of the hero had disappeared along with the Fascists' regime; but not the impulse that lay behind it.

This contributed to an understanding of the elements of the war. The Julia division, like Dolfo himself, was operating on foreign soil, and this fostered that sentiment of primitive man when he finds his enemy where migration has pushed him and wants to get the better of him – like a baby who thinks that what he can reach with his hands is his; and, being men before soldiers, they had another irrepressible instinct, the one that exists in the cubs of wild animals with claws. But more certainly still, they were led along by a thread of illusion. Life shone before them like a perpetual act of imagination, outside any positive theory. Those who listened to my Socratic reasoning, whether beneath the peaks of the Predil or in sight of the stone dam of the Tagliamento, were left resigned and discontented, for there was no getting away from it. Only the 'winged word' was capable of moving them: precisely because it was designed to deceive them.

I got back to Reggio halfway through December. With Pearl Harbour the Japanese had set fire to the other half of the world; and the Rome-Berlin Axis went so far as to extend its war against the United States. The city was covered in snow driven by a tormenting wind beneath the dark porticoes of via Emilia. I saw frowning faces, people walking quickly, warily. An elegantly-dressed woman passed by me staring in front of her, her face slightly withdrawn, like someone who has been offended.

Great changes had taken place at the Command, especially for Nappa; very probably he was one of those who had negotiated his call-up and the best assignment. But his group, which according to the administrative structure was still mine, had suddenly been 'mobilised' – the prelude to a posting as mysterious as it was dangerous. Up till then, the only squadron to suffer had been that of those poor fellows on the Crostolo, for the other three had been quartered in the city. Mobilisation, involving as it did different equipment, weaponry and training for the whole detachment, presented Nappa with many problems, considering how incompetent he was. His subalterns knew even less than he did but, as was to be expected, just as they should have been getting down to work they slipped off to every sort of hiding-place to escape from a body which felt itself to be already under fire. All except four or five of them had ready and prepared some 'provision' or 'circular' capable of releasing them. In the end they dispatched a collective memorandum to the War Ministry then waited the result with folded arms. The major, who earlier had recommended me in glowing terms as a first-class orator, was now urgently pressing to have me restored to him. But he met determined resistance in stubborn Toia and perhaps also in the General, who was against him.

In this uncertain situation, not for any merits of my own but for reasons connected with the defects of those who made a show of caring about my services, Toia dispensed me from almost every task. His dark intentions must have come to fruition in those two weeks, and he did this under cover of the uncertainty of the situation. On the other hand, as he himself was in the last stages of his exile and ready to flee back to the Ministry of Finance at any moment, he did nothing but propose card games, musical pastimes with the gramophone, little meals and diversions, all day long; and always in the compulsory company of his wife and myself. I could not evade these orders, at least for ten hours a day, however unbearable my uneasiness became; but between us was Signora Albertina, a double-edged blade in whatever way I might have tried to take her: for I could neither help her nor abandon her; and my instinct told me I had to pass through those dark Caudine Forks. Even Demetrio's prophecies came back to my mind, for they chimed in so well with what had happened and what was going to happen. 'Before long you will be warned, and then great demands will be made upon you!' Was this the 'warning'?

Though I had observed Albertina closely I barely received a hint that she had so much as noticed me. As an individual, I mean; because of course she treated me with the respect due to an officer held in high esteem by her husband. Toia was about forty-five, Albertina little more than twenty-five; they had already been married for some time and had a small baby who was always ailing and whimpering. When, on Toia's orders, I telephoned his house at a specific hour, it was always Albertina who answered; and I could always hear the baby screaming wildly, so that Albertina hardly managed to get out brief phrases of instructions or receive my report. Then Toia would take over (I imagined him always beside her garnering every word!) and behind his coarse voice emitting the usual outbursts of protest and reassurance, the cries of the baby would fade away into the distance. I could see the impatient wave of the hand with which he would order Albertina upstairs with the wriggling baby in her arms. Once I had seen the baby. He was fat and almost repulsive; I felt Albertina was in some way sentenced to his weight and his appearance, both so like the father's; and, moreover, had to love him; as with a wicked spell in a fairy-story, or like something in a cruel and incomprehensible dream.

Stretched out on the *pec* in those days, I had come to various conclusions concerning Albertina, Toia and myself. Everything about him was so appallingly commonplace, even his captiousness. If he wanted to test his wife's fidelity or, worse, positively push her into betraying him – either so as to get rid of her or (a more probable hypothesis) so as to rage against her, win a victory over her, settle some long-standing account – then his choice of me as guinea-pig, and the abuse of his rank involved in forcing me to comply, indicated the abject level of his mind and his incapacity to penetrate the thoughts and emotions of others. It must have seemed to him that the double-rhetoric of my coat-of-arms and my ancient name, reinforced by the subsequent rhetoric of my romantic scar, my supposed oratorical talents and, now, my probable imminent danger at the front (for otherwise Nappa would not have been so eager to have me) – it must have seemed to him that all this added up to the right man at the right moment where his nefarious aims were concerned; for his was a bureaucratic mentality that judged people according to their 'character notes' which had made me seem a dandy along the lines of the *Segretario Galante*. But even if he did not know me, and had seen me only through the spectacles of his preconceived idea, it seemed strange that he knew Albertina so little. Did he really think her capable of some servant-girl's lapse between the kitchen and the pantry, or of an affair in a train with her neighbour in the next bunk? And, if so, did he then want to cheat with himself and bring down vengeance on her whole life for some casual sensual slip? It was a contemptible game that ought not to have been played, so as later to blame fate for the outcome.

Meanwhile a gust of hope and enthusiasm was sweeping through Italy in the first months of that year. The Reggio paper *Il Solco Fascista*, which up till then had done everything in its power to conceal our many misfortunes, now proclaimed over eight newsprint columns that the Axis had broken through in Africa and that our tanks were eighty kilometres from Alexandria. Those armies had made a huge and generous effort. With their litre of water a day in that parched desert, with petrol a priority over bread, inadequately armed and with nothing to back them up, they had managed to beat an enemy with unlimited resources at his disposal.

In the other hemisphere the Japanese were simultaneously pouring into Singapore, the Philippines, the East Indies and Burma, and we were assembling an army to play our part beside the German effort in Russia. This latter item caused Nappa burning anguish for he did not even dare to envisage a destination such as the legendary steppes that had brought even Napoleon to his knees; he did not even dare to envisage it for his troops or for himself. His difficulties with his unreliable subalterns were already real enough. The General had to resign himself, and I now found myself reintegrated into the Command of the squadron, one unit of which had left the Crostolo and passed with the other three beyond the city gates. It seemed that my perplexities over Albertina would get into focus in the frightful confusion afflicting the squadron and in which I was intimately involved. The adjutant, no doubt foreseeing the need for future good relations, whispered in my ear that the documents dealing with my promotion to the rank of captain – which had lain for five months on the major's desk without his doing anything about them – had been sent off a week earlier with recommendations for urgent attention.

'Here, things are going badly,' he added. 'Nearly all our officers enjoy special exemptions and will make use of them. There are no sergeant-majors and very few senior sergeants left. There are a few second lieutenants, and then there's you who will soon be the only captain and thus second-in-command of the group. But I've noticed that you're declared unfit for service abroad. Nappa will ask for a revision of that – you wait and see!'

Thus things emerged from their earlier confusion. By appointing me his second-in-command despite his antipathy towards me, Nappa managed to throw the whole weight of the mobilisation on to my shoulders. He had seen me spend a winter on the Crostolo, the unhealthiest river in the province, so he had every reason to suppose that I could serve in the devil's own house should this be necessary. But the rush to have me promoted revealed a more far-reaching purpose: that of having a replacement to hand when he himself moved off, as he would when the suitable moment came. In the meantime I had to spend murderous weeks dealing with the troops whose physique and morale had both been seriously impaired by over a year of pointless sentry work. Drawing on poetic memories of Ferrara and the noble shade of the colonel at Pinarolo, Count Dadi, I was just able to pull myself and the lazy discontented troops together. My appointment (that anxiously-awaited glory of a career!) arrived almost immediately. I had to drop in on Toia who had repeatedly asked to see me, and I was met by an ostentatious, almost aggressive cordiality.

'At last we can talk to each other in the second person! This calls for a first-class celebration!'

'I think it'll be the last,' I said. 'Nappa's preparing some trap for me.'

'Nappa won't do anything!' cried Toia, with a threatening eye. 'My case has now been settled. Within a week I'll be going back to Rome and then I'll take care of your Nappa!'

I tried to change the subject for I disliked this way of talking. I had hoped not to have to see that man again. It was difficult to address him in the second person and I did not like him doing so to me. I had to accept his invitation but refrained from mentioning Albertina, even to send her my formal greetings – and nor did he mention her.

Events followed thick and fast within the next few days. On the military transmitter that repeats the same line in triplicate to avoid all possible doubt came the order assigning our group to the Athens Command, thence to proceed to some further destination on that chessboard. The General summoned me. He was a decent man and seemed to be divided between various lines of thought.

'Now that your Command is being sent abroad it wants to retain you at all costs. I don't know what the Medical Board will decide; but in any case I could have you seconded to Captain Toia's post which will be vacant when he goes back to Rome. I've asked him for a full-length report on the work you've been doing in these last months; and if it's favourable, as I'm sure it will be, we could keep you here. You've done your bit in the war as it is.'

I thanked the General; but I felt an ironical happiness stirring within me which presaged a change in my fortunes, as my scars showed a change in time. The following evening was to be Toia's party: a knot in that depressing tangle.

This time the venue was a large room made from a converted courtyard – such as one sees in the provinces. There were dozens of bottles of every type and origin ranged on vast tables; everything was too big, too little used, and too uncomfortable. The Captain had mobilised the whole of the P. Office and a small group of women, evacuated from Milan or Bologna, one or two well-to-do, but most of them of very uncertain means; though it was not actual hunger that would make them potentially dangerous. In defiance of rationing, there were large quantities of mille feuilles gateaux of translucent whiteness; and as for the Trebbiano wine, this time Toia had really excelled himself and bottles were displayed by the dozen. In a rather ill-lit corner of the huge room a corporal was operating a gramophone by hand, but very quietly, for, in view of the war, every kind of entertainment was forbidden. So all those present took on an air of complicity. By the end of the party no less than half of the guests had discreetly disappeared.

Toia deliberately took no part in the dancing. He seated himself at the far end of the room, almost in darkness, behind the cake table, and set to work on his bottles.

For a while at first Signora Albertina seemed to want to stay near him; but as his absorption in the glasses prevented him from paying any attention to her, she gradually started looking after the others – who were after all her guests – and with her formal and slightly weary politeness patiently handed round cakes and Trebbiano. Every now and again she was invited to dance and she accepted with an ease that removed all value from her consent. But she only exchanged a few words with her partners, and certainly generalities at that; no one seemed really interested in her as they all had their own intrigues in hand and were doubtless intimidated by the presence of their immediate superior.

However much it might have pleased me, I did not want to dance with Albertina. Shyness, always the sign of some affection, prevented me from asking her; but most of all I felt that our relationship, which had been rendered impossible by circumstances, would only suffer in such cramped conditions. Moreover, some kind of keen intuition, if not sheer fantasy, warned me that in that almost funereal room only Albertina, her husband and myself were involved in some business relating to real life; this flashed across my mind so insistently that it was impossible to ignore it. After a couple of hours Toia seemed so heavy with wine, and so quiet and inert in his corner, that I could scarcely see him from the other end of the room. At that moment Albertina, who happened to be beside me, put aside two unaccepted glasses and smiled at me wordlessly with her air of gentle patience. I was seated and she sat down beside me. It was the first time we had been able to talk alone.

'Are you tired, Albertina?' And an echo within me seemed to say: 'Are you tired, Vincenzina?' – words of years ago beneath the olive trees of Licudi on the night of that moonlight barbecue. And from that echo sprung many others, as many as the years, and they made me feel sad.

She kept her head down. I expected her to give a timid glance at something or someone, just as Vincenzina had done on that previous occasion. It occurred to me that if I had asked her to dance she, too, would have refused with a 'No, no, that's not for me!' – although she had danced with everyone else. I said nothing. In that attitude, with her delicate skin, her fine hair, her ears unpierced, Albertina looked like a young girl hardly yet awakened.

Our conversation was long, hesitant, uncertain. No one took any notice of us and we forgot everyone else. I knew that she had married very young; and I surmised that for complicated family reasons – of the kind that so often form the dramatic undercurrent to what goes on in certain households – she had been unable to extricate herself from what others had decided for her, and that Toia's overbearing personality had been able to impose itself in some way. There had been no one to save her from someone who, though better disguised than Dr Carruozzo, certainly came from the same stable. Following this thread of reminiscence – she having said nothing – I knew what she would not be able to admit even in confidence, given that she had tried so hard to close her mind to it.

The doors of our big room were firmly closed, with the result that the air had become heavy. Someone had the idea of lowering the lights which were already pretty dim; and in the semi-darkness one could only just make out the couples gliding along in slow dances. All that swaying and squeezing seemed to be causing Albertina more than mere boredom. And now no one asked her to dance any more.

'What do you think about it, Albertina?'

She tightened her lips and shook her head. I could sense her thoughts so well that they might have been words; I saw her as an innocent young girl led lovelessly into the arms of a man whose weight must have crushed her. I stood up and offered her my hand. As I steered her towards the centre of the room I again caught sight of Toia, now almost besotted with wine, his head down, his eyes blank. But I knew how he could disguise his tensions. That he should have wanted to inflict this new kind of anguish on himself; that he

should have wanted his sin against Albertina's life to rise up before
him again, whole and entire, with all the suffering it entailed; that
he should have wanted to be sure that she was completely free from
him, who had broken her without even touching the surface of her –
there lay the mysterious side of his character. As for me, I was convinced that I ought to obtain the answer to this conundrum, and
from him; an answer that he had spent so many years denying to
himself but which was now demanded. And she wanted the same
thing, though she abstracted herself from me. Like all deeply
wounded people, she had an intuition that I was wounded too. Our
sympathy for each other was of the kind that has always obliged
the world to feel in bad conscience when confronted with those
whom it ill-treats and yet battens on. It was necessary that the ulcer
of a problem that he had no right to disregard (and he was the first
to know it) should reopen within him. Yet I was afraid of reviving
those lacerating wounds for Albertina's sake. Meanwhile she
appeared to have awakened – perhaps for the first time for years.
Colour had come into her face; her eyes were afire. As for me, I
realised it would be useless to pursue her, because such pursuits
had already taken their toll in my experience, and it was a risk
because Toia would certainly enter into the game finally. Yet it
was impossible for me to hold back, not because I was unable to,
but because I did not want to: I thought I was fulfilling some kind
of indefinable duty towards her, some right over him, and at the
same time challenging what Demetrio had said should not be called
fate.

At a certain point Toia got up and staggered from the room.
She did not utter a syllable, but sat down beside me again and
waited a long time before following him.

In saying goodbye to her I felt that the moment was over, and
that there would be no tomorrow.

As I had foreseen, there was no further summons from the General.
Toia's report on my conduct as a propaganda officer must have
been a masterpiece; he knew very well what I thought about the
state of things in Italy and of the war in general; hence his praises,
tempered with ministerial wisdom, were certainly wrapped round
in impenetrable veils of doubt. Then something else unforeseen
happened: despite Nappa's assurances, the Medical Board insisted
on classing me as 'unsuitable' for service abroad. Together with

ninety per cent of the other officers in the group – their collective memorandum had won a victory – I was exempt from going abroad with the detachment and was sent back to my original area for an assignment to some other unit at home. The dice, having rolled capriciously over the table, had stopped on a blank. I was free from risk and able to set myself up again as I wanted.

Mobilised in February, our unit had been reorganised as well as could be expected in two months. After so much labour we were as good as ready, when suddenly the men found themselves without officers; worse, they knew their officers were privileged and exempt from common duty. A wave of unrest bordering on rebellion ran through the ranks. In his despair Nappa sent for me.

'Listen,' he said, 'all reason is on your side. But I have nine hundred and sixty men, with six second-lieutenants, and not one regular officer. Who's going to put them on the train? If you leave me too, it will be the signal for mutiny. We'll have the military police. For God's sake, Sansevero, come with us!'

We were outside Reggio in some school buildings in the direction of Sant' Ilario, having had the torment of several successive mobilisations. We were pacing back and forth over brick paving that crumbled beneath our feet with age and use. The sky was already bright with the beautiful colours of the new season. My thoughts were a thousand miles away from the Major and what he was saying, so that I was only giving him formal attention. I knew perfectly well that I would not abandon the detachment, and the Medical Board had no importance for me at all. The only thing that irritated me was Nappa's insistent appeals, for what I really minded was having to fall in with his wishes.

On returning to Reggio, I ran into a poor-looking man who stared at me from beneath the shade of a battered old hat: it was Demetrio.

'Captain, sir,' he said almost humbly. 'May I offer you my congratulations?'

'What for?' I wondered. And his eye gleamed from deep in its socket, made darker by the brim of his hat.

'There's an evil force against you; but it will be atoned for in the future by whoever harbours it in his soul. All you have to do is to carry on.'

'According to the force of things? Or against the force of things? And who will be able to stop it?'

'That's just it,' said the Seer. 'That's just it! No one will be able to stop it!'

On the eve of the day fixed for departure the group's morale was at zero. It was four miles from the village to Reggio station from which our train was to leave at eight in the morning. At the last minute the depot had sent us nine officers, of every age and type, and picked up from every branch of the army, but only so as to accompany the troops on the perilous journey through the Balkans. The staff would be reconstituted in Athens. At the Divisional Command in Bologna the lieutenant-colonel who had received my declaration renouncing my 'unsuitability' looked at me quizzically but countersigned and stamped the form without comment.

At ten in the evening I gathered together a handful of sergeants and one or two other reliable men. More than half the effective troops were missing from the billet. The lancers – whether scattered in wine-shops, huddled in ditches with girls, shouting in bars, or taking refuge in private houses – seemed to be in the grip of a sort of collective neurosis and were giving vent in a thousand unreasonable ways to the nervous crisis into which I had managed to throw them – Socrates apart.

'I am the only person here who belongs to your own branch of the army! I've been at the front already and I'm going back. It's a thing between men. You'll see that, too!'

By four in the morning, under a full moon of fantastic beauty, the trucks had rounded up most of the men and delivered them back to camp. We took the baggage of those still missing, as rumour had it that, by hook or by crook, they would be at the station in time for that train. We came across quite a few of them on our way to Reggio, some in shirtsleeves, some in a feverish state of excitement, some plain drunk. We picked up those who could no longer stand on their feet, and told the others to follow along behind us. The trucks had to shuttle backwards and forwards until the frantic work of picking them all up was finished. At half-past seven the military authorities who were to give us a formal send-off began arriving on the departure platform. Nappa was among them, as yellow as a lemon, and it was to him that I was able to report that the men had rejoined the ranks – which gave me feelings of pride as well as irritation.

From the large group of territorial officers and city authorities – totally unaware of the situation – came sounds of greeting and applause. Fascist women dressed in black clustered round the train bristling with bright or gloomy faces, and from their little plaited straw baskets distributed carnations in token of good luck.

Then the train set in motion. The gentle countryside, already marked with the sweet footprints of spring, fled past us – our comfortable motherland; warm kingdom of waters, of greenness, of peaceful mists. But the pleasure-sadness that soothed my heart came from understanding my country better now that I was about to leave it: understanding how its very essence lay in expressing itself in a continuous emanation of its power and love; but a voice that is not heard unless it is raised, unless it breaks out of the breast and flies upwards.

'Splendid!' I said to myself. 'You were looking for communication with men, weren't you? Well, here you've got an army! Come on now, Sansevero!'

THE SCREECH-OWL

The village of Krano, in Arcadia, seems to hang over the southern edge of the high plain that forms the heart of the Peloponnese, once known as the Morea. From up there you can look down on an endless landscape sloping into greenness, criss-crossed by sky-blue rivers and fading away in torrid haze towards sunburnt Messenia – all that famous land which legend and poetry tell us was traversed by the horses of Telemachus. At that height, what with the steep gulleys and unnegotiable stubble, even malaria loses something of its hold; and the parched heat hanging over the low plain is somewhat calmed.

After moving about for some months, first in Attica, near Megara, then among the pink and graceful little villas of Corinth, it was in Krano that my Command was finally established just as the new season was beginning. During that time the group had been subjected to almost continuous changes and upheavals, but there were no engagements and life was uneventful – it was rather like that period of duty inside Reggio. Major Nappa and his boot-licking adjutant had finally managed to land a soft job in Athens, leaving me in provisional command and with a sea of woes. But after nearly a year, the arrival of a new commanding officer brought about a move to a new destination, and I saw my small battalion of scarcely more than a hundred men extended even further than at Bay in the early months of the war. At Bay we were hardly beyond our own frontier, and nothing very dangerous was happening, whereas here our perilous redoubts were miles away from each other, and covered an arch of gorges from the centre of Tripolis as far as Kiparissia on the coast; they represented not so much efficient defence positions as attractive prey for the guerrillas who were hungry for food and arms.

There were seven of these redoubts, each with ten or twelve men, and their job was to guard the viaducts, tunnels and bridges of the long thin railway line which twists and turns interminably among the folds of those mountains, winds through the entire peninsula, spanning it from the canal to Kalamata. Thus the few lancers who remained at the Command with me had to supervise the stores, the arms depots, and the means of transport – when not replacing the sick or those on routine leave. An impossible task, even if they had not been incessantly on their rounds (as they were), first drawing food from the central stores then distributing it to our guard posts. The roads were bad and dangerous and often blocked; the trains had unpredictable timetables and only went by day; so that once the men had gone, they could disappear for two or three days at a time, and a second distribution of supplies was required before the first had even been completed. Then it was one thing to load sacks or hampers with supplies for a hundred men, but quite another to divide it all up into seven parts and send it off in cans and bottles; a ludicrous undertaking, especially as with the arrival of summer many provisions soon went bad in the heat. I had noticed that up till then the remedy for this untenable situation had been the tolerance of the various Commands towards raids operated by the troops on the Greeks' poultry-yards, orchards and sometimes even markets, each group thus more or less providing for itself on the spot. But times had slowly been changing as the clouds grew darker and darker over the destiny of the Axis. To embitter our relationship with the Greeks and sooner or later to incur reprisals was a risk with which I had to concern myself as a personal matter.

As for my own life, I found myself yet again reduced to almost absolute isolation, though for ever bound down by duties that broke its continuity but not my meditation. From the very first I had been moved by the striking resemblance between the natural features of the peninsula and the natural features I had known in Licudi. There were the same bare austere mountains, the same sparse but impressive vegetation, olives, vines, the reddish sand and, everywhere, the dazzling light and the distant shimmering of the sea. The strength of the plants was amazing; the geranium hedges were as tall as houses and as long as streets; the eucalyptus trees spilt cascades of dusty foliage which became all entangled with the exuberant undergrowth. The sun's silences were hallucinatory; the nights magical and withdrawn.

This filled my spirit with a secret delight, enfolded it in a sort of wide toleration, separated it off. If the Commands in Athens were living in a state of reckless euphoria, for us the war was ceasing to be an inward-looking affair (in which we had nevertheless to defend our essential if minimal positions) and direct and distinct experience was taking over, reaffirming that we alone were responsible for our actions and our lives. Nothing could have been more relevant to my thoughts and my intimate ratiocination than to be led to the places that I myself would have chosen; while my long-ago youthful affections – coupled with the sediment of culture instilled into me by the monks at my school – could be sustained by the sheer word: Greece. And in my fancy transform the whole dangerous business into a pilgrimage back to my origins – a pilgrimage rich in toil and fatigue, like the one I had made to the top of that mountain with the poor people of Licudi.

We had a Group Command too, at least in name. But if I had seven redoubts in my care, scattered over forty-five kilometres, our new major had seen his four squadrons dispersed – one to Patras, one to guard the bridge over the isthmus of Corinth, one to Nauplia on the eastern shores of the Morea, and the fourth (mine) almost to the other end of the peninsula. He was a nobleman from the Marche, a fine fellow with a strong sense of duty but already advanced in years and unsuited for work of this kind. He was decorated with the little black disc of the Cross of Malta and had had too much self-respect to evade the call-up; but his moral stamina was inadequate to the sheer physical exhaustion of his post. Besides which, he suffered beyond measure from the lack of those comforts he had always enjoyed. He had only about a dozen men with him and not a single heavy machine-gun; his liaison with us was very unstable through the spider's web of field telephones; and had he wanted to inspect the thirty redoubts of his group it would have taken no less than six weeks. Then he was in some way linked up with the higher Commands at Tripolis, but these left him in peace. When he had torn himself away from his native Jesi to come and put himself in the lion's den, the good man had provided himself with a case of Lambrusco wine which had been improvidently consumed in the twelve days' journey through the Balkans. So his hope lay in the celebrated Greek wines; though he was well aware that even the water would fail him.

I felt Christian compassion for the Major (that nobleman Costa Oliviero – hence consecrated to peace, if my schoolboy memories do not deceive me) and I relived the anxieties that must have led him to run through his precious reserve of Lambrusco during his (and my) railway journey through the Balkans. From the chaotic sorting-out at Mestre under an African sun, and then across the wild mountains of a primitive people, the disturbing spectacle became more and more apparent, that of a situation manifestly on the verge of total collapse. It was the Germans who kept guard over this railway, the only link between Greece and Central Europe; but as they were more logical than us, they were not going to waste their troops keeping guard over the thousand kilometres of dangerous railway-track separating Klagenfurt from Salonika – the seat of their High Command which was watching over the movements of the Turkish army and the chessboard of the Middle East. The Germans had merely placed large deposits of material and adequate groups of men at various key points, deeming it more practical and expeditious to repair the railway every time it was damaged rather than mount guard over its whole length and throughout the whole year. Thus there was a progressive increase of partisan activity in that barbarous country where war and brigandage were still a normal way of life, so that countless troop trains were burnt, overturned or derailed. Along the track was an unending succession of black and twisted carcasses; the night was broken by gunfire; and during the hours of darkness it was obligatory to stop, take up defence positions and pass weary hours under arms. But what had been worse was our encounter with the first Italian detachments sent to Macedonia – the strange spectacle of those soldiers crowding on to all the stations just for the fun of it and wearing the oddest assortment of clothes sometimes bordering on the grotesque: for there was hardly anything to be seen of their uniforms, nor of anything that a sane person would wear. Clad in shorts of every colour under the sun, pomaded, and chatting away like women at the market, those soldiers seemed to have lost all contact with the dangerous realities among which they lived. Our detachment, composed of veteran lancers accustomed to the iron discipline of war, seemed to belong to another army and another nation; our men stared in silent amazement at those others, while they in their turn stared back at us. It was the period when the African units were fighting in the desert with insufficient arms and their famous litre of water a day. Here was another aspect of the unfathomable vibrancy of our race, the way not only different men, but the very same men, could change direction, be transformed, be stimulated anew, according to their mood, or the situation, or the point of departure. These men were not really different from the valiant fighters in Giarabub or Tobruk; it was just that their malleability had exalted one lot to heroism and pulled the others down into licence. The duality of Italy . . . almost incapable of ordered government, yet harbouring in its bosom the most extraordinary governmental structure the world has ever seen – the Vatican. A marvellous conundrum that I love to try to solve.

As I was overwhelmed with the work of having to watch over all our men – of having to see that they did not leave the train at a halt, or barter any of the squadron's property in exchange for the cockerels or tobacco that the Bulgarian or Serbian peasant women came to offer us at every stop, or run after those easy skirts – for the time being I had almost put my own thoughts to one side; just for once, I had sunk into the way of life of those who no longer work to live but live to work, and finally lull all self-awareness to sleep in the ceaseless grind of an engine turning in a spiritual vacuum. But fortunately Nappa was now making no more demands on me; he had barricaded himself in his reserved first-class compartment, where the red velvet upholstery was, nonetheless, shiny and almost black as the result of constant wear; and anyway he knew I was looking after everything. So that compared with that troublesome business I had become involved in in Reggio, I preferred this risk and weariness for at least I could breathe within it as a man. Greece was about to be revealed to my avid eyes, my spirit knew it, charged as it was with such fantastic expectation as to vindicate even a trace of rhetoric: for it was dissolved and submerged in an utterly genuine wave of emotion. Free from the fear of death, and frequently on the watch from the observation-post at the very back of our train among the trunks and barrels that cluttered it up, I felt ready to rediscover the myths.

But our arrival in Athens excluded any such rediscoveries. Though May was only just beginning, the city was already dazzling white in the sun. Swarming like a beehive, mercantile, disordered, tumultuous, it lay like a vast theatre in which at any moment any type of show could take place. Once the first tragic period of hunger was over, a very complicated network of interests and collusions between the Italian army and the subject people had been established in the capital: a licentious and improvised Mecca of pleasure and intrigues was milked by a veritable myriad of personalities and half-personalities eagerly pouring in from Italy as from Greece itself. Of course those unfortunates who were keeping up the occupation on the rough mountains of the north or the grim plains of Trikkala and Larissa were suffering torments of melancholy and malaria; whereas our central Commands each formed a little court shot through with privileges and secret understandings, where people trafficked either openly or under cover in a hundred ways, and order and conscience were alike disintegrating beneath the hot Mediterranean sun.

For three months our group remained encamped as well as may be on the dusty verge of the road to Piraeus, in other words until the dog days of summer. We were waiting for the outcome of Nappa's manœuvres as he moved towards his twofold objective of profiting by the Command for the time being and remaining in the capital till the end; but great though his skill was for manœuvre in this type of terrain, all he achieved was to stay in Athens alone with his precious orderlies and let the four other squadrons take the road to Megara; and a few months later he handed the group over to the good nobleman Costa Oliviero. He then returned to his old love, the military police, in which he must certainly have provided superlative proof of his abilities. Once we were delivered from his hands we found it much easier to endure the killing labours forced on us by the circumstances. But the moonlit nights up in those mountains were supremely lovely and peaceful. The moon threw back the reflection of her rays as if in a triple mirror, from the one into the other two seas and above the deep shadow of the earth, and she moved in her bright course as if resounding in the skies; or was this Diana's silver bow? Or her mysterious voice drawing events and ideas up into the divine procession?

The sun was rising, its light vibrating on the bare mountain peaks in a blaze more dazzling than the sky behind them. The air was a deep ochre colour. The dark green of the vegetation was pierced by blue shadows. Up there were the heroes; Cybele's drum rolled in the forest. Immediately afterwards the sergeant on duty came to call me for the distribution of the rations, and I spent interminable hours engrossed in the endless crates of preserved foods, margarine and coffee.

The affinity of this landscape with that of Licudi (as it had been before it was corrupted) again held me spellbound in a complexity of thoughts and emotions. At certain times and at certain hours of the day a wave of that former bitterness swept over me as I beheld those lovely aspects of nature whose secret sweetness was already so familiar to me. But the unjust sufferings that we were inflicting on

Greece – we, who should have venerated her – put my own sorrows to shame and helped them to fade into proper perspective; not that those sights and scents that moved me so deeply ceased to have their effect, but I felt that through this unique ordeal at least a part of the past wanted to be restored to me.

A similar thing happened in my relationship with the lancers. I had thought that in moving out of my caste I would re-establish a pact with the common people, but even this had failed. What it did was to distance me from the soldiers. In their servility and devotion I could read the same deceptive appearances that had deluded me in my early years at Licudi. And indeed the same type of nature was to be found in the lancers who were modest country folk like the people of Licudi, obliging and respectful until circumstances – or simply their whim or inconstancy – drove them against me; then nothing would make them revert to our previous relationship. In our ambiguous position it was quite on the cards that there might be a turn or reversal in our fortunes that would put me in their power as, now, they depended on me. But even that thought was insufficient to guide me – either towards making them my friends or towards suspecting and hating them. What obtruded and put up a resistance was that thing deep in my nature which even I was unable to fathom. Thus a scrupulous carrying-out of duties, prompted by my methodical habits and instinctive love for order, produced on the plane of reason what my emotions urged me to deny; and the result was a meticulous concern for which they seemed grateful. The feeling that I had fulfilled my day in a perfect way, like the monks on the Virgo, and was achieving a busy life in accordance with a schedule that I did not even need to follow, but had prescribed for myself, brought peace to my evenings when the pure breath of the breeze touched the Krano hills. Then I stood watching the sun go down, in that same motionless and almost animal happiness with which I used to wait for the sunset in Licudi, surrounded by my household and the animals and the trees; and breathing in unison with them.

Then, though not forgetful of the past, I tried not to think about it. The difficult situation we were in, and the concealed yet certain danger that was now imminent, gradually cauterised wounds which perhaps wanted to be healed. The salt of adventure, the pepper of necessity, the ferment of obligation and action drove away the black turbid water which had stagnated for so long; they spurred on my energy; calmed my diffidence. Now I again wrote to my uncle with some hope; and he understood and answered, also with hope. In this way the slack season came to an end, and the standard of May was again raised in the heavens.

(*From fragments of my diary: Krano, February 1943.*)

One of the soldiers, a peasant from near Sinigallia, needed some tool or other, a billhook or a pitchfork, so went to borrow it from a group of Greek peasants standing a little way off and staring. And since they could not understand him, and remained silent and almost expressionless from his very first words, he began to wax eloquent, explaining that certainly he would bring it back, that labourers should help one another in all situations, that they should try to be friends: and it never entered his head that those poor wretches were unable to understand a word and that the world contained a language other than the dialect of Ancona. This soldier has a happy temperament; his name is Adorno.

Twice a month the local Command offers hospitality to a small group of applicants who are not at all military. The higher authorities, with the pious intention of 'providing for the needs of the troops', have set up a network of brothels all over Greece, and have more or less handed over their order and discipline (a very bright idea, this) to the individual Commands. In Krano the job falls to me.

The local institute is not very well provided: three girls is the usual number; but when the change takes place, between those who are arriving and those who are leaving, four or five present themselves at the appointed hour. Looking as stern as I possibly can, I examine the documents and with a glance satisfy myself that the photographs correspond with the originals. Then I sign.

In the normal way it is young women who come and not at all displeasing ones. The great hunger which followed immediately on the occupation led thousands of needy people to queue outside military messes and offer themselves for a loaf of bread. The extent of the offering explains the good quality of the product which, in normal times, would only have been found in luxury places and now is for the soldiers. But this morning there was an incident.

It was a morning of heavy gloomy sirocco and the whole place seemed frowning and taciturn under the squalls of dust. I thought I heard a sort of insistent wail between the gusts of wind, and soon I was forced to realise that it was a human sob. And we saw a woman slowly walking along against the wind, under the shelter of the wall, in the direction of the church square. It was she who was making that lament to the locked doors and windows and receiving no reply but the swirling of the dust.

Later I discovered her in my orderly room. Her daughter is one of the girls stationed here and according to service orders has to remain a while longer. She was in the room too, standing with her back to the window so that I could hardly see her face.

She had written to her mother telling her she was in regular work – as they often do to hide their real situation – never dreaming that her mother would get a pass, heaven knows how, so as to come and visit her. And the mother had found her (so I heard) in the very room where she plied her trade; which was why she had come along in that distracted way and with that wail that sounded animal as much as human.

And while I was stamping the papers, I saw her raise such a harrowed face towards her daughter, full of an indescribable look of love, shame and pity. The way I looked into my own self. And perhaps the way Mary had looked at her Son's wounds when they brought him down from the cross.

When I was at Megara I exchanged an old cloak for a sucking-pig a few days old. I decided to call him Ciccio, gave him over to the soldiers and more or less forgot about him. But he has not forgotten me. Every time I pass anywhere near his sty I can hear him running out and grunting, almost shouting. In my days in Ferrara and Largita the horses were perfectly aware of a man's rank, and if Lieutenant Binutti was in sight they stopped kicking and biting each other. But who has told Ciccio that he is alive because of my intention and patronage? And does he grunt out of jubilation? Or does he sense the immensity of the dangers, and being so alone in the world, is he trying to make his presence felt and ask for help?

*

If the surrounding woods recalled Cerenzia, and the bare mountains behind recalled Palanuda, Krano itself was not unlike any of the little villages round about Licudi. Built on the final spur of the

mountains, it was like a prow over the huge valley spreading out
as far as Kalamata and the sea, and an adventurous little road ran
through it which, after leaving the church square, ended vertically
over the void. From the two rows of houses, each backing on to the
precipitous slope, there stretched a few lateral paths, not much
more than goat tracks, and then a leap over the gorges. The railway
passed about half a mile beneath the inhabited area. My little
Command, with its small contingent of men, lived in a fine house
just outside the village, and it looked out over the endless panorama
below.

As my rank entailed my being local commander of civil as well as
military affairs, I had established the immediate contacts demanded
by protocol: the mayor Theodosius, a kind of cattle-dealer who only
knew his own dialect hence could only reward me with smiles; the
orthodox priest Zagara who also acted as interpreter; and the
policeman, who was little more than a pig-herd and recognisable
mainly by his ancient muzzle-loaded shotgun which our authorities
allowed him to keep.

The ban on holding arms of any kind was in fact one of the most
brilliant vexations of our Command, because at one time the Greeks,
as keen huntsmen, had equipped themselves with excellent guns
from the famous manufacturers in Belgium and England; com-
mandeering them became a splendid business and the trade resulting
from it flourished on the Athens market. If the Greeks concealed
them, this had very little to do with the activity of the partisans;
but the guns were the subject of equivocation beyond words if
someone interested in keeping them wanted to, and could, get the
lion's share. Even in Krano there had been an obscure incident
concerning a situation of this kind a short while before.

Standing in front of my customary chair-easel in the small
square in front of the church, a matchless vantage-point overlooking
the valley, I had taken up my painting again after more than a year.
The fear and resentment caused by my uniform for once kept
urchins and other inquisitive people at bay. As drawing-paper was
unobtainable at the local store, I had obtained some, after a certain
amount of insistence, through the good offices of the Krano schoolmistress – a lovely young girl but obviously very frightened of me.
When she suddenly withdrew she left me mortified by her fear and
my power. This was why I felt it almost an obligation to let my
paint-brushes be seen in public, knowing that I was being atten-

tively watched. It was another reminder of Licudi – except that now I was watched with the prejudice and acrimony of a Denise Digne.

Through the half-open door of the church came the voice of the priest, Zagara, conducting his service. He was still young, strong, muscular, with intense feverish eyes and long greasy hair. He spoke adequate French, a little Italian, and sometimes helped himself out with Latin. He and the mayor had been cautious at that first meeting; they had examined me with the keen penetration of Mediterranean people. Evidently my predecessors had left unpleasant memories, and I realised I would have to bear the weight, not only of that past, but of a situation that was altogether unacceptable. Zagara, the priest, was endowed with a fine baritone voice, and when he raised it in front of his square altar it could be heard far and wide.

After that first formal visit of exploration, the priest returned alone to see me. His first requests were on behalf of the village and its outskirts because the troops stationed in the area were continually raiding the chicken-runs, gardens and orchards. Zagara was respectful but not obsequious. His bright heavy eyes – like those of a Circassian or an Armenian – were continually alight with requests, hints, concealed irony. In the previous November there had been a tolling of church bells throughout the whole of Germany over the Stalingrad catastrophe. Hitler seemed possessed by incredible contempt and bitterness, almost as if the Russian resistance to his armed forces was a base revolt of slaves against their rightful master. But now the Axis troops were also having a hard time in Africa. The unheard-of strength of the American armies as displayed in Morocco was to lay them low by sheer weight. Each combatant on any given front seemed to disregard, if not positively forget, all the others; though it was common knowledge that once the fire had burnt itself out in one area of war, it moved on to the next. This time it was coming in our direction.

The priest surveyed the whole scene with calculated prolixity and tenacity, but his spoken discourse was accompanied by an important unspoken one. He pointed out that though we exacted a levy on Krano for a certain number of commodities, it lacked enough supplies for its own needs, and it was impossible to go and get them from areas under partisan control. He asked me to hand them back. I told him I needed time to think it over, then sent him away. If I decided to act in the interests of the village, and put an end to extortion and raiding, then this meant scarcity for the soldiers. Yet if I continued to be harsh towards the Greeks, then I would be risking something worse later. The conclusion, after consultation with the senior orderlies, was that we should extract by trickery from our military stores what, out of blind adherence to the lists, they were not assigning to us. As far as the Administration was concerned, the seven redoubts were scattered over three different districts, and I could get provisions in the one I viewed most suitable. We drew from all three the supplies for the whole detachment. With a triple quantity of rations, it was possible to assign double to the redoubts; and with the other third, through the priest, to set up a progressive system of exchanges between our dried foodstuffs and the fresh ones the village was able to barter. Naturally, at the first overhaul, everything would come out into the open. There was no need of the divining power of the Seer, Demetrio, to foresee the epilogue: not a single tin can would we salvage from the African armies; and hardly anyone had survived the tragedy of the Expeditionary Force in Russia, for our hundred thousand fellow-soldiers had been swallowed up by the Russian winter. The same thing would happen here. Cheered by our initial success, we drew extravagantly from the divisional stores at Tripolis – camp-beds, mosquito nets, kitchen-ware, supplies not really meant for us. The redoubts became comfortable, except for the heat and the malarial mosquitoes. Zagara was satisfied. In the village I noticed various signs of relaxation. The way had been opened to greater confidence through the guarantee of man's first need, bread.

'Commander, do you know the case of Spiropulos?' This time the mayor was there too. As I had only two chairs, I was sitting in one (compelled by protocol; I was in an official position), while Theodosius had taken possession of the other, with that wide smile of his stuck on his peasant face. The priest was standing, darting glances at me from his glinting eyes; and his wonderful vocal organs made the walls of the little room vibrate as if by magnetism. Outside, evening was drawing in.

Yes, I did know the case, alas. The house in which our conversation was taking place had previously belonged to the unfortunate Spiropulos before being requisitioned by the Command; I had been shown the walled-up niche in which the anti-partisan authorities had found four valuable fowling-pieces hidden by the Greek. Spiropulos was now in the Derveni prison.

'Spiropulos's wife and daughter,' went on the priest, 'are now at Kalamata. Second-Lieutenant Cedda of the Nuoro brigade, which used to be here, is having them protected, or so they say. And hence their position is dangerous. This would be worrying enough in itself.'

'And what else is there?'

'Look!' Zagara explained. 'Spiropulos was a rich tradesman who had retired after forty years' commerce in the Greek-Egyptian colony, Alexandria. He was totally indifferent to politics. He hid the guns because they were valuable and because he was fond of them, yet he's been imprisoned as a partisan. They say he was subjected to prolonged interrogation; it isn't clear who denounced him, and then . . .' (here the priest dulled the liquid fire of his eyes and lowered his voice) 'and then he had a way of keeping a sizeable reserve of gold in his house, and there's no trace of it. In cases of this kind the Resistance end up by intervening, even if they've been uninterested at first; and they can do that in many ways.'

'And what could I be asked to do?'

'As you know, it's almost impossible for us to move around without passports and authorisations. But someone ought to be able to help Spiropulos in his prison and make contact with his women folk at Kalamata. We know them and we don't view them as bad but only as misguided. For me these are the duties of my ministry. And I must ask you to put me in a position to carry them out.'

My visitors had been gone for some time and I was slowly reconstructing Zagara's words in my mind, retranslating and perfecting them from the mixture of languages in which they had been said, and with each examination they seemed more demanding, more persuasive; compared with this, Carruozzo's intrigues in Licudi hardly existed. Here the stakes were high: the lives of the two women who had followed Second-Lieutenant Cedda to Kalamata (and were certainly marked down in the partisans' black list); the life, the freedom and certainly the possessions of the old man; the complicated relationships between all of us and the Greeks, not only Zagara and not only in Krano; and finally, my obligations; not the ones that I could feel spontaneously as a man, but the ones thrust upon me by my function and rank. These latter were the most tiresome, and I realised that even against my will the natural effort of my mind was intent on evading them.

Our war against Greece had been unjustifiable from the start
and had subsequently become a monstrous imposition. The Greek
army had fought very well, and ours had been badly led, though
the sacrifice of the Julia divisions had saved the honour of the flag.
But in fact it was not Italy that had given Greece 'a kick in the
behind' (to use Mussolini's brutal and rhetorical phrase), for we
had descended on Athens to reap the fruits of the German victory.
As earlier in France, public opinion could hardly be on our side.

But according to the flood of gossip in the Fascist news-sheets,
this was the first experiment of high civic value ('imperial' was the
word used) that Italy was facing as she presented herself as leader
not of a colonial country but of age-old Greece. What was not said
was that the experiment was being carried out with such disorder,
abuse and corruption that it was hardly tolerable even for people
who had behind them four hundred years of Turkish domination.
Thus slowly the Resistance was building up round a Command
situated somewhere among the rocks of the Taygetus, backed by
English aid and strengthened by remnants of the Greek army that
had taken to the maquis, as happened in Italy in 1943; and the
spirit and rights were identical in each case. But there were also
political groups who exploited the situation, vaguely-defined bands
or sometimes mere brigands who subsequently fought one another.
The natural forbearance of the population, the interplay of interests,
and the endless web of erotic relationships (which had given our
army the nickname of the Sagapò – the Love Army) cast a dangerous
fog over everything. Once involved in an intrigue, it was difficult
to get out of it. The Greek Spiropulos, whether partisan or not,
was very badly off in his cell in the Derveni prison. And it was risky
to try to get him out.

I went on to the balcony from which the master of the house
must have enjoyed the beauty of the valley heaven knows how
many times. At the moment the valley was lying in deep darkness.
The sky was veiled by the vapours of summer and only the larger
stars could just, dimly, shine through.

How could Spiropulos be my enemy, and not just a man who
had fallen on adverse circumstances, even though these, if I wanted
to help him, were adverse for me too? Zagara must have been
thinking along the same lines because he was a priest. The motives
and arguments that had led us to oppress a people with the same
sensibility as ourselves and with the same, if distant, origins –

motives incomprehensible to the majority and arguments non-existent to everyone – signified to Zagara no more than one further injustice in the world to be fought mainly for the sake of the justice of heaven. As for me, who had had the rhythm of dactyls and spondees beaten into my head with the master's rod at school, how could I reject that other kind of universality enshrined in the myths which are the seed of all world history? After his life of toil, that aged merchant must have wanted to retire in peace with his women folk and his sacks of gold. He must have lived in well-deserved content until the iron hammer of war came and swept away his home. I looked at the fine olive-wood table that had once been his and I was now using. He had probably poured his precious coins all over it to count them and look at them, coins of every sort, coins such as I had seen being passed over the counters at the *bureau de change* in Athens, but with the unmistakable glint and ring of gold. I had examined the whole house, object by object, detail by detail, recognising the signs of the same labour, the same patience, the same love as had brought the House of Houses into being in the olive groves at Licudi. A sensitive hand, a mind capable of many thoughts, a fulfilled and complex life – all these were written in the choice of objects, the distribution of spaces and the skill of the furnishings. He was a man like me, who had built and lost a house like mine. Perhaps so that I should be forced to remember it? Or so that I should find the answers I needed in the sense of desecration and perfidy that breathed over this half-despoiled and dishonoured place?

Two days later the most distant of our redoubts, a few kilometres north of the ancient Venetian fortress at Kiparissia, was attacked at dusk. It was the first time; but the men were engaged for almost two hours against invisible people shooting at them from the darkness. One lancer was wounded. When morning came they found the footprints of mules in the brushwood and traces of men who had perhaps been hit and carried away. I was on the spot when the 'anti-partisans' arrived in their dusty trucks.

They were a motley crowd of the worst types, the refuse of the detachment; but according to the Divisional Command gazette their duty was 'to make the weight of reprisals felt wherever guerrillas had put in an appearance'. Dressed like real gypsies or brigands, and living in extreme licence, they had no other task but to turn everything upside-down. But this time the nearest populated centre was Kiparissia, the seat of one of our fairly important Commands which had no intention of being disturbed. So these wild men, who arrived ten hours after the skirmish when not even a vestige of the assailants remained, threw themselves at random around the cliffs, shouting and shooting. They crushed a few unlucky vines belonging to God knows who, and ended up by falling on an old peasant who was going down towards the beach with his donkey and knew nothing about anything. The cries of that ill-starred man, who was thrown from his mount and trampled underfoot like a carpet, reached even our ears. Then the trucks went swaying off though not without taking aboard, in the interests of those executors of justice, a couple of nanny-goats found grazing in the neighbourhood.

Some silence followed this episode. Krano seemed to be deserted at an early hour when I resumed my habit of painting in the little square in front of the church. Zagara came straight out of the door and sat down on the low wall beside me. After watching for a while he started to speak, and his voice coming from behind my back made my eardrums vibrate.

'We're happy that you like our village. The schoolmistress had no idea that she'd receive so many exercise-books in exchange for a piece of drawing-paper. We're grateful to you.'

The school at Krano, as I had discovered, was a fit rival to the one at San' Giovanni, above Licudi. But for a couple of years the mistress had failed to obtain even a minimal allowance of teaching materials. So the lancers, feigning a sudden love for evening classes, had got hold of a case of them from the Divisional Command: not bartered against a single sheet of drawing-paper, as Zagara had so courteously suggested, but against sheep's cheese of the most delicate quality.

'I feel sure,' the priest went on, 'that as you're living in Spiropulos's own house, our pressures on his behalf won't be forgotten. We have faith in your Command, and we are sorry to hear that there has been an incident, though it happened far away from here.'

'If it had happened here,' I answered, 'we would have had a lot of trouble in the village. But even so, the redoubt down there belongs to my Detachment; and the fact that I've done my best for Krano hasn't spared me the attentions of the Andartes.'

'Oh!' Zagara answered, 'there are bands and bands; war is war; and there might perhaps be some ill-feeling towards you about this Spiropulos business. But, all told, we didn't suffer any loss of

materials or arms, and only one slightly wounded man. And then...'
Here the priest's voice stopped.

'All right,' I said after I had made three or four brush strokes that
seemed to me good. 'The Command of the Nuoro Division has
summoned me to Tripolis the day after tomorrow because they
want a first-hand account of certain details. There'll be a place on
my transport; but you must find some plausible reason.'

The sun was beginning to get hot, submerging the valley in a
bright haze. And later, when I was in my room looking at that
olive-wood table, the priest's powerful voice came to me every now
and then as he sang lauds inside the church. It was the voice of
prayer but so warm and sunny that you'd have thought it was a
love song. And the war seemed absurd, and to have vanished.

(From fragments of my diary: Krano, March 1943.)

Yesterday morning I went with a section of my men to one of the
redoubts to change the guard. On our way we stopped at the foot
of a hill whose slopes were covered with beautifully-tended vines.
Though the grapes were bitter, there were plenty of them already
showing.

Then a woman came towards me with a look at once timid and
determined, as though she wanted to make some very bold demand
to which she had no right; and she begged me to order my men not
to damage or strip her lovely vineyard.

How many weeks have I been here? I have not yet spoken to a
single child; our dealings are only with the tradesmen who come to
negotiate the exchange of foodstuffs. I spend my days in trains, on
dusty roads, in the dirt of open trucks, among hairy men with
disquieting eyes who do the work on the railway lines. I never
hear gentle voices or laughter. Only Zagara's golden voice raised
in song, and the responses from his silvery choir; though I have
never seen what this consists of. The frightened schoolmistress who
gave me my drawing-paper is always disconcerted if we meet, and
tightens her lips. She is afraid the Partisans will think she is friendly
with us, and shave her head.

Below lies the hump of the Taygetus. When I go down to the
plain towards Meligalà I get a glimpse of it: solid, compact, and
with leafy woods lying thick over its red cliffs. Later when the colour
gets darker and stiller in the motionless enamel of the early evening,

you would think it was a mythical animal covered by its woolly coat and exhaling deep warmth and scents. It is somewhere buried in there that the Greek guerrillas have their headquarters; somewhere there lies the hiding-place of the bands and the sum of all hatred. But all the same for me it exhales 'the odour of lambs and milk' – just like Licudi in the past.

*

General Coi, commanding officer of the Nuoro Division garrisoning the central Peloponnese, was one of those men who had risen from the ranks (as they say). He had attained his lofty position through uninterrupted service since the Libyan war in 1911 (when he was a volunteer before he was twenty) up till the war in Spain, always picking up semi-official but important posts. There were six rows of ribbons on his chest, the first one – blue – bearing witness to his courage under fire. Though short in stature, he was robust and pulsating with life; and vigorous but friendly in manner. Thus did he receive me, later placing me beside him at the mess (like the colonel in Modena so many years before).

Now I have to go back a little. When we reached the Morea our group had had to halt near Corinth, and here a General even more highly placed than Coi had decided to review the troops – who had seemed to him fairly fresh on arrival but were really utterly worn out, what with the Crostolo, mobilisation, the trooptrain and the Athenian suburbs. This General was a heavy ponderous man compared with Coi's liveliness and athleticism. Weighing well over two hundred pounds, flabby, of yellowish complexion, and squeezed into a uniform that tried in vain to bestow on him a military outline, this incredible condottiere was unquestionably living in a dream-world of vanity and euphoria. Even from a distance you could catch whiffs of the strong scent sprinkled on his person – a sure sign that he must have taken full advantage of the erotic adventures that the situation permitted. I was reminded of Omobono, of happy memory: had fate assigned him a Command, he would have interpreted his position in very much the same way. And the General had in his power nothing less than the Army Corps and the magnificent headquarters at Derveni.

Having assembled the men on a dusty plain, he had ordered a rostrum to be improvised from a triple row of benches placed one on top of the other; and from this he intended to address us. But first he wanted a full-size military review, a ceremony that ended in disaster. The lancers had been thoroughly instructed in horsemanship in peace-time, and ever since the war they had mounted guard so continuously that they had positively put down roots. But if they were unprepared for this manœuvre on foot, so were the officers, and more so; and the pitiful disorder of the whole affair culminated in a gaffe as innocent as it was ridiculous – for our major, the nobleman Costa Oliviero, in bringing his troops up to the rostrum where the General was standing, told them at the crucial moment to present arms before he had ordered them to fix bayonets. So while Oliviero, his back towards us and carrying out the order he himself had given, was standing stock still with drawn sword in the regulation position, behind him a farce worthy of a French film was taking place. One man was hurriedly fixing his bayonet, another presenting arms without bayonet, while the majority were consulting with their comrades with their arms held anyhow. The very important General contemplated the whole scene with bitterness, but it did not rob him of his speech.

Unfortunately his words were not only thwarted by the wind which raised high waves of dust (and, anyway, in a vast open area such as this he would have to be a Stentor to be heard), but no sooner had he begun than a column of German tanks passed nearby, drowning all his attempts at eloquence in the infernal clatter of their caterpillar tracks. True, with an air of great arrogance, he dispatched an Ordnance Officer to halt the tanks, but as the emissary did not really believe in his errand it was ineffectual, for the Germans first stopped a moment to listen to him, then pulled down their shutters and continued on their way. So it was our Major Costa who had to bear the brunt of his superior's anger, while the lancers looked on in the worst possible humour: they had seen this kind of thing often before and knew what would follow. The story of our hopeless performance spread far and wide and finally reached the ears of Coi himself; but he assured me that it was when under fire that soldiers proved their worth; that the little guard post had behaved admirably under attack; and he gave me to understand that he was thinking of coming to visit us. I left the mess somewhat relieved. It was impossible to recall the scene at Corinth without laughing; and yet it is in that type of farce (as in the days of that Fascist boss in Milan) that the germ of our misfortunes as a nation lie; even Coi, who was not really a bad man, seemed mentally ill-equipped for a post involving responsibilities that were not purely military. Like the Fascist bosses, the Generals were none of them trained to a complex or political vision of the facts (and how were they selected?). And yet the low rank from which my Coi had risen, and of which he still had a pretty strong smell, was much better than the perfumes of that other man, which made one think he was disguising some horrible disease – following the custom of the ancient Persian satraps.

I went to call on my good Major who had established himself in a withdrawn dead-end of Tripolis, and had even found a way of avoiding the communal mess at the Divisional Command. Alone with his ten or twelve lancers and the only second-lieutenant who remained to him, the Major was living a miserable life, bewailing his Lambrusco wine and his little girl-friend whom he had left in a small apartment in Jesi, well outside the city gate, he said, with a view of the hills and the quiet Esino valley. He was much thinner and the whites of his eyes had become duller. They told me it was hard to find any food that would tempt him; and as for the wine, treated with cypress resin, he found it disgusting. So the poor man was letting himself literally pine away with sadness and starvation, like a prize animal removed from its native surroundings.

'I've heard you're behaving in a thoroughly imprudent way, Sansevero. Yours is a dangerous area, as you've seen. According to regulations, you should go around with an escort, but they tell me you go around alone. What's got into your head?'

'But I assure you the Andartes have no earthly interest in me as a person,' I explained. 'They're looking for shoes, food, and arms. If I go around with four men, that means four rifles, a certain amount of ammunition, a good supply of bread, and quite a lot of clothing. Ten or fifteen of them lie in ambush for us and it's for action. But if I go alone and unarmed, and if they get me, they will only have one pair of boots, while condemning the village of Krano to flames as reprisal. It isn't worth their while. So I go around as I do, not out of bravado but common sense.'

'You mean you go unarmed, Captain? There must be something wrong with your head! I don't even want to hear you say it!'

'Please let me explain. A gun is the main bait and I don't like taking it with me. But I've got two hand-grenades of the pine-cone type from the other war, and I take those with me. Some Alpini gave them to me on the Bainsizza. I don't exactly go around with my eyes shut, and I could place them all right. They're not recoverable afterwards; nor are the men who were in their range. And you can be sure the partisans know.'

Wearily, in a soft voice, the Major gave me explicit orders always to go out with an escort of four men armed to the teeth; and with that we parted.

Meanwhile, General Coi's little court had noticed the distinction with which he had treated me, and inferred that I had personal links with him. Thus the captain in charge of the military information service at the Divisional Command thought he had to receive me effusively; and he was even generous with information that he should not have communicated to me had he been carrying out his duties seriously.

'The Spiropulos case,' he confided to me, drawing me to one side, 'has brought Second-Lieutenant Cedda the distinction granted to those who identify elements of the Resistance by their own zeal. Cedda was more than a year in the Krano redoubt, where your men are now. Perhaps he found a way into the good graces of Spiropulos's daughter, or his wife, or both; perhaps he found out from them that there were guns in that wall, or perhaps he discovered the hiding-place himself. We don't care about details, but results; and the guns really did exist, four of them, and well provided with ammunition for boar-hunting. The law is explicit; Spiropulos is at Derveni, and now it's up to the people there to make him talk.'

The captain exerted himself so far as to look up the dossier himself.

'Here we are! Cedda later brought to our notice that the two women were suspected by the partisans so were in danger at Krano, and this was why he obtained their transfer to Kalamata, where he is now, and it's a big city. I wonder if I could ask you why you're interested in this business?'

'I'm in command at Krano, and things that happened in the past can reflect on things now. I've even mentioned it to his Excellency the General who told me to watch out. I'll let you know.'

I left my friend satisfied with this promise, and became a provisional collaborator of the Information Service as I had previously been of the Propaganda Service. At the appointed hour I met Zagara where I had put him down in the morning, outside the city.

'The archimandrite asked me to thank you,' he said. 'The visit has been useful.'

Those were almost the only words we exchanged during the interminable return journey. We had been told that the roads and railways of the upper Peloponnese had been built by Italian firms over the past ten years. But as they had been paid for by the mile, those thoroughfares twisted like snakes between the folds of the hills and seemed always to stay more or less at the same point. When I got back to Krano I noticed that I did not say to myself, 'Here I am at the Command,' but 'Here I am, home again.' And it was Spiropulos's house that was giving me this sense of comfort.

These events occurred in the spring; but with the advance of summer the fortunes of the war came to a head. The defeats in Africa were now definitive and had closed that round of the match; the Allies were now in Sicily and their control over the Mediterranean could no longer be contested. The fate of our army in Greece – an enemy country, difficult to defend and almost isolated – was becoming precarious indeed. An intolerable heat fell on the country and with it there was a premature outbreak of malaria. The soldiers manning the redoubts in the lower areas of Messina were particularly afflicted but it was impossible to remove the men owing to lack of reinforcements. Then suddenly partisan activity increased. The reckless euphoria of the Athens Commands collapsed at a stroke. The Germans, who had hitherto kept only a few troops in Southern Greece and the Morea, got on the move. But they did not come to Krano because it was hardly more than a village.

And now when I came out on to the church square to contemplate the valley as it disappeared among the fiery eventide mists, I had Zagara and the mayor Theodosius as my almost constant companions. I had performed various other services for those two. I had enabled the priest to recover some paintings on wood from an enterprising colonel who was already getting them packed up to take away; it was said that as a good southern Italian he wanted to offer them to the Madonna of Pompeii for favours received, but a sudden transfer had interrupted this charitable operation. Though the paintings were only a few decades old, the antique style had been recaptured to perfection – so much so as to remind me of the patient work of the novices at the Virgo. As for Theodosius, I was not grudging about permits for his trips to Laconia, Attica and Messina; 'cattle' he always gave as his pretext, while Zagara said 'churches'; but in fact they both unquestionably belonged to the Resistance. A current of secret thoughts had been set up between us as participants in the vast understanding of the Mediterranean, and my classical imagination enabled me to appreciate all that lay behind the mayor's shrewdness and the priest's zeal. Though extraneous to them in practice, I felt myself within their complex of words and deeds and vowed to interpreting them.

'The government,' Zagara was saying, resuming a conversation begun some while before, 'the government made use of a study prepared by an Englishman named Cockerell for the restoration of the temple. But these days the Paulista mountains are inaccessible; a pity, because the monument is wonderful.'

'Why inaccessible?' I asked, for I had pored over maps and taught myself about the area from an old guide-book. 'Our redoubt at the end of the Kiparissia beach is near the mouth of the old Neda. If I went up that valley I would soon find myself in the heart of Phigalia, between Cotylium and Asum consecrated to Black Demeter. And if I couldn't go from that direction, I could try the other, set out from Megalopolis, and reach the high plateau like that. It would only take a day.'

'Perhaps Signor Commander,' said the priest, when he had translated the gist of my remarks to the mayor, who looked on with curiosity, 'perhaps you haven't a very precise idea of the nature of those mountains, and don't realise that to venture into an area controlled by the guerrillas, and without any roads, would require considerable forces – out of all proportion for an archaeological trip.'

'Considerable forces,' I replied, 'or else one man alone. That's how I see it. The Divisional Commander wouldn't loan me a regiment, but you two could find me a guide.'

For both them and me there were good reasons for reverting to this discussion about the temple of Bassae. The emotion that had once impelled me to discover and make contact with Uncle Gian Michele's woods, was now driving me towards this new project; it was a direct challenge to circumstances and good sense, but seemed to me to combine the exercise of a right and the fulfilment of a duty. We were in Greece as an enemy occupying force, and had totally disregarded the obligation to venerate the land that had nurtured every particle of our culture. In the name of Art and Truth I was hoping to redeem the collective sin by this single unknown offering: and thus refuse to accept the sin. If Dolfo had given his life on the Goliko for the sheer exaltation of his power; if the Seer

Demetrio had used up the vital energies of perhaps a whole year of his secret existence so as to dominate weight under my eyes and thereby prove himself as worthy of life; then I should climb the mountain consecrated to myth, and place my being at the foot of Ictinus's monument and do so unarmed. The chant of the nuns uprooted from the world, as I had heard it on that distant Christmas night in the Roman basilica of Santi Quattro Coronati, became fused in my memory with those other melting chants on icy mornings at my school. There was no doubt that the devout voice of the saint alone in his cave had the power to atone for sin in God's eyes.

To these lofty flights of fancy were added other thoughts of a similar kind. A conjunction of things was coming into being, and the moment it reached completion, at that moment precisely, then I would be ready to go; like an astronomer who, at a specific moment in time and point in space, and only then, can perceive the interconnections of a star. I convinced myself that I had perhaps come here for no other reason but to seek out and achieve that unique pilgrimage; and that when I had done it everything would be decided, everything settled; and that I would be able to move off towards other points of rest. These thoughts flowed thick and fast. As night spread over the valley my interlocutors fell silent, and we could hear men's faint voices, and cowbells; and the damp twilight breeze sprang up to blow away the scorching day.

'I've heard,' I went on, continuing the same conversation, 'that Napoleon Zervas is interested in Spiropulos. The old man's fate is in the balance; but if Zervas intervenes it would indicate that relations really did exist between Spiropulos and the Andartes.'

'It's a very confused situation,' said Zagara, 'and Zervas's intervention could mean any number of things.'

Napoleon Zervas, the leader of the Greek Resistance, was naturally much discussed; many people thought he was living in Athens itself under the aegis of the highest protection. The captain of the Information Service at Tripolis had let me know 'on an absolutely private line' that someone had seen to it (heaven knows how) that Spiropulos was at least left in peace in his Derveni cell. At first he had been subjected to the string treatment (a piece of string with knots in it progressively tightened with a twisting movement round the temples) but he had given nothing away. No more was known; but perhaps Zagara was better informed than the military office.

'We've already spoken of the gold Spiropulos may have hidden in his house,' the priest went on, 'but nothing has been found except the guns. It's possible that it was, or is, in a place known only to the old man . . .'

There was a silence in which our thoughts confronted each other, trying each other out like combatants who pause for breath. Then the priest resolutely threw himself into the risk he had to run.

'Let's suppose,' he said, 'that Spiropulos promised those funds to the Resistance which certainly needed them. It would be a good motive for Zervas; and he would then have a way of getting the old man out of prison. But the difficulty lies in getting into his house, which is at the moment your headquarters as commander. The partisans would only be able to do it by force and that would involve reprisals on Krano. Of course these are only theories of my own!'

'Zagara,' I immediately replied, 'I want to visit the temple up at Bassae. Give me a guide. If I get back we'll carry on this conversation.'

The priest got up with a bow, and Theodosius did the same. And they went off without exchanging a word with each other. Mosquitoes came to buzz irritatingly round my face. On the mountain peaks, towards the north-east, an overpowering brightness announced that the moon was rising. And in my imagination there rose the noble sanctuaries sacred to Apollo Epikourios.

Acts prompted by impulse, acts that far outstrip the limits imposed by authority or convention but burn with instinct and passion, acts that challenge us to set out on an adventure, if not to achieve the impossible – these are the ones that stand out in our memory as vivid, real and unquestionable certainties. That was why, in the past, I had so often wanted to go into reverse, wanted what was forbidden, because only there could I find the authentic taste of life, something I almost owed to all the shades that had prepared its course, and to the thoughts that had consumed me. And now, in the torrid glare of July, I felt I was again entering the absurd, if only within myself and before myself; I was again being drawn to that shining point, there to anchor a great moment of my life.

I knew I could be assured of Zagara's protection, but it was he who had told me that there were 'bands' and 'bands'. He could pass the word to the regular partisans, to Zervas's lot, and to the ones

under English command in the Taygetus; but he could not safeguard me against the outlaws infesting the area, nor against the
small bands carrying on guerrilla warfare on their own account,
and those were the most ruthless. So I was committing an action
with risks on two counts; first, I was setting out on that unknown
journey without really being certain of the priest's guarantee, and
at the same time involving myself in helping him as if he had given
me this guarantee; and second, by making it possible for him to find
Spiropulos's gold (and he had not concealed from me that it would
go to the Resistance), my action had the ring of treachery owing to
my uniform; and this could rebound against my own soldiers, if not
against myself. The final knot in the tangle: the life of a man who
had been cruelly stripped of all his possessions and whose desecrated
home I had hourly under my eyes.

Moreover, I had to bear in mind that our military structure was
on the point of collapse; and that, when it came to the reckoning,
we would find ourselves alone; and each man of us would then have
to choose and provide for his own destiny. Here there were no roads
to enable the defeated soldier to escape home. Our army had already
yielded the island of Sicily to the Allies almost without a blow, so it
would certainly offer them no resistance on the coasts of Greece.
Everything was uncertain, and had many facets. And everything
could lead to a crisis of conscience, to yet greater danger, to useless
sacrifice, or to searing dishonour.

These were the arguments put forward by reason. But a secret
instinct accompanied by almost childish lightheartedness and un-
conquerable joy, made me realise that these evaluations did not
really count with me. My sense of honour was profoundly moved
by the priest's trust in me. He had placed himself in my hands and,
what was more, he had tested me with the tinkle of gold. As master
of his secrets I could have betrayed him; whereas the pride of the
Sanseveros made me, in my turn, respond by placing myself in his
hands. Moreover, I wanted him to understand the motives of what
must have seemed like a senseless action; the votive act whereby I
felt I was asking his people for spiritual forgiveness, at least as
regarded myself. It was a reconciliation for which it did not seem
excessive to risk my life, and one that should show that neither
Spiropulos's gold nor anyone else's meant anything to people who
really wished to come together over and above the prevailing hostile
circumstances – that is to say, circumstances that required men to be

enemies when they themselves wanted to be acknowledged purely and simply as human beings.

In the middle of July, after a brief visit to headquarters at Megalopolis, I returned as far as the bay of Karytaena by a military transport luckily going in my direction; and when that had pushed off into the distance I saw in front of me the little shepherd boy who was to be my guide. In the silence that enveloped us my bonds with my country, with the Army, with the whole war were suddenly severed; it was a silence so fresh and free within the scents of the wood that it seemed to belong to another world. I had been warned that the going would be extremely difficult, as all well-trodden paths, roads and villages would have to be avoided. I would have to follow cattle-tracks hidden in the folds of the mountains, and Zagara himself had given detailed instructions to the boy – a kind of Arab with bright bold eyes. And so we walked hour after hour through those deserted expanses. Sometimes I heard the rushing of a stream, the rolling of a stone; and then only the faint rustling of leaves. But as we never met a living soul we were usually surrounded by enchanted silence, and again it seemed to me that I was travelling towards another planet; and always with that indescribable feeling of happiness, so that sometimes I smiled as I went along while the most disparate memories flooded into my mind – prompted now by a hornet, now by the shape of a rock, now by a flower. It was the evening walk at the monastery on the Virgo; it was the cart high against the sky bringing the stones to build my house, with the dazzling sea lying below; it was the people of Licudi hurrying towards their Madonna over the rocky shingle of the torrent-beds, between the gleam of the water and the darkness of the shadows, in the light of the moon.

In the afternoon we rested and only began walking again with the approach of evening. Sometimes my guide paused and listened; and I too sometimes thought I heard the sound of footsteps or of distant engines down in the valleys; or sometimes, perhaps, the echo of a shot. Then silence returned and reached out ever further as the evening slowly spread around us.

And as daylight faded, an immense radiance beyond the horizon heralded the rising of the moon. It was under her guidance and in a sparser undergrowth that we climbed the final slopes; and the temple appeared before us.

We stayed concealed among the trees for a long time without

going right up to our goal, as the place was obviously used as a
reference and rallying point and also as a shelter. But later, when
the moon withdrew up to the heights and grew smaller and spread
her gentle light evenly over the milky landscape infusing it with
peace, then we crossed the clearing and installed ourselves in the
deep recesses of the temple. There were the remains of a bivouac
and a lingering smell of smoke, but the embers and cinders were
cold. The boy signalled to me gracefully to be on my guard with
both ears open for the slightest sound – and on such limpid nights
sounds carried from afar – then rolled himself up in his blanket and
fell asleep. But I communed for long with that silence, that darkness,
that void. On the dark mass of the low pillars I saw no blossoming
of shapes or designs, but I felt the emanations of the heavy heat
that they had absorbed from the sun during the day. And perhaps
because I was so tired I had a dreamlike sense of being nowhere;
of being suspended in some extraordinary entity which was the
sum of all my days, and where I had to lie motionless – like my
little guide, in sleep.

It was then that the screech-owl suddenly let out its shrill cry.
First with that double top note, almost an angle of notes, followed
by a quaver in a minor key, a plaintive echo of the first cry. Through
the chinks in the walls I saw the scorched and holy landscape spread
out beneath the radiance of the moon, prostrate before the altar of
God, whence in return it awaited its own redemption. But the
ominous and most noble cry of the bird of wisdom brought home
to me the pull towards ideal abstraction found in its devotee.
Eyes that see in the night, and the call of a solitary voice – to make
you shudder, yet to set you boldly on your way.

The return was exhausting, an interminable trek through the
desert lands that had once formed the territory of ancient Phigalia.
At last we saw the rim of the high plateau over towards the mountains above Krano; and we arrived there almost at dusk. The
lancers were waiting in some anxiety though I had told them when
I left that I would be away for the night. Zagara was not to be seen,
but my little guide – who had disappeared the moment the village
came into sight – must have informed him. Before I fell asleep – and
for a while weariness held me suspended in a sort of elation where
sounds and lights appeared to be multiplied – I seemed to hear
voices calling me by name. But though I could not distinguish them
I knew they belonged to people I had loved and lost, people

who were watching over me so that I should not lose myself.

About a week later, at the end of July, the Fascist Regime in Italy collapsed. King Victor Emmanuel, who had decorated Mussolini with the Collar of the Annunziata and called him 'cousin', had no hesitation in arresting the man from whose hands he had accepted the crown of Emperor of Ethiopia, and this inside his own palace where a guest should be looked on as sacred, under the sign of Jupiter, and in accordance with a rule that would be followed by the poorest shepherd of our mountains.

General Badoglio – an ambiguous figure for long suspected of treachery, for many years in charge of the army, and to whom were unquestionably due its lack of preparation, its disorder, and that underground disintegration bordering on sabotage – took over power and ordered the armies to 'continue the war'; an absurdity that could not stand up to the most superficial examination. I unfolded a map of the region in front of my mournful major and pointed out the reality of a situation which was precisely one of geography.

'Our links with Italy along the Balkan railway are as tenuous as a hair. Between Morea and Attica there is only the Corinth bridge – another hair. If the Allies appear on the beaches, the Athens Command will have its hands full dealing with the bulk of our army in the north up to Salonika – no more than that. Not one of our group will get back past the canal.'

'So what do you want to do? And what do you want me to do? You're a captain with ninety men and I'm a major with twenty-two. Leave the map alone and let what will be be.'

The good man was suffering badly. To compensate for his loneliness he had found a little Greek girl who could remind him of the one he had left behind in Jesi – at least this was the gossip of the Orderly Room. And this new affection now redoubled his woes by adding infinite fears and anxieties. Furthermore, as a declared monarchist and convinced aristocrat, he saw thick clouds gathering over the throne of the House of Savoy, and at the same time had to turn a deaf ear to the mutterings of his men who were becoming increasingly red and less and less subject to discipline.

'Look,' I went on, 'you're in a better position with twenty men backed up by the Division than we are with ninety divided between seven redoubts in the middle of the mountains. If the Allies dis-

embark they'll take their usual few weeks to reach the high points
from the beach; and if the bridge is closed behind us we'll have the
partisans on our backs, and we'll have to fight, ten men at a time,
against a whole country in revolution. With the Andartes, that's all
right; but with the Communist bands, or worse, the brigands, you
know what lies in store for us. It's my duty to say this because it
concerns the lives of them all.'

'So what? What?' he said restlessly, clutching at the rosette he
wore as a Knight of Malta. It was already pretty bedraggled on
his dusty jacket.

'And then keeping the men scattered like this means condemning
them to a nasty end. There's nothing more to guard now, no
bridges or anything else. Get permission to round up the detachment here, where at least there'll be a lot of us. Or let me get mine
together at Krano. The General would certainly understand this
kind of talk!'

But two days later Coi calmly came up to 'inspect' the Krano
redoubt, as he had promised. He inspected it minutely, made the
most apt observations where it seemed suitable, then gathered
together the little platoon of twelve in a heat that was melting the
rocks, first to regale them with a talk and then to make me exercise
them so that he could judge their training (he, too!). The platoon,
worn out with malaria and the heat, carried out the General's
orders but left him dissatisfied (like the other one!).

'Are you trying to spare your voice?' he asked me. 'Just you see
how a detachment is commanded . . .'

And that Divisional Commander, amused at returning to those
distant times when he was in the ranks, displayed a splendid voice
sending those twelve up and down, while all of us (including himself) had a hatchet at our throats. It would have been vain to repeat
to such a man the arguments that even the good Oliviero would
not have put forward.

The lancers looked at me pitifully. But what could they hope
from me?

That evening I told Zagara that I had to carry out some repairs
in the house of the Command, and could he find me suitable
workmen. Especially as the repairs seemed urgent.

That August was one of anguish. There were persistent rumours
that the war would end soon, and the silence of the Greeks was
heavy with implications; but for them too the hope of liberation

was accompanied by fear of the problems involved; countless was the number of those marked out by the Resistance as collaborators with the enemy, if not outright traitors. Our army on its side was enfeebled and corrupted by two years of collusion and malversation and had no power to pull itself together: a mass without a soul, heavy with burdens and destitute of energy. General Carlo Geloso, rumoured to be King Victor Emmanuel's natural brother, who had been living luxuriously in the princely villa of Cape Kavouri among incredible dissipations and secret extortions, found himself succeeded (after a sensational and discreditable inquiry) by a good man, but not much more; a man, in other words, of the type of my Major Oliviero, who was far indeed from that greatness required for taking control of situations which by their very nature called for the mind and spirit of an ancient Roman consul; and there were hundreds of higher officers who, like Nappa, had intrigued for a post in Athens for their own profit but were now trembling in their shoes; it was they who had reduced our army in Greece (the Super-Grecia) to the weak and bloated monster that it was. The Germans, on the other hand, far from showing signs of doubt, every day brought fresh and powerful troops to Morea and the beaches; on the one hand foreseeing our defection, and on the other determined to hold the country. A new and unexpected danger, as the conflict between these two forces – of which ours was superior in numbers, theirs in readiness and close-knit structure – would have given rise to chaos, especially with the unpredictable attitude of the Greeks thrown in.

From the fragments of the diary I kept at that time, I have found the following:

Krano, August.
Malaria has struck down two-thirds of the men; it is impossible for me to replace the sick at the guard posts; and, consumed with fever in a heat that has reached 40 degrees down in the valley, we live in a sort of hallucination, our arms reaching out to the machine-gun. Most of the troops have been away from Italy for about three years; the desire to put an end to it all has assumed the force of an intention. Fed up with the absence from their families, with inertia, with their own deterioration, the men look longingly towards the oasis of home so as to rest at last and find themselves again.

My contacts with Zagara are rare now. I have given him a mule and it may be that he visits the chapels in the mountains and makes his golden voice heard there. As for myself, I am doing all I can to stock up the redoubts with food and ammunition so that they will be able to manage as well as possible when they find themselves isolated, as I foresee they will.

Lying on a piece of tent canvas drenched with my sweat, in the infernal heat of the valley where I often have to spend the night, stunned with quinine yet aware of the hum of fever in my ears, once again I am faced with a mysterious haze, an enigma of arguments, an obscure turn of events in which no single thought can get the upper hand and no intention really formulate itself.

A few days ago, at a specified hour, I sent four of the nine men remaining at the Krano Command out on a fatigue; three to the redoubt on some pretext; the rest to the village. Then two Greek workmen turned up to do the repairs about which I had consulted Zagara, and they carried them out in less than half an hour in one of the store-rooms, while I remained alone in my office. One of the two saluted me with a nod of the head on departure, and I had to admit he had a certain style. His shining eyes and lean taut face, coupled with the deep eye-sockets, bore witness to a harsh life; but his noble bearing was not that of a peasant. Perhaps the partisans thought I wanted to make friends of them, now that our cause was lost. I know that I was not thinking of myself at all, but of things as they appeared to me, with myself removed: of the ninety men whose fate lay more or less in my hands; of Spiropulos's freedom, paid for after all with the gold belonging to him alone; and especially of Greece, and its ancient face of wisdom which I had glimpsed that night behind the screech-owl's cry. Doubt as to the motives and justice of my actions – that is the highest price I ought to pay. So my glance answered the glance of that man. In the evening Theodosius brought me another piece of drawing-paper on behalf of the schoolmistress. He begged me to do a watercolour of our headquarters which had formerly been Spiropulos's house: to keep, so it would appear, among his records.

Shortly after this there was another incident: the fifth redoubt guarding the railway bridge over a remote ravine can be reached only by the railway itself. I often go there in an antiquated steam train which puffs away when climbing and goes too fast when descending. Sometimes there are crowds of Greeks in the goods trucks; I am often alone with them, in an unlit truck and at night.

Then I have to order them all to huddle up on one side of the truck while I sit on the other side with my torch pointing at them and those two famous hand-grenades within reach. Those faces, white with exhaustion in the beam of the torch, worn out by their wretched lives, return to my memory like ghosts.

When I arrive I stop at the signal-box lying in that remote corner of the mountains, five minutes away from the redoubt and the bridge. I return there to wait for another train to take me back up the line and sometimes the wait is long. The signalman is exactly like our Calabrians; massive build, highly coloured complexion, moustaches like King Umberto, cheerful loquacity. It all reminds me of those little stations on the line rising from the Ionian Sea towards Melito di Portosalvo, around Tropea. I had already got my tongue round a few words of Greek – or perhaps, without knowing it, of dialect. In any case I talked as best I could with that man.

Last time the train was late and deep night had fallen; in the increasingly solemn silence we, too, ended up by having nothing more to say. When at last I reached the Command two hours later a telephoned message from the redoubt was awaiting me. Aroused by gunfire, the lancers had gone down to the signal-box and found the signalman shot by people who had already got away. It was said that the man was involved in some sort of denunciation or spying, but the people who killed him must have waited for me to leave, with the deliberate intention of not touching me. Perhaps I am already in Zagara's debt, and this weighs on me.

Towards the end of August Spiropulos was released; it seems that he is safe in Athens and that his women are now with him. But Lieutenant Cedda has fallen victim to an ambush on some country track, beneath one of those tall geranium hedges that blend so nobly with the cypresses of the Peloponnese. Why is it my destiny to be involved in the destiny of others, when I feel it to be so extraneous and remote?

Yesterday a lancer arrived here from the redoubt on the beach at Kiparissia which has already been attacked once; he had fled from his post. He was trembling violently as he told me a tale of assaults and deaths; and yet nothing had in fact happened. This stifling heat coupled with the delirium of fever fills the silences of the midday sun with frightening spectres. And the night, infected by the malarial mosquito as it may be, is not long enough.

Athens, September 3.

At noon on the last day of August I dropped in unexpectedly at the military command at Meligalà. It had for long been in the hands of a captain who disposed of a whole company of infantry in this small town of little pink houses basking in the sun; he was a stupid man who had committed countless abuses earlier on and now could not conceal the panic that beset him. He had shut himself up in a real and proper redoubt and one had to wind one's way along a trench to find him. My visit and his good manners were decisive for his destiny and certainly had a modifying effect not only on mine but on that of everyone bound up with mine at that time. Fate?

When I left after lunch the captain took it into his head to accompany me outside the trench and towards the apparently deserted square lying in the burning midday sun. We were hardly in the open and taking leave of each other when I saw a dark object plunging towards us from the top of a roof. I leapt into the trench. I saw him fall, and it was certainly to him that the attention of the Resistance had been directed. A few hours later, before making contact with my own men again, I ran into the good Major Oliviero at Tripolis station. Patiently and without irony he made what would also have been Uncle Gedeone's comment:

'You see! They used a hand-grenade on you this time!'

That night I reached Hospital No. 536 in Athens wearing only trousers, boots and a shirt. With commendable perseverance a tiny splinter of metal has again lodged itself in that battered left eye of mine. The other wounds are not much more than bruises. As for the captain of Meligalà, he is dead.

In the torrid breath of the late afternoon the muslin curtains – which formed a very high, threadbare and somewhat dusty wall – scarcely trembled. From beyond the residences disposed around the king's former palace, from the squares in front of it, and from the low gardens, there rose a confused clamour which sometimes grew fainter and then swelled again to fill the spaces, like smoke from a bonfire which now curls thinly and then picks up and swirls thickly around, according to whether the wind clamps down on it or kindles it. And smoke indeed was rising from distant points in spirals and curtains and clouds, mingled with indefinable scents and continually hanging over and permeating that vast tide of shouts and noises which seemed to come from a countless crowd running through the city; a city, perhaps, with doors and windows thrown open, not because of merry-making and gift-offering but owing to abandonment and fear.

The architecture of the hall was of the majestic Wagnerian school where heavy German fin-de-siècle blends with classical art, but the hall itself, though immense, was denuded. Weighty glass showcases contained bronzes, marbles and earthenware, but the collections had been ravaged and decimated, and though efforts had been made to cover up the empty spaces, the dust made them all the more obvious. Mr Niko was standing humbly before me, waiting. His striking ugliness was redeemed by his discreet but penetrating eyes and his exquisite manners; at first sight one would have said that he was a retired don. His French, which he had learnt from books, sounded very pure in as much as it was academic.

'My cousin,' Madame Theodora interrupted, 'is convinced that you should decide quickly!'

Unlike Niko, Madame was large and masculine and unquestionably suffered from diminished feminine appeal owing to the down that darkly adorned her upper lip and cheeks, but to the entire advantage of her energy. Nor did this deprive her of style; and her interests, in the days when she had had them, would certainly not have been of the kind limited to words.

Imprisoned in my uniform, I felt distinctly uneasy in front of them, so said nothing. The black eye-patch over my ill-used eye must have endowed me with a heroic aura – in very poor accord with the circumstances. It was through the good offices of the Archimandrite of Tripolis and Zagara's unexpected solicitude that I had my letter of introduction to these two people. I was meeting them for the first time; and cards needed to be put on the table.

'Look,' Mr Niko went on affably, 'it's impossible to know what's going to happen, but it's certain that the alternatives to be faced will be serious. At least you're in a favourable situation, even if it's against your will, because you have only yourself to answer for and not any troops. That simplifies a lot of things, because nowadays anyone who's alone is lucky!'

'Think it over,' Madame Theodora advised, 'and have the courage of your convictions. We have at our disposal the entire wardrobe of our relations who have taken refuge in Egypt, so why not take a civilian suit for the time being – it could be useful; and then if you prefer to come over to us, who's going to make an issue of it with all this confusion!'

As I was walking up again towards the hospital, the tumult from the city followed me and hung over me, the shouts coming more quickly now with the approach of dusk. The armistice had been announced three days ago and the bottom had fallen out of everything by now; but at least in Athens the outward structures still remained, even if they were tottering and cracking up in unprecedented clouds of confusion and disorder. The huge and already finalised event was crashing headlong all around us, incredibly swift and as if static owing to the immensity of the void: millions of age-old episodes, millions of age-old intentions circumscribed by the occasion. That very simple definition of history – 'how things really happened' – posed the whole problem of it yet again; no mind would have explained, or even registered, a chain-reaction of numbers capable of thus committing the nations. It was so often impossible to verify a single small detail of the communal happening. Who, with such an infinitude of motives put forward to obscure it, who would have been able to bring the truth up from the bottom of its well and lay it bare?

Thus with no regrets I felt my mind turning away from relentless reality so as to find refuge – then as now – in the only authentic history possible to it: the secret, sweet, destructive history of itself; the only one really known in its smallest events, its subtlest motives, its imperceptible links; which was nothing compared with that other history, yet nevertheless was so drawn into the myriad of existences above its own tiny wave that it seemed its source and then its head. An interminable river but made our own again in desire and memory, and if only because of that little trickle of water necessary for our own minimal life.

It was already a week since the eye doctor – a major – of Hospital No. 536 had removed the small splinter lodged in my pupil. As he was manœuvring his instruments he pressed on my eyeball so as slightly to distort it, and this produced a corresponding distortion of everything I saw: a phenomenon usually brought about by nausea, but in me, by association, provoking it. I then fell victim to the well-known chronic pessimism of oculists; it is my opinion that in some obscure way they are infected by the fear and sadness staring at them in close-up from the tearful or bloodshot eyes with which they have to deal; and in any case on this occasion the Major had no particularly cheerful news to impart,

'It's an ill-wind that blows nobody any good,' he said as he went on exploring my eye with his lenses and waving his treacherous instruments about in the air. 'You're now going to get a splendid six months' leave and a visit home before everything here collapses.'

'It's collapsing as soon as that, is it? And what about my men stranded in the depths of the Morea mountains? Who's going to help those poor fellows?'

'Certainly not you!' he said, shaking his head lugubriously. 'You must keep this eye shut for at least two weeks and do as little as possible with the other one. Heaven preserve us from a complication which could lose you both of them!'

Relieved of the splinter but fed up to the teeth with ill-humour and boredom, I had then returned to the darkness of the little room and stayed there for four days like a bat hanging by the feet from the stalactites of a cave. Four days – each one bringing us nearer, though we were unaware of it, to that inevitable collapse. And when the bandage was removed at least from my good eye, I was able to occupy that slender thread of time – having no idea that it would be the last – in writing to my good Major, to tell him it was useless putting me in charge of the baggage as in any case I would first be going to take leave of my detachment. He sent me a phonogram wishing me a good recovery, and before that he had given me an introduction to the personal attaché to the commander-in-chief o our army in Greece. Those were the parting shots of that modest member of the flock of the Cross of Malta, and he wasted them on me whom he was never to see again. It was the 6th of September.

Next day, in defiance of the oculist's explicit orders, I went to call on the attaché. Like me, he was a mere cavalry captain but had avoided military service thanks to protection from on high; he received me in the vast neo-classical building of the General Headquarters, in surroundings that were luxurious but dark owing to thick curtains and lowered lights. He made no mystery of the rumours spreading like wildfire through the town. An important personage had arrived a few hours before on a secret mission from Rome and was still in conference with His Excellency. Something was on the point of happening. I asked him to release me from hospital and send me back to my men.

'Don't move from here!' he cut me short. 'You must leave your

detachment to others. Where do you imagine you can go with
only one eye?'

So making slow progress through the tumultuous crowds throng-
ing the marble pavements of the main thoroughfares, I set off to
find an attaché at the Legation – a contact of my own this time.
He lent me a shirt and a jacket, and when I had exchanged the
ostentatious hospital bandage for a narrow black band I went back
into the street. I was so unused to civilian clothes that they seemed
very light, almost as if I had nothing on. But the weight of the heat
and the intensity of the noise and lights bewildered me. An enormous sense of freedom invaded my breast, as when one goes out
for the first time alone. This detaching of myself from the war, as
the product of active desire and an exercise of my sovereign power
(an action which my mind had anticipated in conceiving the idea
of the expedition to the Bassae temple), was now becoming more
clearly defined. And the immense drama into which Italy was about
to plunge dazzled me as if it was her very liberation that was in
question, whereas really she was about to pass over to the other side,
the side of the conquered and the oppressed, and I was about to
pass over with her. It seemed impossible that my heart should be
so light!

I shall never forget that summer evening! I was as unknown and
unattached as in those early days at the Roman hotel up among
the swallows, and again I was separated from everything, though
not by my own will this time; and with yet another deep dive into
my memory I discovered the resourceful delights of the little boy
intent on exploring and exorcising the big house at San Sebastiano;
the little boy turned into an unknown, unseen spirit, and gifted
with nothing save the mysterious power of penetrating and understanding.

The city was noisy and brightly lit and in a great state of elation,
hot with the summer heat and feverish with the imminence of a
crisis towards which the collective soul was already moving and
preparing itself, like a choir about to give voice. Owing to the ready
intuition that runs through a crowd when great events are pending,
everyone knew that shortly they would be living not as subjected
to a demon but as protagonists in an important page of their history;
that in the narrow space that was to contain the conquered and the
conquerors, their real substances would have to face each other and
come to grips with each other and express some measure of absolute

value that was over and above force: as a proof of mind and civilisation. And the swelling excited throng was already assembling and forming the first and most certain images of that foreknowledge. One's glance slipped behind the rhythm of the footsteps on the marble paving-stones: perhaps they were stained with crimson as evidence of the many who had fought over them in the final convulsion during the famine. And perhaps there was no stain but only the venerable stone washed by water, the sun and time.

And so in my inner transport and emotion I spent perfect hours mingling in that vast tumultuous concourse, abandoning myself to its vital flow, breathing in the pulsating life of others from which I had been excluded for so many months; and from every word, gesture and look, gathering in the warmth of affections which I managed, as the moments passed and in the mediation of the hour, to welcome as if they were my own. Later, in a crowded popular theatre, I felt I recognised in the participation of the people with what was going on on the stage a sentiment well known to our old dialect theatre. The actors' attitudes, their mimicry, the human and complex expressions on their faces, the propriety and gentleness of the women, they were all a mirror of my South. And I could almost understand the words, so close and akin to me were the situations and the plot.

This immense Mediterranean nation – the only one which under an infinite diversity of laws has progressed through the centuries following the same way of life, and spreading from Alexandria to Algiers, Barcelona and Marseilles – welcomed me as a fellow-citizen in that little theatre, as it had welcomed me already in Omonias Square where a beggar-boy, differing from those in our country only as to language, had beaten his brushes on his shoe-shine box in pride at polishing your shoes – not out of servility but so as to earn his crust of bread like a bird and add to his city's lustre through your elegance. When I went back at night – again wilting under the heavy, almost insupportable weight of my uniform – I was followed from inn to inn by the persistent noise of guitars and the rustle of couples in every house, in every street, among the trees: the implacable advance out of war and towards love.

By sundown next day the Italian State had disintegrated. As for the nation, no one could speak for it as a whole, but individual histories were going to be unfolded for several years to come. Silence and alarm had suddenly descended during the night while from all sides the German tanks could be heard rumbling in – they were looking for an enemy, but no enemy showed itself in the darkness. My thoughts went to Uncle Gedeone, waiting at his post in the light of the tallow candle; and I responded to him with an intensity and vigilance of my own, for my courage was due to his. I felt I was ready for anything, rather like the migrant driven across the seas.

Whereas the German forces in Italy, galvanised by Hitler and determined not to give up a single strategic bastion in the peninsula, acted swiftly and resolutely with regard to the Italian army, and to a large degree were helped by those who remained faithful to Fascism and thought it dishonourable to abandon their ally before the outcome of the war was finally decided – it was all very different in Greece. Here, the Commander-in-Chief of our army, if he had had the capacity and the energy to lead, was in a position to disarm the Germans (at least in southern Greece), to close the roads below Salonika to them, gather together the bulk of his army, and treat with the Allies for a reasonable and ordered surrender according to the terms of the armistice and with a laying-down of arms.

Perhaps some time in the future the calamitous history of the secret pacts between King Victor, Badoglio and the Allies will throw light on why the orders transmitted to the good Vecchiarelli should have served to paralyse our troops, throw them into equivocation and then chaos, and finally hand them over, defenceless, to the very men who, previously, far from hoping for an incredible solution like this, had been trembling in their skins. Between those early days when many Germans deserted or tried to escape towards Turkey, and the last ten days of September which saw three hundred thousand Italians dispatched like sheep to Germany and a fate that was to mow down twenty per cent of them, only two short weeks had flowed through the hour-glass of time; but they were of a passion and exaltation that verged on madness.

Ever since the evening of September 11, and as a result of the mysterious treaties ratified between our army in Greece – the Super-Grecia – and the German command, the men of our army knew they had been abandoned. The Germans were already coming forward in small groups to demand the surrender of whole regiments, and if there were individuals who felt scalding tears of shame, everyone could nevertheless see that the bonds of discipline had broken down, that the military stores had become 'res nullius', and that there was no longer any need to render an account of anything if accounts were not even rendered of the arms entrusted to the flags. A process of dissolution substantially the same in Greece as in France, and to a great extent in Italy herself: because that was the genuine 'historical' result matured in its good time. By collective consent – amazing in a people chronically hostile to any sort of unanimity – it was in fact agreed from Toulon to Leghorn and as far as the Piraeus, that rather than hand over anything to the others (whoever they might be) it was better to use everything for one's own greater good. The black market sprawled over the Athens pavements (where I had imagined blood!) with the new vital urge characteristic of Greece's flexible and mercantile soul. Our peaceful dissolution seemed adequate satisfaction for a breed aware of its deep links with us; while allowing it that smile that demolishes honour and avenges the past better than reprisals.

Then over and above all this, individual passions burst out, the lust for money and the thousand other manifestations of an excessive conglomeration of human beings. The slopes of the Lycabettus were crammed with couples making love – the incalculable coin of forgiveness spent to make mockery of the hate between men – while archives were burning at Command headquarters and disquieting hordes of people freed from prison heralded the looting and general uproar. Meanwhile the Germans in silent scorn looked after what was essential, namely that that dangerous mass of men should be removed; and they did no more than put them on troop trains. Only where there was no forgiveness was there a flow of blood. Relentless news reached us from Italy: the Allies were above Salerno; and perhaps that stretch of olive grove that had once been mine was re-echoing to the cannon.

The second time I went to see Niko he introduced me to an important Greek whose credentials, however, he did not vouchsafe. I found the two of them waiting for me in that stripped room among the dust-covered antique collections. I was still in uniform, but had been totally unable to glean even the slightest news of Major Oliviero or my squadron, all contact with Morea and the Islands having been cut off for some time now.

The unknown Greek greeted me with deliberate courtesy; then, while Niko remained motionless with his thoughtful eyes lowered, he said:

'My cousin has told me all about you. The Germans have pledged themselves on their General's word of honour to repatriate your army; but we all know that the General's authority goes no further than the frontier. It won't be him who receives the troop trains or is in charge of them once they're out of Macedonia. And so . . .'

While speaking he looked me straight in the eyes, as I did him. In his greyish pupil there lurked a tawny glow as with birds of prey. His Italian was correct and yet it aroused in me an inexplicable irritation I would find it hard to describe. Madame Theodora came in.

'And so,' she said, resolutely concluding his remark, 'the Italian army will end up in the concentration camps of Northern Europe. Hitler is raging against you and calling you all traitors. So just when the Germans are involved up to the neck controlling the situation in Italy, it's hardly likely they'd agree to hundreds of thousands of disbanded men arriving . . . The Salerno landings have split the peninsula in two. Where do you imagine all the Southerners in your army going? You must sort that one out for yourself, here.'

'The Germans,' put in Niko in a low voice, 'are offering to incorporate in their own army, with equal rights, anyone willing to make a declaration of loyalty to them. This may be displeasing to your ears, but inside information has it that they won't put any trust in the Italian elements, not in any circumstances. They'll leave them unused in some backwater. But still, it's better than the camps.'

'Then there are always possibilities of escape,' the other Greek went on. 'Not as some are doing, by putting their faith in unknown traffickers, which can bring them assassination on the high seas, or as has happened – robbery and abandonment on some deserted beach here in Greece. But the partisans would be very ready to receive skilled and determined volunteers for their operations against the Germans. Or alternatively it would be possible to treat with them and with their help get through, for instance, to Egypt.'

He then felt like a busy man who has things to do, but as he took leave of me he already knew he would never see me again. A light cloud passed over his face signifying both irritation and resignation.

'And you must remember,' added Madame Theodora, 'that your life is worth something.' She and Niko both insisted that I should take a civilian suit with me and she packed it for me in a knapsack. She looked at me from eyes now slightly opaque and melancholy, and I saw memories pass through them that both moved me and humiliated me although I could not quite understand them.

I went on thinking about those two when again entombed in my small dark hospital room – this time not to please the oculist but in order to concentrate. They knew what they knew through the good offices of the Archimandrite and Zagara. The man I had met was certainly a Resistance leader and would have helped me on this occasion for nothing, or so I believed. But then was this really for the best?

Madame Theodora seemed to value my life, but what did she know about it? I had wasted it three times in its brief span: first in Naples, then in my disorderly youth, then at Licudi; always finding justifications and always without remorse. And what had I to put on the scales to counterbalance these turbulent fancies of my mind? My private sorrow? But this in its turn had become bound up within me as a force of inflexible obstinacy and ruthless contempt. All I had needed to quieten my mind for having allowed the partisans to get hold of the gold that went to pay for the Resistance – the Resistance against which I had been called up to fight – was a solitary pilgrimage to the ruins of a deserted temple. Was it an aspiration to sovereignty, or an absurd flight of the imagination?

Hundreds of thousands of men were now drifting and swarming like bees whose hive has at last caught fire. A miserable horde scenting profit, or a scarred and wounded mankind whose sufferings and despair had to be shared and examined just this once? The vast sediment of differences and contradictions deposited within it by the centuries was evaporating like the last speck of foam on a burning rock. Was there a need to forget charity for this reason? St Paul's epistle did not ask for a judgement to carry it out but only concern and affection. And even if Christian warmth were lacking, man's patience could suffice to take its place.

As for myself, I had not risked my epaulettes so that the Andartes should be my friends, but for the sake of that poor old prisoner whose life I understood because it was written into the walls of his house. If I now accepted some kind of reward then I would belie the nature of my action, I would feel some kind of betrayal within me. The man dressed up as a workman who had come to do my repairs and scrutinised me when leaving the Krano headquarters with his little sack of gold hidden in his labourer's haversack had questioned me with his eyes. And he had received confirmation of the answer I had already given him.

On September 18 I went for the last time to visit His Excellency's attaché. It was ten in the morning and the military police on guard at the gates of army headquarters let me pass as though they had not seen me. The ordnance officer was not there. While I was waiting in the half-darkness of his room I saw a German junior officer advancing silently in colonial shorts, revolver in hand, followed by two of his men, walking stiffly and cautiously with sub-machine-guns under their arms. Without a word those three men entered the General's office. A moment later he came out and I saw him. He was a white-haired man but with a strong pink face; a kind of good country uncle on whose countenance I read little more than surprised vexation. He crossed the anteroom under my eyes, always followed by the three. The military police had disappeared from the gates. The general headquarters were empty.

Back at the hospital two hours later I heard voices outside my small window – a window that had been shut for days because of my eyes, so that people in a little inner courtyard of the building must have thought they were alone. From this peephole I could see a group of hospital orderlies haggling in undertones with some Greek women over one or two half-open boxes.

The sun was still high, and as the light fell slantingly between the white walls of the courtyard it lit up with vivid colours the strips of cloth which were the object of this cautious bargaining. It was a business of flags. The orderlies were carefully sharing out the three strips of cloth, the red, the white and the green, and were making them up into compact little bundles to sell to the purchasers. From without came the distant but intense noise of the feverish Athens sundown.

That evening I took Niko back his civilian suit and he presented me with a spoon, a soldier's prime need but a thing I lacked – he took it at random from his untidy table. No words passed between us, but his eyes moistened when he embraced me. Madame Theodora was silent too, and this time her eyes were lowered.

On an open truck among unknown people, and having adequately tightened the bandage over my wounded eye, I left for the North without any reservations and in summer uniform. There had been an absurd farce at the station at the last moment. Two Greek girls disguised as soldiers had tried to follow an elderly colonel who was their protector (towards Italy, as they thought). They were discovered by the Germans, however, and as we left were leaning crying against a wall, amid jeers and jostling, their hair (which had given them away) now falling loose and long over their too-large army jackets.

THE MUSHROOMS

If the story of a life is to be sincere, it must obviously include the story of its areas of darkness – which, in man's moral world, are so vividly intermingled with light, for not only passion but thought itself lives in a perpetual alternation that permits of no monotony. But when one descends from the realm of fantasy and romance, the texture of life as it appears is grey and drab indeed. Modern society has worked so hard to repress the personality that events themselves are hardly marked, and the fury with which the gossip columns are followed merely indicates the emotional poverty of the masses. So from the point of view of its colouring at least, this story now needs in some way to be darkened; for at that time even great events – events tragic in their causes and consequences – took place in an atmosphere of humble greyness. For though the Germans surrounded the destiny of millions of men in an aura of blood, though they brought death to Russian prisoners and Jews and slavery to countless others, the prevailing atmosphere was one of pallid gloom. An infinitude of mankind was extinguished without beauty and with the help of almost mechanical means. And as for the common prisoners, who were excluded even from the glory of extermination, they were left to rot in a swamp. Nothing was less theatrical than that slow degradation against the background of that mournful northern landscape. But in giving the picture of a life we cannot leave out the dark hours, still less the merely dull and ordinary ones – of which our life mostly consists.

I am not applying these maxims to my own particular life, for neither at that time (nor at others) did it follow the rhythm seemingly laid down for it; but sometimes the history of others has precedence over our own; and in the perpetual duality of the mind – which can participate in events, judge them, but also passively endure them – there can occur periods and events wherein contemplation so engrosses the mind as to make it almost forget itself altogether. And so it was with me then. I had embarked on the communal adventure of my own free will, but this was the first time that I was prepared to resign my will to it. And at once I became aware of how easy it was simply to drift with the current and allow it to carry me along. In the past my life had often seemed to others as one lacking either aims or obligations, but I now saw it for what it really had been: a continual struggle. Conversely, others saw this period of the war as one of bitter pain and appalling danger (and later described it as such), whereas to me it was an endless time in which my thoughts could grow more deeply and my eyes see more truly – owing to my freedom from any complicated involvement of the mind.

At the same time I made a more searching examination of my behaviour. At first I had thought that in sharing the communal fate I was making an act of humility and mortifying my pride, but perhaps this explanation was not quite as genuine as I intended it to be. Like a strong high-flying bird who lands in a barnyard of domestic fowls, I was torn between a certain sense of duty – because I could easily have helped the others with no trouble to myself – and the desire to lie low and remain at the communal level and position. I looked for other points of reference: the saint who is a pastor and figure-head to men yet out of self-abnegation wants to make himself last when he is obviously first; Diogenes in his barrel, yet nevertheless passing judgement on Alexander; Socrates' resignation which brought the worst accusations against his judges – all these examples pointed to the same thing, namely a humility hardly distinguishable from pride. I was not sure whether I should ignore my faculties (and thereby fail to perform the duties they entailed) or exercise them by putting myself forward as a prop to others, and thereby again move into leadership. I felt that in the whole business of teaching or preaching or even setting an example there was a point of balance very difficult to find: between serving good in the abstract and imposing oneself as a person. This was why Christ commended the poor in spirit rather than saints, thinkers or poets. I was familiar with emotional duplicity, with confusion of thought, with the near-impossibility for a cultivated mind to reduce itself to elementary purity – the only kind that has value. I lay inert on the hard wooden floor of the open truck as it climbed with dramatic slowness towards the ambiguous North, and half-masked by my bandage which for want of any other possible treatment I had decided not to remove from my wounded eye, and as I lay all these thoughts passed through my mind; while all the thoughts that were ravaging my companions – regret, indignation, homesickness, hope, fear – were indifferent and extraneous to me. And I felt I ought to reproach myself for this, while realising there was nothing I could do about it.

Meanwhile, having been enlightened by Niko and Theodora, I knew full well that the whole army was on its way to captivity, but I had to keep this knowledge to myself. The Germans had behaved with fox-like malice. Nearly all our soldiers had been away from their families for at least two years so were only too ready to believe the promise of repatriation (which had been given), for nothing is more easily believed than what is ardently desired. The Germans knew this. Thus our troop-trains crossed the Balkans free from any kind of guard; the immense illusion of our men was quite enough to keep them chained to their seats. Tito's partisans came up to the trains and told us that we were heading for the barbed wire in Poland; but no one believed them. And in any case, who would have left a troop-train to all appearances on its way home, and leapt out into those barren mountains to throw in their lot with the partisan bands – as little to be trusted as any other kind of betrayal? Perhaps it was the need to cleave to their illusion that drove many of our men to throw foresight to the winds and get rid of their belongings – food reserves, blankets, overcoats. It was mid-September and still hot in the land that had once been Serbia, and many of the men thought it pointless to hold on to their unbearable uniforms; or was it that they wanted to burn their boats in a vague hope of overcoming their fears? So for two weeks hundreds of troop-trains rolled up towards Austria, and once they had crossed the frontier there appeared the barbed wire, with the searchlights, the machine-guns on guard-towers, the police-dogs; and such shattering disillusion that no one dared to admit it even to himself on that first night. There was silence.

But when morning came the new reality had to be looked in the face. The other ranks were immediately sent off to hard labour in appalling conditions, while the officers seethed with indignation. In Greece – as in France, where things had happened in the same way – they had handed over their arms in return for a promise of repatriation, so they now saw the Germans as betraying the word pledged by their commanders in military honour. But these promises had been made in distant territories by local authorities and no one seemed to have heard of them in the Reich. Here, the Italians were regarded as traitors to the alliance and had to answer for it themselves. Those first assembly camps and sorting-out centres in Lower

Bavaria were run by low-grade troops and highly politicised young officers who tested our sincerity, with typical northern simplicism, by asking us if we wanted to go on fighting alongside them. To our negative reply they responded with contemptuous silence or dark threats, while among ourselves the chorus of argument and lamentation reached the rhythm of Babel. The equivocation was basic, but after pressures and exhortations which sometimes reached the grotesque, a modest percentage was persuaded to join the German cause, and these new collaborators took the way of Innsbruck and North Italy (their lives thereafter to be fragmented in their various destinies); while the others were told that they would have to pay the penalty of their unwarranted obstinacy. This time terrifying trains with sealed coaches moved off towards an unknown destination in the silence of a landscape already grey with impending snow.

The journey from Athens to Moosburg, not far from Munich, had lasted thirteen days. I had known no one personally in my open truck and there had been no one from my regiment. My possessions were minimal both in clothes and money (though I did have one gold sovereign which I had collected for touristic interest in my early days in Athens) – so already in that first period my material conditions had been somewhat harder than the average. But from Moosburg – after about a week's stop spent in complaining and quarrelling – our train ground on for another fortnight during which the cold and other privations became worse and worse. Incomprehensibly to us, our train followed a loop of thousands of kilometres between Vienna and Berlin; we turned off towards Warsaw; we rolled north-east between deserted plains and desolate heaths where we could see nothing but spectral huts on stilts in the marshes; we touched on Lithuania. Then our erratic train decided to reverse its route and it turned southwards along eastern Poland. It came to a halt at Lemberg, the former Lwow.

A journey not easy to forget! But the multiplicity of adventures that have befallen people in the last two wars has robbed stories such as mine of flavour. The episodes that made Pellico's diaries famous a century ago would not interest anyone today. The eccentricities of our guards (and there were some!), the daily incidents of that journey without any knowable goal, the Kafka-like hallucinations of those ghostly landscapes where the frightened prisoners conjured up a new Katyn at every turn, with ourselves as the slaughtered – all this would be small fry indeed in the gigantic explosion of the collective adventure through which the world lived at that time. And yet on that October dawn, when forty-five of us were packed like hens in a coop in our asphyxiating coach, when we had not the faintest idea where we were being taken, and as the train ground relentlessly on with its cargo of fear and lamentation – I have to admit that I felt that silent smile reawaken within me, the smile of elation in danger, of pleasure in experience; a completely irrational happiness, and its keenest moments corresponded with the sharpest craggiest peaks my life had known. My bandage had not been touched since we left Athens. Beneath it I could feel the scab over my eye, painful, and flashing with little stabs of light when I touched it. I had had to risk my 'good' eye being open all this time, and though it had watered and swelled up it had survived over a month of dust, damp and dirt – this time on 'extraterritorial service'. But now, after the second part of the journey, I had no means of knowing whether the sight of the bandaged eye had survived and I just had to trust to nature. When those two interminable weeks came to an end and we realised we had at last arrived, we were at least sure of our lives. We crossed a city inhabited by people whose furtive glances showed us they were friendly; and once we were under cover and breathing freely, without the obsessional rolling of the train, we felt a faint hope trickling into our hearts. That first night we did not stay in the city but were convoyed to various huts put up outside it. Worn out with fatigue, the company collapsed into torpor almost at once, and from that confused mass there rose only the sound of animal breathing. A cold shaft of moonlight came in through the small windows.

My right hand had been burned and was hurting – the result of an incident at the last food distribution. As I had no mess-tin I had had to use a container lacking a handle, and the Russian prisoner on duty had poured in a ladle of boiling soup right up to the brim where my fingers were holding it. He viewed me as an enemy owing to Mussolini's efforts on the Don, and his act was one of intended hostility – what he hoped was that I would drop my ration so as to avoid the burn. But I was determined to hold on, and for once a German corporal came to my help, removed my bowl from my hands and put it down. It was the first kind act I had encountered in Germany. So now I was sucking my thumb like a baby and finding a certain pleasure in it. In fact, I was glad that the pain should keep me awake for I had planned to carry out my experiment in practical medicine, and I didn't want any witnesses. So when there was perfect silence, and the gleam of the moon had slightly brightened, then very very slowly I removed the bandage. It was far from easy as I had no water to soften the crust of blood and dry pus that had formed during the past five weeks and was now as thick as cardboard. I was afraid of tearing away some sensitive part; and knew nothing about what the reactions of the epidermis would be after such a long separation from air. But finally I squeezed my eyelids tight together and, saying goodbye to my lashes, ripped off the scab; then waited, not daring to open the eye.

But a gentle moonbeam came to visit me, and gradually, through a great cloud of joyful tears, I saw it and other trembling forms floating about in the pale blue light. When I used to wake up at night in the dormitory at school I felt hemmed in, abandoned, cruelly sad. Now I was calm, free, and almost happy.

Mussolini never really stopped being a journalist, and in his final polemical essay entitled *In the Days of the Stick and the Carrot* (it was circulated in our prison camps by the republicans of Salò) he described September 8 1943 as the day of the 'pulverisation of Italy' – thereby using a word that implies that the material smashed was already rather fragile beforehand. In the flood of diaries and histories describing that period, this famous event is usually glossed over, due, I think, to a misunderstood love of our country. The event represented a panic crisis of which the military collapse formed only a part. There may be some truth in the infinitude of circumstances brought forward to justify the crisis, but it is also true that 'where many reasons are brought forward none is really valid'! Yet had a returning prisoner pointed this out after the war, he would have found himself reduced to silence by the detailed accounts of all the agonies endured by those who had escaped from the German and Fascist round-ups: as if the fear of something – a fear lasting a few weeks – was worse than the thing itself which had been endured for two years. But the fact that the shadow of that fear still lingered on in people's memory showed that their primary impulse at that time was not the desire to defend their country by risking their lives, but (always excepting the peace of the just) the desire for personal escape, for getting out of it all as quietly and quickly as possible. Though Italy has always been rated very high on the level of deeply meditated values, seen as a national structure she gave clear proof at that time of being dominated by a centrifugal rather than a centripetal force. Indeed, everything appertaining to the State was attacked and destroyed, almost as if it were a question of the goods of a loathed enemy. A lesson little understood by the political levies that have followed, and have been determined to lead a country that hardly knows them, hence so tepidly follows them. And a country that remains indissolubly Catholic because in Catholicism it has found its measure and its rule: 'For,' as Machiavelli said when speaking of the 'antique orders of religion', they 'have subjects and DO NOT GOVERN THEM !'

The most varied remnants of that dissolution met each other in the fortress at Lwow – about two thousand officers, the majority from Greece and France, the rest rounded up by Rommel and Kesselring in Italy. Whereas friendships are natural and spontaneous in war, they were difficult in the camp, because these men – who were a tiny mirror of the decay into which the country had fallen, a country already, and by its very nature, in discord and socially divided – these men had not in any sense found their common denominator. Usually one becomes a prisoner as a result of surrender after battle. Fighting forces have a unity through their common experiences, hardships and dangers, and this homogeneity persists among the prisoners and forms the basis of their dignity and solidarity. This was the case in 1915 with the Italians who honourably endured the famous camp of Mauthausen in Austria. But it was not like that with us.

In Reggio I had seen how the call-up worked: equivocations, confusions, injustices; infinite intrigues to avoid military service or to go into it for non-military reasons, with every kind of equivocation and favouritism. In France and Greece – occupied countries where it was easy to practise abuses – whole gangs of profiteers had gathered who were even physically unsuited to the rigours of war: the tradesmen and businessmen dressed up as soldiers with whom Athens, for instance, had been swarming; and the first people to leave the Greek capital that September were two hundred Field Officers who suddenly became aware that they were 'supernumeraries' simply because they hoped to get back to Italy, and who, in fact, were the first to set foot inside the camp. So the mass was made up of every kind of element: men of a certain age who had wanted to be called up because of the pay and the rations when

times were difficult in the cities, and who had occupied cushy jobs
in the administrative services; boys from the Leghorn military
academy; others fresh from Modena; men with a thousand thoughts
and ideas of their own and following a thousand different directions;
legal men, ruffians, neurotics, the sick, the rich, beggars and snobs.
Yet the Germans pretended to see some kind of unity in this motley
crew and stigmatised it as 'anti-Fascist' and 'pro-Badoglio'. Whereas
there were as many monarchists and Mussolini-men among us as
there were convinced republicans and ferocious haters of Badoglio
and the king (I, for instance, was one of these), all mixed up with a
crowd of others who had no sense of being soldiers at all; it was these
last who complained the loudest when they saw the undertakings
they had embarked on with very different prospects in view coming
to such a disastrous end.

The stories related by all these men were generally vague or
yawning with gaps; and very few of them had actually fought – if
only because the Germans, in view of the defection of the majority,
had been able to crush the small pockets of resistance and had
ruthlessly left few witnesses to the facts. It was said that at the
moment of our surrender they disposed of a good 300,000 of their
best troops in Italy alone. Now if the legend of Garibaldi (and it
really is a legend!) presents him as conqueror of the whole of Sicily
with a band of barely 1000 red-shirts; and if it was true that
Mussolini took over the country by marching on Rome with 40,000
black-shirts, then the 300,000 very war-seasoned Teutons must
surely have been an excessive force even for a country of 45 million
souls. But it is also certain that the Russian bear did not exactly
find honey when it pushed into stoical and thinly-populated
Finland, for ferocious fighters rose up against it from every cove
of its thirty thousand lakes and from each of its countless birch trees;
and it is also undeniable that, much later (and back in Italy again
now), the whole police force and authority of the state could not
capture one man, the bandit Giuliano, when they found he was
really determined not to be caught. Considerations which I kept
strictly to myself, while observing the singular and pathetic spectacle
of our tumultuous billet in those first days.

Protected from the winter's cold not by our inadequate little
stove but by walls three metres thick – freshly white-washed and
equipped with two-tiered wooden bunks – our billet looked like
any other military quartering. Contrary to the conditions of those

of us who landed up in makeshift huts in swamps, imprisonment in the fortress of Lwow did not for the time being entail excessive hardships – a fortress majestic as to outline and on whose stony projections the snow conferred a delicate moulding rather like the elegance conferred on a human face by a powdered wig. True, our 'detainers' took delight in subjecting us to endless roll-calls and keeping us standing for half a day at a stretch (and once for a whole day) on the sheet of ice that already covered the courtyards – but that was the only real form of tyranny they inflicted on us. For the rest, short of putting his morbid fantasies to practice on them (as, alas, sometimes happened), what could a gaoler do with his prisoners except count them? And that was what ours did.

Food was short too; but we were not subjected to any hard labour and we did not suffer from the cold. The Polish people looked on us as victims of the hated enemy and so were on our side, and it was not impossible to bribe the guards, many of whom were not Germans but came from the areas incorporated into the Great Reich. So it was enough to have some money or some objects to exchange, and many of the men had stocks in their baggage that at that time seemed enormous.

It began with those of us who had come from Greece 'showing' cigarettes, and those from the Côte d'Azur – who had cornered a market in perfume – displaying their bottles of scent. But by degrees everything that had been taken from the military stores at the time of the collapse was produced, ending up with the considerable sums filched from the departmental cash-boxes. These had certainly not been destroyed, as the records relative to them would have us believe. Indeed, in the last days in Athens (so I had heard) the entire funds for the army's needs for a month – 50 milliards of drachmas – had been drawn with praiseworthy foresight only to be mysteriously spirited away at one stroke. Not only this, but many of our men who had been in our army in Greece had substantial hoards of gold coins on them that they had had no time to send home (between two pieces of cardboard); and a certain Lieutenant Quero, an unscrupulous adventurer but a likeable person, had as much as a kilogram of them. He made no secret of the fact that most of his haul came from trading in fowling-pieces – the type of gun that had been at the bottom of the Spiropulos affair.

'With all due respect to your rank,' he said to me, 'I can see you're absolutely destitute. May I ask you, providing you use equivalent articles of clothing as stakes, to partner me in a game of poker against Lieutenants Fabbricatore and Mozzillo? They've already cleaned out two or three of our company. But with your personal coolness and knowledge of the game, plus the strength of my capital, we'll bring them to their knees.'

Such a proposal would have horrified my good Major Costa Oliviero, Knight of Malta, but to me it seemed so ridiculous that I accepted it. Playing poker in partners was absolutely not the done thing but was openly practised by our two opponents; besides which everyone knew that I had no money and would stake minute percentages of an equivalent – in thick socks and Balaclava helmets. So the great game took place but turned out to be a disaster, for those bandits Mozzillo and Fabbricatore, to the dismayed incredulity of the many men standing by, produced 'four queens', a 'full house' and a 'royal flush' – all the best possible poker hands – almost in succession, thereby accumulating on their side of the green baize (unearthed who knows where – could it have been a piece of flag?) a single pile of thousand-lire banknotes of the last Kingdom of Italy, black-and-green dollar bills, slim French banknotes, and gold coins of every stamp and type. What with the heat and the noise and the smoke, you might have thought you were in a gaming-den in any part of our unhappy world. That stolen money obtained once again by theft reminded me so much of Madame Julie's diamonds in my Milan boarding-house. In the matter of men's sins it seemed that the imagination did not range far.

Quero belonged to the second brigade of Grenadiers and was a tall, carefree, very vivacious Venetian. His father was a cattle-dealer and had directed his son's speculations in Athens by means of detailed letters – a fact which Quero himself frankly admitted to me. Attached to the Divisional Command, he had enjoyed the whole golden age of the Sagapò in Greece and knew all about it down to the last detail. But he never passed judgement on the confusions, collusions and malversations of the army, confining himself to merely narrating the facts with a slightly mocking air and facetious tone.

'Every day had its marginal profit,' he would say, 'and now and again there was a jackpot. You see what I mean? There was a fabulous one in Greece. Quinine made of wood! Little wooden pills put into pink sugar! Sold their weight in gold!'

For Quero a situation like ours at Lwow was simply an opportunity for triumphant profit-making, inasmuch (he insisted on explaining to me) as plenty of money could be made from the misfortunes of others once one knew how to go about it. At least I appreciated the frankness of his behaviour, well outside that real sink of complexes within which the others toiled. He gave himself no rest but was perpetually going the rounds in top boots and a three-quarter-length jerkin lined with sheepskin, conferring in corners with people of every kind, then returning to me with a small smile of triumph – scoop after scoop.

Soon others were also taking part in this activity, until it finally grew into a kind of stock exchange where the basic measure was not gold but cigarettes, and on this index were priced commodities such as watches, skin bags, margarine rations, and even diamonds. The richest among us were not necessarily the cleverest, and we knew an airman who arrived with a good million lire in banknotes concealed in the bulges of his jacket, and not long after was reduced to penury through misplaced investments. Before long a struggle flared up (as it would in any society of men) between the rich in order to do each other down or impose their wealth as power; between the rich and the poor for reasons laid down by countless theorists before and since Marx; and between various sections of the economically weak for reasons of greed or jealousy – altogether a disheartening repetition of my last days at Licudi. There were cliques, there was patronage, there was competition; the information services marshalled their forces so that an unexpected distribution of soap or salt should produce immediate variations of price in these provisions and others linked with them, as happens in playing the import market. And the infiltration of foodstuffs smuggled in from outside corresponded both in its risks and its profits to real frontier operations. My mind went back to the rules of Stuart Mill and Adam Smith, laid down in economic manuals in the days of the Pensile. Cut off as we were from the world, we could only listen to each other: complaints, squabbles, deals and, in the depths of the night, fear. Those were the days when the Russians were overcoming the desperate German resistance on the Dnieper and reoccupying Kiev. This might mean our early release, but anxiety stepped up rather than slowed down the rhythm of our lives. I thought of Binutti, who long ago had given himself up as prisoner to a Mantua cavalry patrol so as to 'see better', as he put it. His phrase acquired a melancholy depth. Was it true that he who thinks detaches himself from life? And that there is less pain when one knows no history?

'I'm still convinced,' Quero whispered to me, 'that Fabbricatore and Mozzillo are a pair of cheats. But their trick must be an unknown one if the two touts I put on their track to watch them, and who are two veterans at the job, haven't been able to catch them out. That was why we had that fine "slaughter"; I don't mind about the paper money; but I'd really like to have back the "double eagles" they got off me.'

Like France, Greece hoards gold; but being more archaic and adventurous in business, and situated eastwards, Greece collects the most disparate coins: from the Chilean 'condor' to the George IV 'sovereign'; from the Bavarian 'double thaler' to the Russian 'fifteen imperial roubles'; and sometimes one came across others that were much less familiar and more ancient, such as the Turkish 'mejid', the Tibetan 'mohur', or the Persian 'two tomans'. Quero knew to perfection the weight, relationship and value of all this coinage. The American 'double eagle', worth twenty gold dollars, is a coin out of a Western; and he had lost four of them.

'At home Fabbricatore is a wine-merchant and Mozzillo a shoemaker. But they certainly know how to *do* us. Instead of fighting them we must take them into partnership. I'm getting new ideas!'

These new ideas had to do with drawing into the black market the supplies that the Germans had begun distributing to those who had finally decided to collaborate with the Reich, under the very nose of the rest of us who were kept on short rations: a novel aspect of our eccentric situation. In obedience to Nazi orders, envoys from Mussolini's North Italian Republic of Salò were undertaking journeys up north to try to convince glum and hungry gatherings where their effective good lay. But once the prisoners had weighed up fear as against hunger, their troubled and confused minds got lost in a whirlpool of arguments, tangled emotions and open or concealed motives. If the Germans were to withdraw from Poland, as was now being whispered, we would have to pass over to the Russians: a thing obscurely feared by everyone. To sign on meant the Front once more, in Germany or, worse, in Italy, or even for civil war. To stay in the camp was certainly the best, provided it would not be for too long, but who could guarantee this? There were Fascist bosses among us who were trying to clear their name and achieve political virginity; there were swindlers afraid of being called to account; amateur lawyers who held forth at length about the Geneva and Hague Conventions with an avalanche of facts. Someone unearthed the concept of military honour, and those from Greece shouted to deaf ears about the agreement reached by Vecchiarelli. No one knew that that General had died in obscure captivity. I recalled his face, that of a healthy countryman. God knows how his life must have been broken – like a straw in the terrible storm that he unleashed without even having an idea of what he was doing.

With all this, not more than fifteen per cent of the prisoners had come forward to sign the act of allegiance – or commitment to collaboration with the Germans; but instead of being immediately sent off elsewhere, these men were kept almost next door to us so that we should see the groaning loads of sausages taken in to reward them. Our tough ones spat fire against such blacklegs, while concealing the fact that, in many cases, their spirit of resistance was based on reserves of money. Quero, on the other hand, deaf to any kind of polemic, and without the faintest hypocrisy, looked on those sausages exactly as a Swiss *rentier* (for instance) might nose out an imminent option on preference bonds. He gazed covetously, and in no time had set up a unique enterprise which included the monied and masterful Fabbricatore and Mozzillo.

'You should join us too, Captain!' In addressing me, he always kept up the correct formalities and I believed him to be sincere. 'You haven't got a shirt on your back and you've every right not to die of hunger. As far as your scruples are concerned, remember it's not a matter of you entering into the partnership but just of being employed as book-keeper. What could be more natural?'

I interpreted his words as a possible desire to create for himself the very alibi that has led brigands to do good to the poor, and notable pirates of big business to found hospitals and schools. Or perhaps a darker instinct led him to detect in me, and in my detachment, the witness if not the judge. And then there are those who are incapable of raising themselves up of their own momentum so try to drag those who are above them down – a phenomenon as old as the human race. And a vast quantity of our literature, following the Italian publicist Longanesi, has been based on the idea that a personal disgrace can be justified by a communal one. But Quero was of a simpler breed. The evil actions he went on committing served (I think) to prove to himself that he was still the same man as he had been before; that nothing had changed; that he was not walking in a void – which would have terrified him. Then I thought that being like others meant not having only their weaknesses but their actual baseness. In worthy memory of the bookseller Pagano, and of the card-index of comrade Chiurico's Fascist bible, I accepted the office of book-keeper in the partnership, rather as I had consented to take part in that game of poker.

The strangeness of this type of enterprise brought me in touch with a lot of the prisoners. Hypocrisy was the worst possible sin in the camp, because those who protested against the black market were incapable of freely giving to others even a crumb of what was theirs, whereas had they done so they would have automatically put an end to the black market. The black market could only be founded on an exchange of goods having an initial proprietor, and here lay the root of the evil. For instance, it was said of so-and-so that he had more than a hundredweight of dried foodstuffs in his possession, but he would rather have been skinned alive than freely give away a crumb of it. When one of the young Leghorn students was discovered to have the tuberculosis from which he soon died, it was impossible to obtain the necessary help for him; and that crime to which I was particularly sensitive (in memory of Nerina) passed unobserved. They answered that they had their own lives to protect. But for many of them it was merely a seething hatred for anyone whatsoever. As they were the victims of injustice, why should they not participate in it? But as for myself, I did not agree that we were victims of a really unjust punishment; in my view we had all in some way deserved it. But the majority simply did not want to accept its austere warning or the truth it indicated.

When I retired to the double bunk of which I occupied the upper place – so as to put in order the accounts of the weary day's affairs – I noticed absent-mindedly the sibilant Latin esses of Captain Téolo, Venetian nobleman from Lake Garda, my fellow-tenant, who at fixed hours recited his Office exactly like an ecclesiastic. To this end he had fixed up a little cotton curtain as a kind of confessional behind which he retired when he wanted to pray, and this was often. At first Téolo had avoided me as a man who kept bad company; but when he saw that I went laboriously gleaning a packet of razor-blades here, a tin of powdered milk or a packet of small cigars there, then he unfroze. I respected Téolo's devotions and his spirit of recollection and climbed up into my bunk without letting the soles of my shoes touch his. Though he did not tell me so, I was later convinced that he had included my name in his ejaculatory prayers – among those to be led back on to the straight and narrow path.

By the beginning of December, just two months after our internment in Lwow, the organisation Quero & Co. had realised such profits that the Italian Command of the camp was moved to intervene; but Quero & Co. pointed out that they had introduced into the camp from outside a huge and indispensable quantity of food, and that the collaborators had charged their weight in gold for the sausages so Quero & Co. had done likewise. However this may be, we were surrounded by the hostile whispering, the suppressed rancour, the back-biting and the insults to be found in the needy soldier confronted with profiteers and the new rich. But the partners continued to ladle out the goods. They were in a position to provide a full dinner, starting with some kind of pasta served with butter, followed by beefsteak and fruit, to anyone who could pay a price calculated at around four or five hundred times the ordinary one. Quero also provided a special pasta meal for the partnership, to which I was invited. But owing to lack of space and the inadequacy of the containers, it happened that while he was cynically serving out the *tagliatelle* under the hungry gaze of our companions, the dish slipped from his hands and the total steaming contents fell on to the filthy floor. Then I heard a cackle of laughter which made me realise what the joy of the devils in hell must be; and, looking up, I saw one of our comrades watching us from the height of his bunk with an expression of such malicious glee that I felt myself freed from my scruples – more even than by a papal absolution. Then some of the poor wretches threw themselves on the remainder of the pasta and fought for it. However, the climax of the dinner was still to come, a vast cup of strong coffee which, taken on an empty stomach, produced the same drunkenness and torpor as wine.

Before Christmas the situation came to a head in Poland too. But as the Germans were worried about the local unrest, they were afraid to remove us by daylight under the eyes of a population already cherishing ideas of revolt. This made them very polite during our last days at the fortress; they gave us, for instance, a free hand over our equipment which would otherwise have been left to the enemy with everything else. So Christmas week was lived with an extraordinary intensity in the camp where alternating hopes and fears were reborn; but even this time the wheel of things turned in an unexpected way because the prisoners in their turn – out of fear of being absorbed by the Russians, or into their legendary and interminable country – displayed such a favourable attitude to their gaolers that it bordered on the grotesque. And our departure was truly grotesque. The old German colonel in charge of the camp, a type taken straight from Elisabeth Werner's romantic *San Michele* (Cristina's books!), waved to us almost as a father to his beloved sons; and we replied! We crossed Lwow in full daylight and almost without surveillance, as had happened in our journey across the Balkans. The Poles were looking out of their windows, silent and thoughtful, and every now and again a large white loaf of bread would fall beside us in the snow. The column reached the trains intact. Quero was concerned to find a place in a carriage where he was little known or not at all. He was afraid of some hostile reaction on the part of his clients. I was with him; but my mind at that time was filled with a keen pity for the flock in which I included myself.

The sufferings of that journey were severe. German comprehensive planning for the removal of vast masses of people – through an enemy country and with the Russian army at their back – gave yet another proof of their incredible efficiency; but this did not detract from the hardships to which they, and we, were subjected. This time we were crammed in fifties into sealed coaches for a journey lasting eleven days, getting air only through narrow vents – except for two short halts to take aboard fresh supplies of water and empty the stinking wooden box converted to man's needs. A number of men were ill, and in our carriage a doctor had to operate on an abscess with a penknife. The slightest movement involved a fight with the others, and the sense of suffocation reached such a frightful pitch that there were fits of hysteria. Suitably anchored to Albero's memories and his frequent sallies on the subject of warfare, I persisted in regarding these torments as the natural concomitant of a checkered campaign; after all, we were at least starting our journey back to the centre of Europe: notions not shared by all the others, to judge by the chorus of laments. It is quickly noticeable that the people least able to endure pain and privation are those who at first sight would seem most inured to them. People who have never known comfort or luxury, farm-labourers for instance, give to their physical being an attention that the intellectual disregards in times of trial. The majority of the officers came from the lower middle class, and I took it badly that they groaned so loudly at being huddled together, as if they had previously been used to princely expanses. These personal eccentricities of theirs, echoes of ancient feelings now largely obsolete, helped me on my side to behave correctly; and I was not unprepared when there finally rose up before us the ominous barbed wire fences of Siltau.

If you came to think about it, it was not difficult to guess what would be in store for us. The Republic of Salò was trying to moderate Nazi severity towards Italian prisoners, but the Nazis were standing firm: if we were not traitors to the Axis then we should at least adhere to Mussolini's new government – if not to the Wehrmacht then to our own republican army. Lwow had been the last testing-ground for this end, and in that short period the choice had been made and we ourselves had made it. Those who had opted for the Fascist Republic went from Poland to Italy by normal military transport; the others were now to know the rigours of punishment. Thus with groans and curses that condemned mass of men passed through the spectral gates of the new *Lager*, while both captives and captors prepared themselves for new trials of strength.

There were ordinary pedestrian reasons too, besides the dogmatic ones, but of unhappy augury for us. When we were first directed to Poland, new and adequate installations had been prepared in advance, at least at Lwow: work which had been destroyed after four months and there was no means of renewing it. In German national territory there were no available establishments or suitable sites. But in this the Germans perhaps saw Wotan's hand of justice. However this may be, in that vast camp where up to seven thousand officers of many different origins were gathered together, it was not difficult to 'lose' Quero and all the others from Lwow, except for the pious Téolo who had prayed the whole length of the journey. Together we hid ourselves in one of the most distant huts, a terrible hole where slatted wooden bunks rose five 'storeys' high right up to the bare roof. Almost two hundred of us were piled in here; and I read at the top of my place, cut with a penknife: 'Boris Dragouliub'. And a date.

The flatlands extending from the mouth of the Elbe over the coast of the North Sea and as far as Frisia in Holland, are neither very cold nor very damp; but the low heath spreading out from the undulations of sand is the kingdom of the wind – a strong and

perpetual wind that blows over the undergrowth and rips at the
fleeting processions of clouds, and at night howls over the desert
land as it does over the sea. Everything in that endless landscape,
under the high interminable sky, is a dark tiny detail; and the land
a network of burnished steel, glinting here and there beneath a shaft
of light from the sky or because of a stream. In that space men are
less than insects and wander about as if without direction. Seen
from above, our huge encampment must surely have seemed no
more than a speck of greenish lichen on the bark of a tree.

Téolo and I took it in turns to get the measure of the place,
without gaining much reassurance. Siltau, we were told, had a few
years earlier been the macabre setting for the death of about sixty
thousand Russian prisoners as a result of exhaustion and disease:
they had been kept out of doors within the barbed wire until they
died. Some French prisoners in the Bavarian camp of Moosburg
had told us that Germans never dared enter the Russian camps
because those indomitable warriors were ready to die so long as
they killed. The Germans had tried to guard them with specially
trained dogs, but as the Russians were used to fighting wolves they
simply faced them and ripped open their bellies with wooden
knives. So the German system for eliminating the millions of men
they had captured in the first thrust of the war between Riga and
the Black Sea had become more simplified and more cruel. As the
soldiers were impossible to feed or use or hold, they were abandoned
on the bare earth to a calculated hunger whose outcome was sick-
ness and death. In the matter of deciding on our new billet, the
Germans did not make use of the huge gruesome quadrangle over
which still loomed the sinister watch-towers, but the huts which
had then been for the service, if so it can be put, of the compound.
Two winters had considerably impaired them; and they were our
home for seventeen months.

Unlike the Russians, we were given old decrepit soldiers as guards,
ones with one arm or a wooden leg; so that what with the mud, the
disgusting swarms of insects, the abominable *Stube* and the rest, the
Lager, from the sentries down to the latrines, was unquestionably in
the poorest possible working order. As all contraband from outside
had ceased, and personal reserves were much depleted, hunger
made itself felt at once – aggravated by a psychological factor that
hastened its risks and consequences. Anyone who had deluded himself that the war would be over by Christmas, after a mere four

months' imprisonment, now had a much longer period of hardship to fear. For many the spirit of endurance now wavered – based as it had been on that early and mistaken conviction – and meanwhile the complex feeling of irritation and spite against the Germans had grown stronger. The Germans were weak in Latin psychology and did not understand this new wave of obstinate refusal any more than they had understood it before. And the camp shut itself up in pig-headed silence, everyone reviewing his forces, anchoring himself to his rights, trying out his obligations, among shattering onslaughts of grief, rage and bitterness.

The interplay of these thoughts and feelings was so complex and changeable that the ironical intolerance I had felt in the train towards my fellow-officers and their lamentations now underwent modification: I developed a genuine interest in their attitudes, rather abstract and scientific though this interest was. The condition of imprisonment is wretched of its very nature (though not worse than the conditions endured by some of the very poor throughout their whole lives). Though prisoners may not have a hand or a foot or both (for good measure!) cut off, as in Plutarch's stories, we seldom hear of prisoners in a state of well-being. With the removal of position, rank, privilege and qualification, there remains only the man, stripped of his identifying marks and sometimes even of his hair – truly naked and how defenceless! The style he has forged for himself so as to become a precise social entity is necessarily swept away, leaving only inborn faculties and deficiencies in adverse circumstances. It seemed to me that in this situation our officers should have constituted a chosen and hence homogeneous élite. But in the September crisis what had literally sunk headlong was the ruling class of Italy, in other words the middle class – and its flower (or what should have been its flower) was with me here in the camp. So just as I had been able to examine the upper stratum of Italian society through my father Gian Luigi, and the lower one through the simple people at Licudi, I now made a minute examination of the middle one as represented at Siltau. What did it reveal?

To begin with, hatred of the Germans. This arose from the particular circumstances, just as it grew up in India against the English and in Algeria against the French. But however theoretical the hatred was, it was much more ulcerating to the haters than to the hated, for it had to be externalised in attitudes of protest that sometimes verged on the lunatic. A few of the officers shaved every day and kept their uniforms decent – at some cost to themselves – for they maintained that you had to put up a façade of dignity and pride in front of the enemy. But most of them went about looking like tramps and were indifferent even to personal cleanliness. Many of them refused to salute the heads of the camp, which threw the latter into a rage; or else they deployed laborious slow motion in bringing their limbs to attention, as they had to do during roll-calls: schoolboy trifles, whereby the Germans managed to discover who would be prepared to become informants on the others. Then there was protest activity in the matter of our barbed-wire barricade. This was over four metres high and five metres wide and could only have been crossed by a bird. In spite of which there was a subsidiary wall of wire two or three metres on its near side – this was called the 'warning wire' and it was forbidden to go beyond it under pain of death. Lacking other ideas, many officers longed with passion to go beyond that wire as a sign of defiance. But the one who put his longing into practice was killed by a burst of gunfire from a sentry on duty for the purpose. The camp went into hysterical fury. They pointed out to the guards that crossing the wire in full daylight could mean nothing at all. But as there were notices along it at every twelve metres laconically announcing that 'anyone who went beyond it would be killed', the Germans maintained that in broad daylight the prohibition was more obvious.

As for myself I regarded these attitudes to be wrong-headed, pointless and often ridiculous, and I found no interest in wasting time with the warning-wire. To begin with, if one escaped into Germany what would one have solved? Where would one then go? Secondly, once I had made my act of presence at the roll-call I had nothing more to do with the Germans, they gave me no more trouble and I forgot them. My difficulties were produced by the Italians themselves, by the circumstances, and preparing for the long haul of the slowly passing months. But on the whole things were not desperate: any intended threat to our lives would have shown itself in Greece (and indeed many had died there); but once we had got to Poland and survived the subsequent crises, it was difficult to suppose that within German national territory a cold-blooded action would be performed openly against us. Yet the Armistice was ambiguous; and if the Allies had not finished the war in a final effort at that time they must have had good reasons, and the war could not be brought to an end so soon. I felt prepared to

withstand the winter in the *Lager*, and then more easily the spring
and summer, and hold out at least until the following autumn.
But it was important to measure out every particle of energy with
the maximum of economy, to obliterate oneself so as to be forgotten.
I and Téolo – who shared my ideas – and two other like-minded
men took possession of an independent four-tiered unit and settled
down to a respectable social life modelled on that of the woodworm.

It was a featureless landscape, a confused mass, a monochrome
drawing after the manner of Callot, relieved here and there by
more sharply defined figures: my Téolo in the foreground, with his
book at his breast like the Bestower in altar-pieces now in some
museum; then the other two – Pannuzzo, very young, of modest
circumstances, brought up by his grandmother who had taught
him to sew, hence very good at mending; and Valente, a submarine
officer, who had invented a stove that could function with small
twigs. If I put the proportion of kind souls in our company at around
two per cent, I think it corresponded to what was defined as 'Italy's
lucky star' by the more shrewd majority who always knew how to
exploit the patient few for their own purposes. Pannuzzo sewed on
endless buttons to help the elect to maintain their dignity, though
owing to his own small blue administrative epaulettes of a very low
grade, and his clumsy ways, he himself remained at the level of an
outcast. Valente provided an infinitude of little stoves and no one
shared with him the meals they were thus enabled to cook. Téolo
did most of all by praying for everyone, but no one even knew it.
As for me, I must have appeared a maniac, no less, for I was
absorbed in my incomprehensible notebooks for hours and even
days on end.

We had acquired a good many of these notebooks from the office
of His Excellency General Vecchiarelli on that famous day of his
arrest. Blessed foresight, for paper was scarce in the camp and
bread was needed as exchange. Another stroke of luck was our
lightning decision, on entering the hut, to take over the four-tiered
unit at the far end near the small window – the only source of
feeble light in the place, for the anaemic little lamps were useless
and the hut was more often than not plunged in darkness. Our
chosen position was extremely cold, being next to the outside wall
and far from the central stove; but wrapped in all the woollies
that I had gained through my work for Quero & Co., I was able
to write for many hours each day; while the others, lying on their

bunks like mummies in their burial niches, could only stagnate, think, and suffer.

From a certain point of view my life now reminded me of my schooldays. But my present condition was much easier. I had been a prisoner then as now; but then I had been a child in need of affection, whereas, as a man, I could do without it. The monks, not to mention the Prefect Cirillo, had seemed much more tangible and frightening than the non-existent Germans. My companions both then and now came from the same class; but now I was prepared to defend myself from them. As a child I had sighed for my medlar tree and my sister Checchina; whereas now Naples, Licudi and Italy were more foreign to me than Germany itself. What else? I found peace of mind; and freedom, because I was removed from everything that had made me suffer so much. Against that there was only the scarcity of food. But no scarcer than the food that the raven had carried in its yellow beak to St Benedict in the desert. No! I saw nothing in imprisonment of what the others were lamenting about. Imprisonment gave me total purity of mind, unlimited freedom of concentration, it absolved me from the past, rescued me from servitude to the flesh and, by obliging me to abide by the rules, it put iron into my will. It made time stretch out like a harmonious ribbon on which no external voice could register a discord; it put me adrift on the water of things; disposed me to the contemplation that gives rise to wisdom and to the recollection that is the mother of poetry. I felt my mind was liberated and safe. And so was I.

(From fragments of my diary: While travelling . . . December 1943.)

Our first halt was on the fifth day, at an ordinary station, not far from the main platform. The contrast was striking. On one side there was us, reduced to mere numbers, locked in like wild beasts, grey and hairy inside those animal cages. On the other side a peaceful normal life was going on: students, tradesmen, young people on holiday, decorated officials. We encountered vacuous glances, expressionless faces, uninterested gestures; people moving around, talking, greeting each other as if we did not exist; and yet we were men too.

The troop-train shunted back a little and stopped alongside a civilian one. At the window two ugly graceless girls began giggling at the sight of us, with a kind of ridiculous coquettishness to which only our sad eyes responded. In the next carriage a good German mother was pointing us out to her small sons, teaching them. And further along a solitary woman dressed in black gazed at us with a heartfelt expression of loss and sorrow; she was very pale. She saw the truth; she saw in our faces the pain of her own loved ones, of those who had gone off and were dead, swallowed up by that ambiguous monster that has no motherland: war.

Siltau, February 1944.
The rations so ardently awaited for eighteen hours had not arrived that evening. In the frozen silence of the *Stube* one of the young men suddenly pulled from his palliasse a bottle of rare French scent; he opened it with a malicious grin and then with a yelp of hysterical laughter poured it all over his filthy hair. That was ten days ago, but a hint of that delicate scent still hovers around in the fetid atmosphere of the hut.

Siltau, February 1944.
After our bath they shoved us stark naked into a room adjoining the showers where there were already many other poor souls trying to keep warm at the one cast-iron stove. All those shivering men stood around in circles displaying their under-nourished limbs, their secret physical defects, their forsaken privates; all reserve gone now, but a certain uneasiness remaining. Because their shrivelled arms, their shoulder-blades and breast-bones sticking out beneath their skin, their white lifeless legs and their feet misshapen with swellings and frostbite – all were in such flagrant contradiction with the defiant attitudes that some of them still felt compelled to assume.

And so much wizened emaciation, and the pale sagging skin of the older ones, and the rare grace that still marked a few of the youthful figures, created a strange visual concerto, some mute canticle that passed description: as in those primitive purgatories where the painter's origins and Christian feeling – inexpert though he may have been in design and perspective – bring together naïve ugliness or sheer clumsiness with an instinctive compassion for human frailty.

And we were frail indeed: stripped of clothes, of action and of pride. And thus taken back very far indeed in both time and species by the tepid sickly odour that our bodies gave forth: a human odour and an animal odour, very ancient and yet new. The odour of milk and of the lair; the odour of dung and of the cradle.

If a well-born girl can play tennis, be a beautiful dancer, know in detail the kinship between the 'good' families of a given province, and yet at the same time be devoutly religious, no one is very much surprised. But for the same attributes to be combined in a man is rather rare, yet by chance I discovered that Téolo had not only been runner-up in his regional tennis championships in 1938, and a winner in several waltz competitions, but also had a detailed knowledge of the aristocracy not only of Venice but of many other parts of Italy. As we walked up and down together for the daily fifteen minutes included in our health schedule – between that funereal quadrangle where the Russian prisoners had died and the filthy camp trenches that served as latrines in Siltau – we discussed the work we planned to undertake, I as a civil-court judge and he helping me with his specialised knowledge in matters sacred. Educated by the Barnabites, Téolo came from an old comfortably-off family and had been able to stock a memory worthy of Mithridates in a library such as Leopardi's father, Count Monaldo, would have loved. He could wander back and forth among the genealogies of the Bourbons or the Medici (which are like forests) without confusing a single datum. As my only books were the Bible and the Gospels, I was naturally led to seek some personal theme in these supreme works, the compendium and matrix of countless others; and my choice fell on the story of Esther.

Situated beside the hut's small window, our four-tiered bunk was the only one standing by itself and thus looked as high as a tower. As the most senior, I occupied the bottom place; Téolo was above me; then came the sailor Valente, and then poor Pannuzzo, who got the full benefit of the bugs that poured down from the roof and thus protected the rest of us from them in proportional scale. On the other side, across a narrow space, there rose the wall of the collective bunk tower, ten bunks, each five storeys high, and taking up the whole of that wall. Thus each of us had an enforced contact with the storey corresponding to our own, and to me fell an irritable captain who was always at war with the four who slept above him because they put their muddy boots on his blanket when climbing up to their places. The never-ending sight of feet hanging in the air corresponded, in our town planning, to the operation of lifts in modern buildings. I got used to regarding Pannuzzo's lean dangling legs as a sign of daybreak, for every day at dawn – when a scarcely perceptible gleam of light began to pick out a shape here and there from the heavy evil-smelling mass breathing in the darkness – he let himself down into the gangway, trying hard not to disturb me, so as to begin a strange operation he imagined he was undertaking unseen.

Pannuzzo, one of the poorest and always patiently engaged in sewing on the buttons of the rich, was a figure from a Gospel parable. His jacket had been the object of an incident when nearly a whole bucket of fatty substance had been upset over it, the more unfortunate as it was already too long and almost worn through. Since that time three-quarters of it had consisted of a single blackish grease-stain that gleamed rather like a coat of mail when in the light. He also (as I noticed) possessed a shoebrush, a black one, with its bristles worn down to the wood, and every morning as soon as dawn broke he took his venerable jacket and set to work to brush it with infinite care, especially over the wide surface of the grease-stain, and kept busily at it for a good twenty minutes.

While pretending to be asleep I sank into contemplation of that intent emaciated face seemingly immersed in some extravagant dream, while the hand mechanically sent the brush up and down with a low regular rubbing noise. No part of that jacket was left free from this scrupulous rehabilitation. Then, as the light grew, and someone began coughing or tossing, Pannuzzo would clamber up again to his fourth storey; his legs disappeared and there was no further news of him for quite a while, but meanwhile the whispering of Téolo's prayers would start up.

Attention to needs like Pannuzzo's jacket will give an idea of what the possible occupations in the *Lager* were. The timelessness of time, when one does not know the measure of it, alters all other relationships. The civilian prisoner knows how long his imprisonment is going to last, however severe his punishment; even if he has a life sentence he can measure its hatefulness with fairly accurate precision. But military imprisonment is conditioned by the war being waged and, like the war, can go on for years or end tomorrow. This gnawing uncertainty creates a shapeless spectre in the mind, a mixture of impulses, doubts, crises. The punishment the Germans

meted out to us, with a system of shortages, that tested to the utmost
our physical even more than our moral endurance, put us into
competition with time. Certainly the war could not go on for ever,
but neither could our capacity to survive; and if the war could go
on a single day longer than us, then it was all over for us.

Thus among the officers there was an obvious confusion of ideas,
a lack of method and discipline, a dispersal of reasoning into moods
and of moods into reasoning; but the truth lying behind every tiny
incident in the camp was that minute calculation between ourselves
and time. Each man became very knowledgeable about the quantity
of vitamins, proteins, carbohydrates, salt and fat needed to maintain
a minimum of life in a body. All knew how many calories they
needed and how many were contained in our diet; they weighed
up the reserves of their individual organisms and measured con-
sumption down to the last millimetre. That famine in Greece when
so many of the civil population had died under our army's eyes
returned to people's minds as an experience to be learned from: the
Greeks used to remain absolutely motionless on their pallets so as to
save up every scrap of vital energy; so most of the prisoners followed
the same method, and in the first two months of 1944 the dormitories
at certain hours were as still and silent as cemeteries.

'If only they would examine their consciences!' said Téolo,
pursing his lips. He had a pretty low opinion of the upper and
middle classes; he summed it up by gesticulating with both hands,
with a glance upwards: 'If there weren't the police . . . we'd be in a
bad way!'

And it was true that there was no talk about examining consciences. The suffering men, wrapped in their rags so as to conserve
their meagre warmth, lay in the darkness of their bunks and dreamt
their headlong dreams; they thought the same things over and over
and over again; they surveyed the whole of their past lives, the
intimate memories, the joys, the sins. But no sound ever broke that
silence save for egotistical remarks and angry lies: the very ones
which, multiplied by millions, had brought us to the present
disaster and were keeping us there. The Italians are naturally
evasive, querulous, and impatient, and now they were facing a
simple challenge: to last out in the camp longer than those others
could last out at the Front; a game by no means decided and the
zero of the roulette was in our favour, for anyone could get out of
the camp at any moment by consenting to work. But as a surviving

expression of all human kind, their nature reacted by showing itself obstinately hostile to every explicit truth and they preferred to cling to certain external forms of self-delusion (if not to error) as if it were life itself. Hence, beneath a veil of words and international law and other Byzantine subtleties, and with unending quarrels and litigations and threats of future vengeance, the other fundamental characteristic of our people presented itself, a people believed by half the world to be one of fiery passion and dashing exploits; and it really did possess the former and perform the latter, but always accompanied by consummate diplomacy (so as to be able to 'put into effect', as Machiavelli said) and a very cold assessment of the facts.

Thus, while two per cent – or perhaps five per cent if one took in the whole company – remained inviolate, poor and honest like the hungry Pannuzzo, the others with an eye on the reserves and an ear stretched for the slightest hint of news from the clandestine radio, gave themselves to nothing but scrutinising the calendar which worked through its little two-coloured pages with exasperating slowness.

Though convinced that I was acting differently from them, I did exactly the same but in another direction: I ousted by means of a total chimera the depressing reality that was stifling us. I even refused to believe that I was hungry. Insupportable though my hunger was as twilight fell, I made out that it was non-existent or, if it existed, was no worse than a common headache. Perhaps guided mediumistically over extra-sensory waves by Demetrio the Seer (or even by Thirteen's unforgettable eyes), I set out to detach myself from matter and, by means of will-power and imagination, to replace the degrading spectacle in which my days dragged by with another spectacle and a fantastic one – of the epoch when proud spirits performed great feats under the fierce African sun. Esther held me in her thrall – passionately so – first because she was a woman (and women had been lost to us for some time); then because she represented pity (from which we were excluded!); then because she fought to liberate her people from slavery (of which I now at last understood the reality and not just the concept); and finally because, amid the regal pomp in which Pharaoh lived, she remained genuine and pure: as I myself intended to be.

On that heaven-sent paper, valued in the camp as highly as bread which was life itself, I found my way back to the dignity of

writing – like the ancient illuminators on salvaged parchment when
they repainted over the invisible trace of the Hebrew, Greek or
Latin texts, like treasure upon treasure; texts that would later
flower beneath the researcher's magnifying glass, a hundred times
more precious than an alchemist's formulae. Once I had started
work I never gave up as long as the faintest glimmer of light remained, but went on noting and commenting: real code-writing
(in which I revelled) over half a page, while the other half served
for footnotes. Indifferent to any kind of annoyance, oblivious of cold
and hunger, I relived every smallest vibration of the doings of
Assuerus, Mardocheus, Aman, and the unconquered daughter of
Benjamin's tribe, the complete heroine, for she combined beauty,
courage, sweetness and virtue.

It was certainly the wisdom pouring down on me from Téolo
in the bunk above and the extraordinary serenity he derived from
his breviary, as well as Valente's patience in making his burners
and Pannuzzo's care in polishing his jacket that gave me strength
to follow my path in imitation of their fervour and renunciation.
But as in my Paris period, when I discovered the Borgognas, the
Medici, Rubens, and finally Goya, and experienced them not as
external facts (which people still want to call Culture) but as expressions of my immediate feelings and will, so did it happen again
now with these new objects of inspiration. I recalled how, when I
had decided to leave Gian Luigi's house, Ulysses' 'little speech' to
his companions in the *Divine Comedy* meant more to me than any
other advice. Both the old and the new circumstances of my life
were stirred into action by the turbulent fantasies of a story continually melting into poetry. The spirit of Paolo Grilli brought me near
to the fire of Aman's troubled passions; the women I had loved
were embodied in Esther: Incoronata with her dedication, Arrichetta
with her beauty, Nerina with her regal bearing, and Cousin
Dolores (in her wreath of orange blossom) with her desperate
courage. And James Murri's rarefied mockery helped me to understand that in that universe starry with emblems and privileges,
ruled by the golden rod of the demi-god, it is the impious one who
submerges himself in the end – submerges himself in sacrilege so as
to bring death from it. In Aman stretched out on the Queen's bed
so that the eunuchs could pierce him, I saw the nemesis that guilt
brings on itself: that of Capaneus and Argante; and I saw how, by
virtue of the funereal quadrangle bounding our horizon, justice

would resolve the war on the side against evil, like a divine judgement.

Pompeo Pompei had called me a fakir in my Milan period, but my exercises in those days were mere trifles compared with these present ones; in which Téolo, Pannuzzo and Valente all took part up to a point, at least for the evening reading: Téolo sitting beside me on my bed, and Pannuzzo and the submarine-man Valente standing unobtrusively in the narrow space in front of the little window – Valente, I think, only out of group affection. Valente was a native of Castellabate del Cilento and had been rescued with one or two others from a submarine that had sunk to the bottom of the Otranto channel – delayed assistance had arrived after seventy-two hours. All bones and sinew, he spoke little; but no one picked a quarrel with him because of something disquieting in his russet eyes. With Pannuzzo, whom he protected against the tyranny of his clients, he even shared a cigarette stub.

The conditions of the *Lager* towards the end of winter were bleak indeed. Through the action of some spy – bribed, perhaps, by a tin of sauerkraut – the clandestine radio was discovered and with it went the basic element for calculating one's resistance: which in fact was deteriorating rapidly. But those who died were replaced by others, brought along from areas taken over by advancing armies. Many had already collaborated with the Germans, but they did not say so, and they also knew various other things which they kept to themselves, wanting to blend in with the crowd as if they had shared their destiny from the beginning. Every day clouds of Allied planes passed overhead making implacably for Bremen, Hamburg or Berlin, and various frightened remarks of the guards let it be understood that ours was one of the safest places. Meanwhile, after the confiscation of the radio and the subsequent grotesque threats meted out all round, the Germans – imagining who knows what signalling system to enemy planes – deprived us of electric light during the night which gave rise to episodes grotesque in their wretchedness: for the many sick who could not find their way to the latrines and for the many who were continually woken up as a result of this. There usually followed furious quarrels that condemned the whole hut to sleeplessness, for the din soon became infernal. To get round the darkness problem, and after endless referenda, vote-countings and ballots, it was agreed that each man should sacrifice a tiny quota of his weekly ration of fat so as to make night-lights. But after three attempts the experiment fell through: there was always some hungry person to put out the little flame at dead of night and to gulp down the night-light, so that we were plunged again into darkness amid the muffled beating of hearts and the earth's vibrations as distant explosions tore cities apart.

The final contrivance of the '*crucchi*' (as we described the Germans of the *Lager* in a word of uncertain etymology) was that of leaving us without matches – perhaps still motivated by some fear that we were signalling to enemy planes; so that finally there was not a single matchbox in the whole of Siltau. Every evening thirty delegates from thirty huts came to a certain place at a certain hour to get fire with a single wax taper for the thousands of people who would not otherwise have been able to smoke or cook on the patent Valente burners. Many were already limping on legs swollen with hunger; a malady which generally afflicted the tall of stature to whom fate granted the same rations as to the small. Many were harbouring that tuberculosis which was soon to kill them; but they refused to give way: some of them sincerely bound to a duty that was hardly known or understood; others believing themselves tied by their oath to the King, although the House of Savoy, in its usual way, paid not the slightest attention to those who were wearing themselves out on its behalf (nor did it show, later, that it had even been aware of them!). But as for me, I was so distrustful of human nature in general and in particular that I remained pitiless towards others, just as I was drugged into a total indifference towards myself. I suffered the same hardships as all the others; indeed, I had freely accepted them, almost chosen them, out of humility and expiation. But it had not been given to me to modify my character and still less to restrain my thoughts. I felt that the communal ordeal had no meaning for me, and that it was on the point of reaching its term.

It was on some grim evening about that time, when we were at the very limit of our deprivation, that we saw Pannuzzo arriving at our private area by the window with something voluminous concealed beneath his vast jacket. As soon as he felt he was safe he knelt down and cautiously extracted handfuls of mushrooms from his bosom, and piled them up on the floor under the stupefied gaze of Téolo, Valente and myself. He smiled in answer to our questions and revealed that he had found them all precisely beneath the watch-tower at the far end of the *Lager*, in a corner to which no one went so no one had noticed their existence.

'Under the tower? But what do you mean?' asked Téolo. 'The fatigue patrols pass it every day by the dozen to draw their rations!'

'Yes,' he admitted, 'but the mushrooms were a little further on, towards the main stretch of barbed wire, right up against the tower. No one's noticed them.'

'D'you mean you got them from the other side of the warning-wire, Pannuzzo? Under the sentry's eyes? He must have been asleep not to have seen you! Don't you realise he could have shot you?'

He looked at us with a confused and aggrieved expression. What we were saying did not seem even to penetrate his mind, much less convince him. He tried to explain that the sentry could not have seen him in the concealed spot where he was, and other absurdities. He apologised for having run the risk of death – he certainly had not realised he was doing so, or else (which seemed to me strangely possible) he somehow knew that he would come out of it unscathed. We did not know what type the mushrooms were and they could easily have been poisonous – but this did not so much as occur to Pannuzzo. So, trusting in his trust and his angelic innocence, the four of us ate those mushrooms (which were excellent) together; together to live or die in the best possible way. All they gave us was the deepest sleep we had had for months.

I awoke in the morning even before Pannuzzo got down to brush his jacket, and found the idea for a new work, perhaps a full-length book or play. If Esther were a dazzling heroine like Brandimarte or Erminia, then the immense figure of Jesus breathing in the Gospels should be raised up and explained on the level of poetry. Pannuzzo's humility, and the simple gesture with which he had placed the mushrooms on the floor and stayed kneeling in front of us, showing and offering them with a look that seemed to ask forgiveness for his very devotion – all this was like the blooms on a tree of revealed sweetness whose seed had been sown two thousand years before on the shores of the Lake of Genasareth. I had never meant to meditate on the figure of Christ; and every time it imposed itself on me I had put off receiving his message till some other time. Perhaps the time had now come. I pulled myself up in the darkness and shook Téolo's curtain above me. But he was not asleep.

'Listen,' I whispered. 'Perhaps I've had an idea. Supposing I wrote a book that was different from all the other books? Supposing I wrote about Jesus as the greatest of all poets? Supposing I could show that this is what it means to be the Son of God?'

He didn't answer for a while. Then:

'Go to sleep,' he said slowly. 'Go to sleep, it's still night. We're already atoning for our sins in this place. It's important not to commit any more!'

Above us the distant drone of the plane-formations going to mow down the cities of the Triangle made the small window-panes vibrate imperceptibly. I buried myself in sleep. And it was now the glass of the skylight that shook. There were a few slow sighs and a deep throbbing organ-like snoring from a few, but interrupted now and again and then starting up again as though in a series of nightmares. They were being afflicted by endless intimate memories, desires and loves churning around in the depths of their hearts; as was happening also in mine because I partook of their troubles without wanting to, but I knew them so well. The rhythm of solitude and companionship did not stop. I heard Téolo's quiet breathing above me; and that of the other two, my family. Perhaps I would be able to detach myself from the world only when I had left this one.

The psychosis of hunger far outstripped its physiological reality and drove the prisoners to various forms of strange behaviour. For instance, they had built with great ingenuity a huge quantity of scales of every size on which it was possible to measure everything down to half a gram. They had originally been constructed as a black market outfit; but later they served to measure out our infinitesimal rations: margarine, sugar, salt. And people even went so far as to weigh cigarettes when it was a matter of exchanging them: just as usurers used to do with florins. As for the method of eating their rations, there were those who ate them up immediately, those who nibbled at them taking at least ten bites, and those who put their bread on their blanket and looked at it for at least half a day saying that this gave them security. In default of real meals, the prisoners enjoyed imaginary ones to the utmost. A thriving literature of cookery flourished in the *Lager* to the comfort of the more fastidious palates, and one saw pitifully muffled-up figures running from one hut to another in search of new recipes to add to their own well-filled scribbling-blocks. Then they would read out menus of gargantuan meals and everyone else would listen as if hypnotised. So there was nothing very extraordinary in us four operating in a contrary way. With Téolo's help we established theologically that the pain and gnawing of the stomach could not act as fateful portents of illness or death, but were more like ordinary neuralgia or the spasms of a common wound. Pannuzzo, and then Valente too, humbly accepted this thesis, and once we had quickly eaten up our communal meal not a word was said in that connection by any of the four of us until next day. On the other hand the monastic rule of fasting showed its powerful logic in that no one in the hut ever spoke of women; and perhaps, for many, this final chastisement was not entirely undeserved.

As spring approached the rhythm of the air-raids on Germany became terrifying. In clear sunsets we saw high up above us the swarms of flying fortresses that had shed their bombs over the region and were returning to the coast in hundreds, in waves, having lost their formation while in action. But seen all together like that, and shining brightly so high up in a sun that had already withdrawn from the earth, they seemed more terrible and invincible than ever. One followed in one's mind the flock of airmen returning to their comfortable shelters; and it meant nothing that they had risked their lives and that many of the men flying up there were wounded or dying. They were the masters of space and that was worth any kind of anguish. Then the camp turned its eyes back on to its own inertia and the night brooded over the heavy breathing in the cattle-shed.

At the end of March the Fascist Republic of Salò conveyed a van-load of biscuits to us. Shortly afterwards it obtained permission for Northern Italian families subject to Mussolini's regime to send food parcels to their relations. So half the camp was cared for, and the persistent malevolence of history regarding the South left all the rest, from Cassino downwards, fasting. However, the Germans then distributed request cards to every prisoner. Immediately the firm of Quero, Fabbricatore and Mozzillo sprang up again – it bought up the cards of those who had no one to send them to and gave cut-throat percentages in return. This business was not run without endless intrigues, arguments, brawls and betrayals; but we, being associated with Téolo, the only Northerner among us, placed our cards at his disposal and got ourselves back on our feet: only just in time, I believe, especially as regards Pannuzzo who was the youngest

and in the worst condition. As for me, I was beginning to suffer
from fevers that later grew more intense and turned out to be
malaria of illustrious Greek origins. While these things were going
on, my work on the Gospel, inspired by Pannuzzo's virtue, took
shape.

It was a work unquestionably weak in its scientific and logical
context, yet strong indeed from the point of view of love. It is
impossible for me now to reconstruct what I felt and saw in it; and
how I thought I could avoid the innumerable shoals which in the
eyes of a punctilious and cultured academy would surely have sunk
such a doubtful thesis. But I certainly buried myself in it with all
the power of my mind; and if I was unable to give the work the
depth it deserved, I certainly drew extraordinary strength from it
which made me impregnable to every pressure and blow from
without, and allowed me hours of peace and oblivion such as I had
not known since the happy days of childhood.

Before the arrival of June with its shattering events in Europe,
and July, so crucial in Germany, I had elaborated the greater part
of the work and was already embarking on the final section – the
death, resurrection and reappearance of Jesus to the women and
the apostles. But here my fancy, unchecked by any critical impedi-
ment (which I would have found restrictive and out of the question)
and resting only on the bare lines of the Evangelists, took flight
around a theme so fascinating that it became the focal point of the
book instead of leading in to the conclusion. And if that work had
not been destroyed as a result of subsequent events, together with
the story of Esther and my notes on the thoughts they both produced, I would certainly have chosen to put the finishing touches
only to this last part: the unspoken drama of Pilate's wife when
confronted with the passion and death of the Redeemer.

That woman was a patrician and a Roman confined for a time
to a sun-drenched province, like the wife of a modern diplomat
posted to some undesirable embassy, and she formed part of that
world that had its new-style poet in Catullus and was rich in feelings
and scruples adverse to the ancient republican roughness. And in
the fantastic novel that I went on weaving in my mind I believe I
almost caught her character; and thence the intimate reactions and
events that were to flow from it. The figure of Jesus was known to
her through the many stories and almost the legend that surrounded
his name; and throughout his cruel trial before Pilate, the Nazarene

must have appeared to her unique; magnetic in his silence and
resignation, and giving rise to disturbing and indescribable emotions.

Though it is not documented, it is reasonable to suppose (following St Matthew's Gospel) that his wife's opinions played some part
in Pilate's hesitations when those of the Temple were a crowd of
seditious fanatics in the eyes of the presiding judge and the Other a
politically harmless man. She must have anxiously followed the
doings of the Just Man to whom the crowd insisted on preferring
the assassin Barabbas; she must have heard from the servants about
the scourging, the mockery, the crown of thorns. The blind and
evil forces that struck the messenger of universal love would have
been nameless and infernal symbols in her mind, hands without a
body, scourges brandished by Evil against Good. And in the same
way she would have conceived the Son of Man to be greater than
anyone else not so much for his august bearing as for the greatness
irradiating from his mantle, as white as that whiteness of soul whose
only counterpart is the flaming sorrow at the foot of the Cross, the
cry of purple as Masaccio intuited it.

When the Passion was over and Jesus was dead there was the
man from Arimathea to take him down from the Cross and send
him to a humble tomb. But on the third day it was empty. From
this point starts the prodigious story of apparitions and revelations
which would grow from century to century and flower into the huge
tree of Christian tradition. But the last certain act of the Passion
remains the placing of Jesus in that tomb. After that we leave history
and enter the domain of faith.

But it was perhaps beyond faith and within poetry that I then
searched for the Man of Sorrows, dragged from the tomb not by
a divine act but by human passions and emotions. It was mankind
and mankind alone that could claim the remains even of God,
inasmuch as he had made himself Man and to mankind alone the
Poet belonged: if this was what being the Son of God meant. To
whom, then, should be assigned not only the idea but the power of
moving away the stone from the tomb – so as to receive from it
the most holy remains and transfer them almost into one's own
heart? From the point of view of the Roman prefect's wife, Jesus'
disciples were simply a group of workmen and fishermen who had
denied him and left him alone to torture and death. The service
rendered to the Man brought down from the Cross was – in its
methods and in the persons involved – the final residue of a be-

wilderment and fear that would later disperse them for ever. For this reason I saw her staying up late, making provisions; through her agency other devoted women whose names are not preserved by Time though they are noted in the march of the universal spirit, through her agency they reopen the unhonoured tomb, take out the martyr, give Him oils, as Magdalen did, and new bandages; then leaving the winding-sheet stained with blood and water, they carry him to her because, as she was the only one to defend him, she now wants to be the sole guardian and repository of the desecrated body of the Man who had understood Love, had flayed hypocrisy, had exalted charity, and had forgiven the men who knew not what they did.

These were the thoughts by which I was totally penetrated and profoundly moved, and I communicated their dangers to a thoroughly upset and almost panic-stricken Téolo who let me talk on and opposed me only with the unbelieving look in his eyes; and throughout all this period the Anglo-American forces were entering Rome and landing in France. The Russians were occupying Vienna, and in Germany they were preparing that *coup d'état* which culminated in the attempt on Hitler's life on July the 20th.

The ferocious reaction following that deed – which in the Reich cost the lives of around two thousand important people including members of the Stauffenberg and von Hasselt families – produced in the *Lager* a new wave of punishments and restrictions that made our conditions very much worse. The dispatch of parcels from Italy was suspended, and inspections multiplied (in which the Germans confiscated whole heaps of our possessions). Once again fear took possession of the camp as persistent rumours circulated that we were to be eliminated before the Nazi surrender. Furthermore, at this time Mussolini dissolved the old Royalist armies by official act of his government of Salò so that we reverted to civilian status and were placed under the rigours of German law – and this prescribed work for any and everyone who found himself within the Reich. This greatly benefited the other ranks who, working as prisoners, were already subject to slave labour and by becoming ordinary labourers they were made equal with everyone else. But in German eyes all possibility of the officers refusing work collapsed. So the struggle became bitter between the two theses though in the end it was the facts that had to be reckoned with.

Once hope was lost that the war would end at least during those months, once supplies had been cut off and restrictions set up, the chances in favour of resistance diminished; many men decided to leave the *Lager* and go over to manual work in factories or on farms. But in September after Paris had surrendered and the Allied armies were heading towards the Rhine, the numbers in Siltau reached alarming proportions owing to those who poured in from the newly evacuated areas, and those who had gone out to work in these same areas and now flocked back to the camps. As confusion reached a peak so did people's needs. A cigarette cost a thousand times its normal price. The prisoners had to smoke tea-leaves, lime-leaves, any leaves, even potato peelings; then came the bark of trees; after which those frantic men resorted to the sawdust from their palliasses, a delicacy that was dubbed 'the lung-splitter'. Many declared consumptives, to whom smoking was lethal and nourishment indispensable, nevertheless bartered a portion of bread in exchange for tobacco.

This was the period of my greatest concentration; but following a system already applied on many other occasions, I allotted myself some exacting and painstaking manual task to alternate with my mental work when reflection on some point had not come to fruition; and this time, strange though it may seem, I devoted myself to washing my two sheets; a thing held to be impossible in our conditions, and it took me nearly a week.

For the cleaning (if so it may be called) of the *Lager* and ourselves the only provision was the fortnightly disinfection of our clothes *en masse* in the gas chambers. The latter, which have played a large part in post-war literature for the last twenty years, were installed in all the camps for the purpose of exterminating insects and providing essential safeguards against contagious typhus; and it was only after the war that we heard they had been used against human lives. But there was no facility at all for doing one's laundry.

To begin with water was scarce in the camp and measured out by a hand-pump, a mess-tin at a time, after interminable queuing. Then there was the scarcity of soap. Finally there was no line and it was forbidden to go near the barbed wire. Could one dry the laundry by holding it out to the wind in one's hands? Or by laying it on the ground to get dirty again? Or by draping it over the dormitory to the indignation of the others and where it would get

covered with smoke from the stove? Or by leaving it on the roof
for the wind to blow away or someone to try to steal? Under these
conditions, and with a cunning and dexterity far greater than were
deployed by Casanova when escaping from the Piombi, I washed
those sheets – extremely rare articles, incidentally, and not used by
anyone. When they were dry I made the bed next to the window,
and the whole block, composed of six huts, came to admire the
marvel – as when there is an international exhibition and the whole
city comes to revere a masterpiece.

Lying between those fragrant sheets I overcame the daily attack
of fever that lasted from six in the evening till around midnight –
although this was during the coming-and-going to and from the
exhibition; then the fever abated and I suffered from a crippling
headache till about two. Then I fell asleep and slept peacefully until
early afternoon. The return of the fever was heralded by a sense of
blissful torpor similar to what I had experienced at Lwow with
those drunken bouts of coffee on an empty stomach. It was during
those rapturous hours that I had my sublime fantasies about the
divinity as incarnate in poetry; but it seems that sometimes I
became delirious, and Téolo had to get me into the infirmary
which was always in an appalling condition and lacking medicines
(beginning with quinine), but perhaps slightly more airy and
restful. Autumn progressed. When it became plain that the war
was going on and that we would have to endure another winter,
the *Lager* fell into a frozen and sinister silence. Once again nothing
was to be heard in the hut but the heavy breathing of those who lay
motionless, blankets over their faces, desperately conjuring up
ghosts. But it also happened that as the situation came to the climax
and needs became more pressing – especially as regards clearing the
rubble and burying the dead in the cities pulverized by the air
offensives – the Germans resorted to force. They sent off a whole
company, complete with baggage, on the pretext of transferring it,
but in fact handed it over to forced labour. The exhausted and
divided prisoners were no more able to react than ants, and when I
returned from the infirmary I found none of my friends left. Téolo,
Pannuzzo and Valente had disappeared; others were occupying
our four-tiered bunk; and no one could tell me anything about
them.

That night I slept on the ground with the ghost of Boris Draguliub
as sole companion. The bases of our beds were made of fir slats, and

most of them were lacking as they had been used for firewood. So the prisoners slept on four or five slats instead of fifteen, each man intent on defending his own and stealing everyone else's. Places left empty were immediately stripped, and this had happened to mine. An examination of conscience was simple this time: my imprisonment was due to an effort at humility and a debt of honour. But I now knew that it was impossible to force one's nature; that I had not really been prepared to accept the communal attitude and had even rejected it. Though convinced of my good faith in making the attempt, I was equally convinced that I had failed. The price paid for an experience of this kind mattered nothing to me, but it suited me to be free again now and to separate my fate uncompromisingly from that of everyone else.

I took less than no notice of all the various arguments; I did not feel bound by oath to King Vittorio or to anyone else; the casuistries of international law were for me merely laughable – the Hague, Geneva, the Red Cross; the laws 'prevailing' for the republicans of Salò, for the king's men, for the Nazis; the 'status' of the prisoner, the internee, the officer, the civilian, the worker. I could not hold out in the *Lager* for another winter, protected from the bombardments raging over the whole of Germany. I did not believe at all in our elimination at the last minute. And the argument that henceforth kept all the others clinging to that kind of rock, bleak indeed but safe, was the absolute imminence of the German collapse. The Allies were pressing on the Rhine; Finland had obtained a separate peace; Florence had fallen and Bologna was about to do so. Hitler's fate was sealed and his days numbered. But what was there left for me to do in a camp whose life and motivations I knew so well? My friends had gone; my book was finished. The tension of my mind would never have been assuaged in the repetition of useless days; with bandaged eyes in the midst of the vast tragedy that was about to reach its climax, a moment such as had not been seen for centuries: a whole proud powerful nation being brought to account amid unutterable events and majestic conflagrations. As a lonely traveller in a land that was not my own, I preferred to take my chance in the open and pay the price of consciousness; I wanted to know and understand.

So one morning towards the end of November 1944 I presented myself to the German sergeant in charge of recruitment. There was a small squad ready to depart and he merely added my name to the other four. An hour later, after the shower and disinfectant, and with the first horse steak I had eaten for fourteen months as provision for the journey. I withdrew from those particular tribulations.

THE GEESE

I looked without much curiosity at my four companions with whom chance had decreed that I should share an extraordinary experience and the risks that could bring it to an end at any moment: a second lieutenant of the *bersaglieri*, of coarse appearance and with a marked Apulian accent; a fellow-countryman of his of the same rank, but flaccid and sleepy; a lieutenant of athletic build, but whose completely shaven head together with the blackish complexion of the declared consumptive gave him the look of an escaped convict; and finally a lean and quarrelsome captain, the only one who took any care of his appearance insofar as this was possible in the circumstances. They were dazed by the open air, and their miserable aspect and frightened awkward movements made me realise that my own were certainly the same.

The journey lasted half a day with two or three changes of train. The coming and going on those little provincial stations, where normal people seemed to be busy with everyday affairs, was utterly astonishing to us after the length of time we had been cut off from such things; it all seemed like a play on a stage. The Germans deliberately pretended not to see us; but the suffering written on our faces must have made a mark on their uneasy consciences now that catastrophe was becoming evident. At one of our halts we happened to have a front-row view of two departing SS soldiers being seen off by their families. Those powerfully built young men belonged to a distinct class and were certainly sincere in their fanaticism. Their mothers and fiancées – respectable women from solid families – were talking gravely with them as befitted the solemn occasion. But our silent group left its mark on those farewells. Twice the eyes of one of those soldiers met mine; and I felt neither aggression nor conviction in them, but only a dark determination.

None of us knew German, and at the many control points all explanations were given by the man accompanying us, an old soldier who had lost a forearm and was in charge of the documents: new aspects of a specious freedom for the deaf and dumb. The refine-

ments of the German mechanism produced its phagocytic effects by
the use of both material and psychological elements, exactly as it
had operated when dispatching our army to the barbed wire
without the help of guards – knowing that owing to our absurd
desire for repatriation we would go there. This time we were kept
under guard by our ignorance of the language which curtailed
any possible contacts; we knew nothing of where we were being
sent; nor with what obligations, and still less, what rights; nor on
whom we would effectively depend. Our ignorance of German laws
in general, and wartime ones in particular, had handed us over from
one imprisonment to another; but it surprised me that as soon as he
saw the two SS men surrounded by their families, our one-armed
soldier did his best to get out of their view; and by his frightened
manner rather than by his few inarticulate words, he intimated that
those were people you had to keep away from.

We arrived at dead of night in a place whose nature we could
not identify. We crossed a wide clearing smelling of the country
and entered a brand new house fragrant with fresh wood. It had
six places, and as once again I was the senior man two of them
were put at my disposal. The dark sky was resplendent with stars,
and high up in the midst of them Orion's belt was shining with a
brightness I had never in my life seen before. While I was preparing
my bunk I saw a spider escaping, black and hairy and as big as a
nut. But though I took it as an evil omen, I fell asleep in this
knowledge without the slightest sense of bitterness; like someone
who has already willingly offered himself to destiny.

In the *Lager* I had always opened my eyes the moment dawn
touched our little window, so now again I awoke while the others
were still asleep and it took me some time to realise where I was.
My heart plunged into an unexpected void in my inexplicable
homesickness for the furtive sound of Pannuzzo's brush over the
indelible stain on his threadbare jacket. And the value of a period
that at the time had seemed static and useless suddenly swelled
within me, human warmth and depth that all Croesus' gold could
not have brought back or reproduced. We had not really known
ourselves, just as we do not recognise emotions which, nonetheless,
will form the basis of our lives for years to come; and in the concentration of captivity there had been a priceless and indefinable
aroma whose last trace I breathed in that early morning blueness.
But I shook myself: because after all, the present time was of the

same quality and rarity and measure; each drop of it being worth the one that had just passed.

On going out into the pristine and mysterious splendour of the dawn, I took my first breath of our new world. Our hut was on the least used side of a vast clearing where I saw great piles of timber geometrically placed. On one side I saw the outline of an antiquated workshop. Further on and situated exactly between two piles of planks was a medium-sized two-storey house; with a doll's-house window, already lit by a brighter light than the dawn's, set in the sloping roof. Behind me, on the further side of an old mossy wall on to which our hut backed, there was the sound of running water, and the tall grass bore witness to the peace of the place. From the direction of the house there came the occasional clucking of hens and one or two streaks of already switched-on lights: an orderly scene waiting to spring to life and re-echo with sound.

The first person to appear on it was a servant-girl – such a ritual entry as to confirm the stage-set illusion. She was about eighteen years old with fair hair and a large bright apron, and she exhaled health and wholesome eroticism from every pore. She was the first woman I had been near for fourteen months and I gazed at her as at an object of great curiosity.

She curtsied to me, pointed to the house, and with other gestures of universal validity was unquestionably inviting me to come and get something to eat. As I followed her I breathed in the damp smell of wood put out to season; our footsteps made no sound on the grass; and as for the house, it seemed to be coming towards me in the still bright morning. The noise of the running water behind the wall was hardly more than a murmur; Orion's brilliant lights had vanished, but not their magical aftermath which still seemed to vibrate on that enchanted portion of the world. As in childhood the first day of a new life seemed to be suspended in time: a shining drop quivering at the tip of a leaf; poised yet not falling.

When the small side-door for which we were making opened, and I saw the cheerful light from the lamps and heard the rumbling of the stove and the frying of the *Speck* that was being prepared for us – all in the warm glow of a traditional German kitchen; and when the mistress of this little world came forward to greet me – so conventional in her ritual part of organiser and dispenser (as the girl had been in her role of servant) – and with many small gestures and rudimentary French displayed a courtesy I had not seen for nearly two years, then the enchantment of that morning came to a climax and at the same time broke. That day was Sunday, and we were left to find our way about and make ourselves at home: we arose from the depths and I truly believe that our lungs swelled out in our painful effort to return to the surface.

The disposition of the mind has a bewitching effect on our thoughts and even our sensations, just as the incidence of light modifies the tone of colours and the key of a musical work transfers its melody. My four new companions clearly did not share my ideas, but then I was not tied to them by any previous links and they were inspired by bitter rancour towards the Germans. All four believed they themselves were somehow to blame for accepting manual labour, so they talked on a level of open-minded superficiality, always ending on a laugh, which was their only way to play down the facts and diminish their personal bitterness. Finding ourselves immediately separated in our work, we realised that the Kurt sawmill had no other function in our regard except to provide us with our lodging; just as the women of that family, though obliged like all German women to do almost military work, had also to provide us with our food. So it was that the *bersagliere* from Apulia had to cart sacks at a farm every day (and very heavy they were, he said); his fellow-countryman, Gifuni, was employed in the stables of a brewery where he had to look after huge horses of the kind that can still be seen in the streets of Munich or even London; the herculean lieutenant, whom I knew to be a Roman and the son of a man in the legal profession, was coupled with me at the goods station to see to the loading of coal and other raw materials. As for the punctilious captain who in civil life was a provincial functionary of Chieti – we had some trouble in finding out his new job which was that of a cleaner in the local fruit market, though he never neglected his habitual care in his dress. At night they recounted the events of the day and made heavy mockery of everything, which did not prevent each trying to fix himself up on his own account, developing relationships and hatching thoughts that the others did not know; though before all this process came to a head there remained an apparent unity between us.

But that poised and motionless moment in that isolated little place was an extraordinary anachronism in the drama that was shortly to consume the whole of Germany. The Allies were marking time in the Rhineland; the Russians were waiting for the winter to end before striking their last blow on the Eastern front; while in the country itself the ferocious Nazi reaction to the attempt on Hitler's life plunged everyone into a deep fear that took the place of enthusiasm and ruled everything with a rod of iron. Of course the war was pouring relentlessly down from the sky; but it had not yet penetrated remote country places which in the Reich are like the dust of the Milky Way. Berg was a secluded village about ten kilometres away from one of the great bridges over the Elbe, and it had hardly even been aware of the war. Depopulated by conscription, it had (as was customary) the old, the wounded and the unfit at its disposal, together with an excessive number of women and a group of forced-labour prisoners from France and the Ukraine who had been there for nearly four years, were simple soldiers and by now rather boring. So that the Italian officers, who had obviously been preceded by a good deal of gossip in that quiet and withdrawn atmosphere, were observed with intense curiosity.

And with equal curiosity did I observe the Germans, indeed with delight, feeling concealed beneath my workman's clothes like a periscope-watcher in the hull of a submarine. In 1912 (the year I began my seclusion at my boarding-school) Italy had been bound to the Triple Alliance by the political pact with Austria and Germany, which she then broke by intervention on the side of the French and British. At that time Italy was by and large pervaded by pro-German sentiments among the two cultivated classes. The monks themselves had close ties with the Berlin court – prodigal as it was of bequests and suggestions to the abbey – and had decorated the crypt with that angular stylisation of Byzantine motifs which, with a somewhat debatable magnificence thrown in, goes under the name of the Bayreuth school.

Encouraged by the enthusiasm of the learned and particularly the philosophers, Germany wanted to retain the compelling good-tempered and largely romantic image outlined by Madame de Staël more than a hundred years earlier – despite the not insignificant novelties that could be read into Bismarck's actions and the Wagnerian postures of Kaiser Wilhelm. Thus little weight was given to vague rumours concerning the self-styled archaeologists, geologists or naturalists with professorial beards who straddled half the world on a mission of wisdom as ambassadors of German *Kultur*; and who were often later reckoned to be special agents if not downright spies. Public applause for the scientific accuracy of everything that bore

the German imprint kept the masses silent. Precision compasses
and Faber pencils camouflaged the Krupp factories. The univer-
sities, Hegel and Beethoven did the rest.

In Gian Luigi's household family tradition maintained an attitude
of deference, if not of expiation, towards the Baroness von Egloffstein
who had been insulted by the Sanseveros. So out of disrespect
towards my elders I always made a point of showing an overall
scepticism about the Teutons (condemned also by Mario, I added
to myself!) and sought to disclaim any satisfaction over the Nie-
belung blood that might flow in my veins. These were distant
memories and lacked any connection with Hitler's Germans as I
had seen them in Greece or in the *Lager*; nor had I attempted to
establish a connection – it was as though they were two different
races. But no sooner did I cross the threshold of that hut in Berg
than I felt the thread of a forgotten thought and secret commentary
coming into motion, unwinding and weaving together again in the
complex texture of my mind.

Just as I had gone down to Calabria to take possession of my
Uncle Gian Michele's inheritance and had found a loved and
familiar face there, so on that early morning in Berg – with the long
grass on one side and stacks of wood on the other – I had felt a
natural inevitability about settling down in that peaceful setting.
All its aspects harmonised within me and were immediately familiar
and understood. The servant-girl's curtsy to a prisoner-of-war
doing forced labour (but in whom she nevertheless did not fail to
recognise a 'Herr Hauptmann') was all part of the meticulous care
with which the timber had been stacked for seasoning, part of the
respect for the trees in those remote woods, part of the fairy-story
house, the gleaming pans used for our food, and the mathematical
precision of the slices of bread that accompanied it. In the space
of a single moment it seemed to make up for all the confused anarchy
I had suffered over the past three years. The French spoken by the
mistress of the house (whom henceforth I called 'Madame') was the
sole means of entering into contact with her and the others. In my
heart I regretted not knowing German, which would have done so
much to crown our concord. I remembered Paolo Grilli and James
Murri and how they used to use this language long ago when, with
Faustian cries, they lost themselves in the musical works of the great
geniuses born on this German soil.

Whereas I spent my first two weeks in that country loading coal with the strength of my bare arms – utterly exhausting work though enabling me to savour a totally different life: that of the labourer whose attention is focused on the mass of manual work he has in front of him, and who measures his capacity and apportions his movements according to a technique born of necessity. The play of the muscles then becomes automatic, but the outcome is all the more efficient as the effort is properly organised. To gain a fraction of a second in time or a few centimetres in space means that you emerge victorious at the end of the day from an ordeal that would otherwise leave you prostrate. It was a sportsman's technique, but applied by us to a vital need. And it pleased me to create a vigorous harmony in my physical being, in the rhythm of my arms and legs, in the swinging of my chest as I wielded fork or shovel, so that I could congratulate myself each time I made the coal fly a little further or land in the place I had intended. When I had passed the crisis point well known to all athletes and realised I was the master of my material, my limbs seemed possessed by fantastic energy and capable of anything. Returning home along the street and across the main square of the village, I walked quickly and self-confidently under the furtive eyes of the people; with a studied nonchalance that certainly bespoke some kind of defiance on my part.

In a village of general kindliness and an ingrained sense of social values, it was impossible for the blatant injustice and inhumanity of our situation to pass unnoticed. The Ukrainians and few Frenchmen who, as prisoners, were already doing work of this kind had been peasants and labourers in civilian life, so were physically adapted to manual work and knew all about it. But as always happens in small centres, the people of Berg held professional men in high esteem and they knew that we were officers and had academic degrees; moreover, our evident malnutrition had done nothing to help our somewhat frail physiques as men of the pen rather than the spade. Only two of us had remotely rustic complexions, Penne, the *bersagliere*, and the herculean Magaldi, my Roman associate in the coal-yard; but even he was clearly a man of education and good breeding despite his convict's appearance. Moreover, the Army – that constant object of worship in Germany – had given us as officers an ineradicable halo. Here, where a sergeant was in charge of a barracks, the captain was really a 'Hauptmann' or 'head man', following the etymology of the word. Not to mention that when my documents had been checked there had been that small

matter of the 'von' (as with the Fascist boss in Milan, that time!) –
a monosyllable highly revered in Germany; so much so that one of
the Ukrainians had mysteriously whispered to me: 'You! Baron!'

So the exhausting toil of carting sacks, of cleaning out stables or
shovelling away like a machine not only had an effect on our arms
but also on the consciences of others. In the early days Magaldi
and I used to be working in the freight-yard for ten hours on end,
in intense cold, and having – just the two of us – to unload thirty-
five tons of coal wholesale then reload them in retail. I don't know
why Magaldi threw himself so desperately into that back-breaking
work – perhaps because he wanted to show his contempt for work
he had accepted to his disgrace, or so he thought; but as for me, I
endured it with clenched teeth. Neither of us knew that this frantic
work was in no way dictated by law, and that as workers we were
entitled to refuse one sort of work and opt for another more suitable
one. So it must have been instinct that drove me on. When at the
end of the day Magaldi wanted to go straight back home, avoiding
the eyes and comments of the people, I decided to walk straight
through the middle of the main square, covered in black dust, my
eyes red and swollen, and my trusty shovel on my shoulder. I told
him that it was salutary for the local populations to see us, and it
was for them and not for us to feel ashamed. And indeed that is
what happened, helped by fear and the existing circumstances.
Once the Germans realised the situation, it was they who found a
way of pulling us out of our slough of despond from which we would
certainly not have been able to pull ourselves; but I think it came
to an end for this reason, the last move in the game, but not the
least important one for that: apart from the fact that the time of
reckoning was at hand and many of them thought it a good idea
to make friends with us pending X hour, it must be remembered
that as we were Italians the feminine element of Berg was establishing its romantic claims – and about this it is pointless to speak either
ill or well.

I had been lucky enough to salvage my few manuscripts from the
Lager – the one about Pilate's wife and the one about Esther. So no
one was better able to understand why it was women who freed us
from our slavery; and were even ready to take us, resurrected, to
the warmth of their hearts.

So while we were being subjected to the devilish gymnastics prescribed by the Todt organisation, the women of Berg were devoting a whole mass of observations, reflections and gossip to our case. They laid the gunpowder, as it were, and all that was needed for it to burst into flame was for my team-mate Magaldi, together with the administrator Gifuni, to dare to go to the local cinema. This happened at the end of our second week. First the girl at the box-office and then the usherette – both slim and lithe – established a relationship, and after the show was over both were in nocturnal dialogue with our two among the timber stacks, seeking those assurances and investigations that the situation demanded. As for Penne the *bersagliere*, he had not set his sights so high, but wishing (in deference to my rank) to save me the morning chore of breakfast, had entered into a very explicit relationship with the servant-girl who, I forgot to say, was called Kate. Nor did the mistress of the Kurt household seem to object to the situation.

This woman answered to the provocative name of Lore; she was about thirty and while not endowed with any particular attractions was healthy and solid with a glowing complexion and rich brown hair. Her eyes were of a variable grey and slightly squinting, her manner a bit laboured and mechanical – but this was a result of shyness. The Kurts were in a flourishing economic and social position; they owned many woods and a sawmill and rivalled the Krauss family, owners of the brewery where neighed the horses groomed by Gifuni; and Lore was reasonably cultured having studied at the Ilmenau in Luneburg, hence her fragmentary knowledge of French. But, as she told me later, she had brought out and dusted her old exercise-books on that first morning, and by degrees relearnt the words and idioms of that enemy language that disturbed her. At the time of our arrival Herr Kurt was away in hospital, or so it was said; and his wife was devoting herself to her only child, a boy of five, whom she idolised. During the two weeks that she saw us crossing the square every evening with our shovels on our shoulders, Madame Lore must have taken steps which were subsequently discussed and approved of by her husband when he reappeared; for shortly afterwards the *bersagliere* Penne, returning one morning with breakfast, informed Magaldi and myself that the coal-age was over and the wood-age was about to begin: and this at the sawmill of the benevolent Kurt family. We were about half-way through December.

The sanhedrin of our little hut came to the conclusion that

Lieutenant Magaldi, my team-mate with the unprepossessing, almost disquieting appearance, had benefited from an attention directed to me as senior Captain and 'baron'. Those Germans knew full well that the war was lost, and that before long they would have to make some kind of accommodation; so that Herr Kurt, approving his wife's initiative, brought the most senior in rank amongst us to work on the premises, thus hoping to put me under an obligation so that I would act as protector when the time came. Suppositions confirmed by the fact that Magaldi was forthwith sent off to the woods, in a temperature below zero, to load '*die grossen Baüme*', while I was left under cover assigned to the light machinery.

So the characters peopling this new stage were: the secretary of the firm, a poor relation, still young, her face horribly burned by the incendiary bombs which killed countless civilians in Germany. This was the last word in Anglo-Saxon hypocrisy, for this type of weapon was not considered unlawful inasmuch as it could not strictly speaking be called 'gas'. All the incendiaries could do was produce a heat capable of melting iron and they roasted people in their shelters like ants.

Then there was Karl, the foreman and a Prussian, a man of few words and stiff as a ramrod. He had been a prisoner of the French in the '14–'18 war and knew what it was all about. He had certainly received his orders in our regard.

Stephen: who worked on the big eight-blade saw. He was said to be a Cossack officer, but he denied this, though he was the undisputed leader of the other five Ukrainians who worked with us. One of these, Kolya, had belonged to the Siltau 'administrative services' when all those Russian prisoners had died. He filled in one or two details of that episode whose import could perhaps be better appreciated in retrospect.

Finally there was Herr Kurt, a weak-looking man with a greyish puffy face and bovine eyes and unquestionably suffering from some deep-seated illness. Those eyes, behind the heavy circle of black spectacles, looked like dead oysters. Yet even in that degree of cold and in deep snow, Herr Kurt got up at five in the morning to keep an eye on the workers as they took up their posts. Then he disappeared – I think so as to get back to bed until nine. German-style punctuality was not belied even by a second at the sawmill: at half-past five there was a siren blast and immediately all the machines started throbbing. When the siren blew for break the men stopped their movements in mid-air, put down their tools or whatever they were holding on the nearest surface, and off they went. Work always started again to the sound of the siren, whereupon the men would pick things up where they had put them down and complete the second half of the interrupted movement. And so it went on for nine hours, with two breaks.

Ten minutes after the mutilated secretary had entered us in the register and a small truck had borne Magaldi off into the cold woods, Karl accompanied me unceremoniously but not unkindly to a bench at one side; this was fitted up with a small saw to break into pieces fit for the stove all the bark left over from the main cutting operation. He showed me the very simple mechanism of this tool which I could carry on with perfect ease; he watched me sawing half a dozen or so pieces, gave a brief nod, then took no further notice of me for a week. During which time I worked with such unbelievable regularity, being deeply absorbed in the general overhaul of my thoughts, that I cut up a formidable quantity of wood. In the evening the two lieutenants and Magaldi disappeared, one of them after Kate, one after the usherette at the cinema, and the third after the box-office girl whom he had nicknamed Kitten. So I was left alone with Captain Ceci who was not at all talkative after the humiliations of sweeping the market. Our mutual silence in the warmth of the hut was pleasant to both of us and established an imponderable friendship between us.

I found Captain Ceci's little personal drama moving. Cavaliere Ceci, as he was known in civil life, was provincial secretary in Chieti, dignified in his ways but frail in constitution, which was perhaps why the Germans had allotted him a broom; seeing he was not strong they had been humane in their fashion. But the cavaliere was neither old nor displeasing to look at and must have suffered a thousand deaths among the housewives of all classes who were buying their vegetables all around him; and imagining that they were thinking and feeling what he himself was thinking and feeling (which time would show not to be the case), he suffered torments. He found his situation especially intolerable in front of the two lieutenants; he suffered less with me, his senior in the same rank, especially as I was tolerant and detached. But how to live down the episode of the pump?

On that second Sunday, while we were standing around in the main street waiting to go to the cinema, the cavaliere was sum-

moned imperiously by the foreman of the market. And to our
astonishment a few moments later an archaic but gleaming hand-
pump appeared, rich with red and green varnish and martial
brasses and pulled at the trot not by horses, as it should have been,
but by four of the market sweepers and among them Ceci dressed
in his Sunday best. The job was to clear out a drain that had suddenly overflowed. The whole village was at their windows, proud
of their pump and of their emergency service; but an ineffaceable
blot had fallen on the life of Cavaliere Ceci. So he passed those
silent hours mending and ironing his clothes in whose faultlessness
and finish reposed what remained of his dignity, as formerly with
Pannuzzo's clients. As for me, I was completing my work on
Pilate's wife; he never asked me about it, nor did I tell him what it
was that kept me so busy.

But though it was an instrument of torture for Ceci, that venerable
pump had aroused old memories in me; of the happy time I spent
playing with Checchina in the house in via della Solitaria, after we
had metaphorically scaled the Family Tree. Our toys at that time
were in fact German: little carriages, little trains, all kinds of tiny
objects that imitated the real ones, and they were bright and
varnished with the same reds and greens and gleaming with the
same brasses as adorned the Berg hand-pump. Added to all these
metal toys we also had painted cards from which to cut out highly-
coloured little houses, cocks with handsome combs, trees with rich
foliage and romantic entanglements of roots; a complete German
village just like the one we were now experiencing. And now our
real village (like the one in our games) was enlivened by teams of
little yellow goslings waddling around in the grass and under the
reddish piles of timber; and when pools of water like blue eyes
appeared in the meadow from time to time, sometimes covering
large parts of it, pairs of geese could be seen, looking as though they
were carved in marble, real Hanoverian *Gänse*, as large and bad-
tempered as swans.

This Germany from which even the memory of the *Lager* seemed
to be banished and whose only knowledge of the war was the passing
of very high planes, with its harmless cottages of wood and clay,
and inhabited by meticulous and thrifty people – this Germany
easily took me into its humanity; and my condition as a worker,
however odd this may appear, completed my sense of sweetness and
peace. 'Slavery' as I had experienced it in the freight-yard faded

further and further away in my daily relationships with all the others engaged in the same work as myself – mostly Germans who were unfit for military service owing to being too old or too young. They were poor people, no more no less, doing what it was their life work to do, like the labourers in Licudi; the circumstances were exceptional only for us, and only we saw them in a bad light. And if the people of Licudi had laughed and sung together with the women while carrying those weights in the depths of the olive grove, the methodical and conscientious Germans affirmed the value, the dignity and even the beauty of work by humbly bending to its laws: the happiness or unhappiness of their state thus depending only on the spirit they were able to bring to it. A lesson beyond nationality, rank and uniform that I needed to learn; a rhythm in which I could take part.

So while contemplating with genuine pride the piles of wood I had so neatly cut for the Kurt stoves, I felt sorry for the self I had been in those days in Milan when I had let myself nearly die of hunger through not having – I would not say the courage, but even the faintest idea of presenting myself as apprentice in that first shop. To have learnt to put trust in my own two arms multiplied my possibilities of freedom in the future; and submission was enlivened by the revival of the innocent subterfuges of the schoolroom – the older Germans with their good-tempered sense of humour being the ones to indicate with a wink when I could get away with something. I recalled the little work-site at Licudi; now I would have been able to understand their most simple thoughts and judge much better who should work for me.

It was Herr Kurt who provided the only blot in this eclogue. As in all natural and simple societies, the mere fact of his obvious physical disabilities set him apart, let alone the fact that he was boss. So when he withdrew after his formal appearance early in the morning, not to be seen again until closing time, we all breathed more freely in our work huts. As from that first Monday, he had always come along with feigned friendliness to the corner where I worked and bestowed a sort of half-smile of welcome on me. It was only natural that for the next ten minutes I should wonder why on earth Madame Lore had married him. But as I had stopped fetching my breakfast and hence no longer had any direct contact with her, I think she looked on the tenuous thread of her husband's abortive greeting as a way of maintaining a friendship that she did not want to relinquish.

The backwards and forwards movement of my saw, which gave a well-turned bow as it came towards me and then flew back with surprising lightness, fitted in very well with the yes and no of my eternal reflections. I recalled the woes that had arisen from the people who had wanted to make use of me, Mavì, Catherine and, more recently, Toia at Reggio Emilia. But this time I was encountering greater loyalty, because Madame Lore wanted to make advance payment on what she was not at all sure of receiving afterwards. True, Magaldi was still in the heart of the forest deploying his splendid muscles in the felling of trees – like a ram knocking down a wall with its horns – but even so it had been she who had removed us from the coal and the *Dreck*; and she also had to reckon with public opinion as well as the Nazi work bureau.

So as I was unable to make her understand that wanting to put me under an obligation only complicated things, and that I would certainly help her in any circumstances out of sheer courtesy, I distracted myself with thoughts of Denise Digne and generalisations about the incommunicability of lives; and so, lost in my thoughts, I reached record heights in the amount of bark I cut for the stove. So the future unfolded itself, like the whole of history, from its own womb. Because when my output was seen to be excessive and had completely overflowed the corner assigned to it, I was ordered to carry it from the sawmill to the attic in the Kurt house. Work that obliged me to traverse the whole building from the kitchen to the roof and remain for a good quarter of an hour each journey so as to stack the logs in an orderly fashion. Inevitably I met Madame Lore innumerable times, and she did not fail to give me smiles considerably wider than those of her husband; to which I civilly responded. Politenesses, however, that did not prevent the women of the house from availing themselves of my services once the wood had been unloaded; with the best will in the world, and where Kate was concerned with the usual curtsy, they gave me buckets, baskets and even refuse bins to deal with in the area behind the house: and this put me in touch with the poultry-yard, and more specifically with the respectable pair of geese of the Kurt stock.

Far away in the distance, and hardly more than two white specks, were the geese of the Krauss stock; so that it was borne in on me that these gentlefolk kept their pair of *Gänse* rather as Renaissance princes kept their peacocks. Our two were of a superior breed, mighty and solitary in that green meadow that stretched as far as a distant stream from which the water fancifully ebbed and flowed in a multitude of varied and shimmering pools; it was here that our geese were really happy, but only when they were alone together and there were no interlopers; indeed, you only had to look in that direction to provoke angry reactions from the gander who would throw a hoarse hiss from his throat, open his fearsome beak and spread his wings as if to fly at you. On the advice of the Ukrainian Kolya, who had preceded me in these household services, the only way of inducing the gander to relative respect for people's calves was to show him the stick. Whereas all I wanted was to love those easily offended bipeds. Squatting beside the gentle eye-blue lakes that had formed themselves out of nothingness, those geese held my spirit suspended in the distant expanse of sky extending over that huge body of land from Ostend to the China Sea, inviting me to endless flights in space. They set a seal on that watery, airy and vegetable landscape, as once Geniacolo's green boat had set armorial bearings on the sea of Licudi.

Oscillating as I was between Georgics and Bucolics, the hut in the evening rather went against my mood as it degenerated from facetious humour to increasingly doubtful farce. Recently in Italy (and following a very ancient evil) there had been some confusion between love, jests and licentiousness, a confusion from which Mussolini himself had not been exempt, as he too was ending up among skirts; while first the Fascist squad leaders, then the Fascist bosses, with the four chiefs at their head, had regarded it almost of political merit and completely inseparable from soldierly and revolutionary behaviour to be (or appear to be) assiduous woman-isers and diligent frequenters of brothels. The *bersagliere* Penne and Gifuni the administrator, who had been welcomed as latin lovers in that first fervour, were now accepting readily all the rest – supplemented by other more positive reasons. But though the Nazi laws were extremely severe regarding German women who had relationships with prisoners, they did not take account of Italians who were looked on as free workers and civil collaborators. So the only available and valid male element was concentrated in them, that is to say, in us, given that all the local men were old or ill like Herr Kurt. This love-making without risk was a great relief after the infliction of so much abstinence, moreover it promised a support for the future, and could be endowed with the flame of romance.

Against all his expectations even Captain Ceci was captured almost by force between the cabbages and the turnips in his market, and by a very young girl. As he was as scrupulous as he was dignified, the poor man touched heaven with one part of himself while with the other he suffered agonies when thinking of his wife; and being already a mature man, this passion burnt like fire and was a fore-taste of the pains that would afflict him later. As for Magaldi, far from exhausting his energies in the woods, and while still looking on the Kitten as his 'little pillow' in time of war, he found himself in great demand; to the point of being involved in sensational episodes.

'When my woman,' he told us with seeming boastfulness not unmixed with a certain uneasiness, 'realised that her jealous neighbour had put a chain on the door and that I couldn't get out until the morning in full sight of all the other tenants, she asked me quite seriously whether I'd jump from the third floor into the canal to save her reputation and get away by swimming through the ice. Finally as I was passing between two rows of neighbours making impolite remarks, she unfortunately saw her own daughter in the crowd, just back from her night-shift.'

The mother and daughter involved in this incident were Dutch, evacuated to Berg heaven knows how, while their husband and father had continued to fight with the Allied fleet ever since Dunkirk. They disappeared shortly afterwards, overwhelmed by the shame of it; and only Captain Ceci had consideration for that other man who for four years had been risking his life at sea and thinking of his women (like the Greek Spiropulos!). The small group of French prisoners seemed not to want to have to do with these episodes. They were simple soldiers and had no respect for us, seeing that we had accepted labourers' work. In Madame Lore's smiles I seemed to detect (and perhaps in more senses than one) the reflection of all the gossip that must have been circulating. But having been educated by monks, I had the trace of their system for ever in my veins and a leaning towards a certain spiritual narcosis. My long imprisonment had led me to get over that crisis point beyond which the suffering of chastity is transmitted into freedom and mental clarity. Having paid a lot for it, and without wanting to, I had gained a very rare value: a better one than I could have gained in my youth and in the passionate renunciations of those days; and why barter it now for almost no reason, when that very clarity showed me what was demanded of us and why?

On Christmas Eve, when the waters seemed to have been stilled, Madame Kurt forewarned us of her coming and then set foot in our hut for the first time, accompanied by her son and Kate and laden with cakes and good things such as we had not seen for two years. The branch of mistletoe and the Christmas tree were not lacking. Madame made a little speech and seemed not a little moved. As I was the most senior, it was for me to answer, while the others stood to attention and for a few minutes recovered their ranks and, I believe, their memory. Then Madame Lore withdrew and I was held by the others to be responsible for her act of courtesy.

Before the end of the year, when I was emptying rubbish in the freezing cold behind the Kurt house, I thought I observed something odd in the attitude of the pair of geese in the distance. I went over, always armed with my stick, and noticed that the gander not only did not hiss or turn round on me, but was squatting beside his companion and clucking plaintively while she lay absolutely still. So I approached near enough to look at her properly; she was lying on her side, her eyes half-shut, her claws frozen and numb. I put out my hand to touch her and the gander let me do so. Then I decided to pick her up – though a residue of fear and her great weight and a certain reverence made me walk back towards the house very slowly.

Of all the many episodes I have relived in my memory, this is certainly one of the strangest: the rigours of winter, a deserted meadow, an enemy country, and myself walking almost on tiptoe holding in my arms the rigid, heavy yet gentle mass of that curious creature, while the other followed after me step by step, wiggling his behind and muttering to himself. Yet at that moment I was moved by the most diverse and long-distant emotions, not to say passions: affection, pleasure, almost inexplicable pride. When Madame Lore saw me coming she waited anxiously while, for no reason at all, I openly blushed as though I were holding a girl in my arms. Perhaps it was then that for the first time since my arrival she woke up from the fixed idea into which her fears had thrown her for the past months – thus removing her from reality. I had the impression that at last she saw me.

It was Kate who took charge of the poor benumbed goose. I left them to it, and meanwhile the gander, providing an example to all us males of self-control and devotion, waited anxiously in the door-way without moving a muscle.

January had hardly begun when the bubble of that impossible equilibrium burst. The Russian offensive reached the Vistula; millions of Germans abandoned Pomerania, East Prussia and Silesia. The *dies irae* was at hand for stricken Germany, the day of reckoning that Stalin had solemnly promised Hitler when he let him know that he would want a settling of accounts for every soldier who had perished in places like Siltau down to the last man – and the day came with the thunder of enemy armies, if it was not the gallop of the horses of the Apocalypse that made the whole earth tremble. From Bucharest to Lwow, which had already fallen, the front groaned and gave way; Warsaw and Budapest, after epic outbursts of heroism and ferocity, were on the point of collapse, as well as Tannenberg, the former glory of the Reich. Sorrow fell on the little village of Berg which up till now had remained untouched. The refugees from the East flowed back beyond the bridges of the Elbe towards the interior of the country in their disorderly and almost macabre tide, and brought the stench of spectral and muddy defeat which rose over the terrified countryside like Goya's *Giant*.

Those amorphous masses of fugitives whispered fearsome stories of the Russians and the hail of iron hard on their heels – in open disagreement with Goebbels' speeches who even in such extremity continued to guarantee unquestionable victory. But Hitler's obstinacy, razing the whole country to the ground in its effort not to surrender, was surely based on the possibility of perfecting the atomic weapon and hence resolving the war with one fell blow and *in extremis*. The Germans were said to have been after the atomic bomb since 1940 when they had 'heavy water' in hand in Norway; and the whole story of the Second World War (including Mussolini's intervention) will only be explained when it becomes possible (perhaps never) to learn the true story of the bomb; of the game played by the belligerents' secret services; of the part really played by the scientists' scruples (the Germans long before the Americans) in accelerating or delaying the perfection of a weapon which meant that the world would be in the Führer's hands. They were terrible stakes that were being played at that time, perhaps among a few unknown brains. But the Allies must have been certain that Hitler had been deluded. Slowly they strangled him and punished him by making use of his own illusion. And every inch of German ground was marked out for its share in the reprisals.

With the solid common sense of country-folk, the people of Berg carefully collected every piece of information, together with the other news that now began to arrive from the Rhine Front, and without going too far they extracted from it all the pith necessary to prepare themselves for the disasters soon to come. With the onslaught of the fugitives, there began to flow in almost Asiatic types with strange attire and customs, in long processions of biblical carts dragged in every conceivable way and loaded with every sort of utensil – as if for a departure viewed as final. But given the length and danger of a trek like this, numbers of them got scattered or fortuitously grouped themselves together; so that more and more unusable and abandoned vehicles were to be seen at the edge of the roads; then oxen were slaughtered and horses left to die. Everyone did what they could to alleviate the horrors of this exodus or at any rate to help with its various stages; the country was transformed into one huge camping-ground of tents, straw and hay. But the milling crowds did not pass unobserved by the enemy fighters, and these did not distinguish (or did not want to distinguish) between military and civilian targets but dived down to machinegun them, and for the first time blood was spilt even in Berg.

Meanwhile the German women – including those who had so far been hesitant – came over to our side; not only to ours, but also to that of the French, because by now the Nazi racial laws were just a joke. As for the Russians they were too much feared for anyone to try to get near them, and in any case doing so would not have mitigated their hatred or diverted their vengeance. As the days passed they assumed attitudes of open defiance. In the sawmill Stephen pushed the tree-trunks against the eight-blade saw at maximum speed in an effort to break it. And when he succeeded in doing so, one of those steel serpents flew through the air and cut off his arm. The mocking smile that I caught on his face while they were carrying him away was terrifying.

For some time Lore Kurt had been living in a state of great anxiety and this episode threw her into a frenzy. There were already good reasons for her fears because the sawmill had been working flat out for the war effort and was obviously approved of by the Nazis; and the fact that Herr Kurt was a sick and almost disabled man gave his wife no safeguard for the moment of crisis nor yet was it a defence against the opposition of foreigners; Berg was so small that nothing could be expected from the authorities, and it was impossible to disguise oneself or escape. But if Lore feared for her husband, herself and her possessions, what made her totally irrational was the thought of her little son being exposed to so many dangers. She had been appalled by the machine-gunnings happening so near; she saw nothing but threats from land and sky; she was convinced that the refugees who had lost their own children would steal hers, or that he would get lost in that throng of tormented people, or that the Russians led by Stephen would pick on him to wreak their vengeance; and in her despair she turned to the only point of protection and support she felt she saw – in other words, to me.

I could understand Lore's way of thinking; it had been plain to me from the first. Having married – heaven knows why – a man like Herr Kurt, she had knowingly (there could be no doubt of this) forsworn love in exchange for a position of authority in which, like so many other women, she could fulfil herself and lavish all her affection on the child. All this was normal, as it was normal that her thoughts and repressed longings should have settled down in a life governed entirely by habit. But once this methodical existence had been shattered by circumstances, and in view of her dissatisfaction in such an unsuitable marriage, tumultuous impulses had come flocking back into her mind, and perfectly natural ones given that she was frustrated though still in the full vigour of her thirty years.

Up till Christmas Day she had still retained a relative control over herself however much the dissolute spectacle provided by the other Berg women must have affected her. If the second-lieutenant *bersagliere* Penne had contented himself with the servant-girl Kate, and, moving up proportionately, the Roman lieutenant Magaldi with the cash-desk girl at the cinema, the rule (however absurd it was to want to apply it to this case!) laid down that the first lady of the village should have a certain right over the most senior in rank among us. Without at that time seeing more in me than a kind of hostage, she was prepared for a holocaust for the sake of her own safety and that of her dear ones, without even wanting to examine whether it displeased her or not; she wanted to prove – to herself rather than to anyone else – that it was the circumstances that were obliging her to acquire at such cost what she would not otherwise have been able to obtain from an unknown officer, and an enemy at that. The great drama of Tosca and Count Scarpia, which had moved half the world to tears, was there at hand to prove the thesis true. But the only authentic thing I found in her was a great fear and a certain pardonable hypocrisy, and moreover I knew something that she did not suspect: that I would be able to do little or nothing to help her, so that if I accepted her sacrifice – whether it was real or false – I would be deceiving her. This was where matters stood that morning when I took her the unfortunate goose in my arms.

Can a single drop of pity cast into the ocean of the soul bring about its total change? It was this that I had given or asked from Denise Digne, and she had refused it – perhaps instinctively knowing that this single drop would have undermined her memories and her rancour, both of which she needed for survival at that time. For Lore, who had always lived among the trees and animals of the country, it meant much more to see me with a *Gans* in my arms than if she had seen me rescuing a man, for this would have been no more than the duty of a good citizen, in other words nothing. So this episode, by causing her to divest of its discouraging positivism the relationship she had dreamed up between us, upset her moral quietude through weakening her alibis. And she did not realise how in my eyes the only real obstacle to going out to meet her with an open heart had thus broken down: the obstacle being her desire to pay me for it.

As for Herr Kurt, at the first signs of the breakthrough on the Eastern Front he removed me from the handsaw and assigned me to gardening work around the house: a sinecure which meant that we were always tripping over each other, he with a multiplication of painful smiles which moved even me to compassion. To tell the truth, I did not see that Herr Kurt, as nature had made him, could be considered responsible for anything. Then the child, Martin, was always round my feet – to the joy of Lore who felt safer at those moments; he was a pretty boy though he had a slight squint like his mother. In a very short time I had established a better understanding with him than with any other German, though the mother had made great strides in brushing up her French. Halfway through January, after the first machine-gun attack on Berg, I again fell victim to malaria – unexpectedly as it was not the season for it. I remained alone in the hut during the hours of work. Lore came to visit me, bringing me various delicacies to eat and fruit-juice for my thirst. And in my warmth and inactivity and feverish elation I began to respond to her.

With the advance of February the confusion in Berg became alarming. There was one crisis after another; either water was lacking, or electricity, or essential supplies, so that work was in a constant state of suspension even when the foreigners, from whom nothing was now expected, would have liked to be getting on with it. We had developed the habit of spending several hours a day in the high meadows outside the village, where the approach of spring and the mild weather renewed the whole idyll of nature once we were beside the quiet river. There, stretched out on the grass, listening to distant explosions and the confused murmur from the camps, we watched the Allied formations passing, bright in the sun, and no larger than an ant making its careful journey along a stem – it was like those romantic prints where you see the tender greens of the countryside between the squadrons drawn up for battle, and the smoke from the bursts of fire is indistinguishable from the clouds. Sometimes an enemy fighter would unexpectedly plunge down to earth level, shave the railway lines, swerve, and then straighten up after the surprise attack, and finally disappear, before the crack of their gunfire had melted into space. There were curls of smoke over there; why should it not come from a peasant burning his stubble?

As Herr Kurt found walking painful he took refuge in the cellars of the sawmill while I took Martin on my shoulders and carried him off at a trot, followed by Lore. Her slow approach towards me in those anxious hours, and her scruples which I divined more and more clearly as she felt herself led not by reason but affection, governed my own emotions. German morality, though fairly open with regard to unmarried and independent women, is strict where married women are concerned, especially if the husband is present. But if it was difficult for Lore to surrender herself, it was also preferable for me not to be hurried. It was hard to violate the abstinence that I had forcibly observed for two years. I understood better the reluctance of virgins before their senses have really been awakened, and with many of them the awakening does not happen for quite a while after contact with a man; the weight of a man can be disturbing and even irritating to them, and they need an impulse of the heart to help them endure it. And this was how I felt too, with the additional aid of Lore's doubts – the doubts that made her pause and that chimed in so well with my own slow liberation, for though she aroused me, she did not provoke me. So we quietly followed the path of Spring; the *adagio* eased off into the *pianissimo*: over which there hovered the *a solo*.

But the boys brought up on baseball in the colleges of Kansas or Ohio, encased for the duration in their airmen's jackets so as to hit a target merely called 'the objective' by their powerful bosses, were now directing their inexorable formations against us, and what could they know about these evanescent thoughts?

(From fragments of my diary: Berg, December 1944.)

We had only just come out of the *Lager* and still carried around with us the smell of prison, hunger and hate; and in the streets everyone turned their eyes away from us; or we felt cold looks on our backs when we had gone by. But once we met three Ukrainian women, and someone who knew us told them briefly who we were. Then all together they looked at us with their six brown eyes as mild as a young heifer's. And for the first time our disarmed souls were suddenly mirrored in those eyes and found rest in them. As the green meadow finds rest in the calm eyes of a flock of sheep.

Berg, March 1945.
Now at the very end of winter, while the whole of Germany is streaming with blood, and the nights are torn by explosions, and the days by the groan of sirens, and the sun over the countryside is extinguished by the constant nightmare of danger and the endless news of death; and while nevertheless the people here go on with their work (or seem to) and their daily habits in an orderly way, impassively, almost absently, I fell in with two women on the road when I was returning late one night – one of them old and dressed in black, the other certainly her daughter, and both weeping bitterly.

It was a shrill mechanical weeping alternating between the two of them, like the groaning of a pulley or the howling of an animal (as indeed I had heard it once before in Greece). And as I followed them, other people who were coming towards them glanced at them for a moment and then quickly looked away, as if preferring not to have seen them. And they continued to walk on, the one supporting the other and repeating those piercing lamentations.

And everything all around seemed motionless and listening. The dark ground, the cold water, the dry wood. All the harsh land of Germany, from which, however, and for the first time, I was seeing tears flow.

The old Latvian never speaks; he moves slowly and stiffly; he seldom even looks up, and when he does it is furtively. He seems to want to avoid everyone, and not to want to be seen. He has lost his possessions, his country, and even the flower that was his daughter. He has seen appalling massacres. And nothing is left to him but fear. I have been working two days with him, with no word being said. Finally, to test him, I said I would like to visit him at his house. He looked at me dumbfounded, as if such human contact seemed impossible to him or as if it could only present a danger. So I added: 'Later on, in the summer.' He gave a brief contemptuous smile. Then he put down his axe, took two pieces of wood he had just chopped and laid them on the ground in the shape of a cross. 'In the summer,' he said, giving a furtive glance around, 'you and I and all of us will be dead.' I asked him why. 'Millions,' he said, 'millions are dead.' Then he picked up his axe and went on cutting wood.

*

'*Schweine!*' This word, whispered over and over again by a nearby shadow, came back like a moth into the small area of light that was my consciousness, then was taken back again into the shadow. I could also hear a faint sound of running water, rather as on our first morning when we went our way silently across the grass in the glory of the dawn. Certainly my eyes were shut, but I could sense a faint light beyond my eyelids, though this soon became clouded with dark forms which in their turn suddenly became an unbearable scarlet. I thought I was asleep and just about to wake up. But the voice of that shadow changed its word now, and said quietly and firmly as if it had found something: '*Frakture.*' Appalling pain stabbed me at some point on my face and I opened my eyes.

The face bending intently over me was a good-natured one but marked by deep dark lines. Glancing beyond the small white form of the nurse, my eyes fell on a disgusting confusion of dirty buckets, soiled and blood-stained clothes, shapeless objects under sinister shafts of light. The doctor was holding a pair of forceps high above me, then he lowered them and that atrocious pain broke out again, affecting every portion of my body: a fraction of a second and then darkness again. I learnt afterwards that this operation carried out by an old dentist assisted by an inexperienced girl lasted at least an hour. This emergency 'surgeon', who had been operating for fourteen hours already, had no vestige of anaesthetic left and was doing his best simply to keep people alive. So the spasm brought me back to the light of day only to plunge me back again into darkness. But image after image passing in my mind with the swiftness of a dream – which suppresses all intermediary ideas to concentrate on a few that seem without connection – found me in the noonday sun after I had taken Lore home, standing with a group of French and looking up towards the sky; then the terrified expression of someone who put a handkerchief over my face; then clusters of trees passing by; then a nun crossing herself, solicitous but recollected in God. All this must have covered quite a few hours. I knew that the *Schweine*, swine, referred to the Allies who in a few seconds had torn Berg to pieces and killed or maimed a third of its inhabitants. And I knew I was not dead: a matter which seemed to me of total indifference; as if neither pleasure nor pain had ever existed within me and thus I did not know anything about them.

So this was how things were when another voice (and I felt its breath on my ear as it spoke) said: '*Eine schöne Spritze!*' thus promising me sleep in the paradise of morphine.

From then, and for an undetermined period, I had to rouse myself, only for a second or two that first time but long enough to realise there was snow outside the window – the last snow of that year, I think. The stillness, the silence, the torpor of the narcotic and the shock prefigured for me the blissful contemplative and perpetual peace of paradise. Then I went to sleep again perhaps for two or three days, and when I woke up properly it was deep in the middle of the night.

My mind was clear and rested like that of someone waking from serene sleep. The suspension of thought, which had lasted possibly for a week, must have benefited the depths of my organism more than the trauma and the haemorrhage had harmed it. The elusive nervous current active in our every tiny particle was flowing out within an essentially whole entity. I felt that the crisis was over and that my vital forces had returned. I tried clenching my fist, and as it readily responded I moved up my fingers to an exploration of my face and head. I found them swathed in a mass of gauze which left only my eyes and a corner of my mouth free. I contracted the muscles of my legs and they were there, both of them. I tried to move to one side; a violent pain rose from my abdomen; but I realised I could overcome it. Slowly I dragged myself to a sitting position.

The ward was small, tidy and dimly lit. I could hear someone breathing regularly. Based on my experience with my bandage in Poland, I decided to verify these first favourable discoveries about my condition with a supplementary experiment. As I fought down the pain and in so doing recognised fresh energies, I moved inch by inch into successive positions until I finally found myself on my feet clinging to the bedstead.

I took a brief rest so as to concentrate all my powers now in my legs, and passing from one small bed to the next I managed to do the whole circuit of the little room. None of those sleeping figures moved, and when I was able to recuperate between my sheets again, no one heard the lively eulogy that I dedicated to myself for the happy outcome of my test, nor the self-congratulatory speech I made for having saved my skin.

The action carried out over Berg had no military justification whatsoever but belonged to the final solution with which to punish Germany: a thing rendered possible by Hitler's persisting obstinacy when he had no effective defences with which to back it up. The Allied air fleet, with clear skies and from a comfortable height and without in those last days encountering either anti-aircraft fire or fighter planes, was stripping the oak of the Reich leaf by leaf and with it all that remained of old Europe; a kindness defined by a linguist of the High Command as 'carpet-bombing'. Berg had forty-eight thousand-pound bombs dropped on its small surface. The Kurts' house was unharmed, but the sawmill had a direct hit on its machinery and was a headless body; our hut disappeared together with the administrative second-lieutenant Gifuni, the only one of us in it at that moment; the *bersagliere* Penne had got out in time. As for Ceci, he left three fingers of his left hand at his devastated market, while Magaldi had the huge tree-trunks to thank just for once because the 'carpet' did not reach that far this time.

As for me, I had been talking that morning with some of the French and was the only survivor of a group of seven – we had been thrown into the air from the crater of a bomb which must have burst underneath us after penetrating the earth obliquely for the usual four yards. A leafy but indiscreet tree ripped off all my clothes and a good deal of skin but served to soften my fall. A fractured jaw, a massacre of teeth, a mournful series of wrenches and minor gashes and the abdominal injury following the headlong fall – these were my rewards for sawing the Kurt wood. I reached hospital (thanks to Lore, as I found out later) with no covering other than mud and blood, and they put me among the desperate cases who – as happens in such crises – are the last to be attended to. That was when I saw the nun piously indicating heaven with her eyes. In that first moment she could not identify me; and the *schöne Spritze* with which she assured me an immediate paradise, pending the final one, was an impersonal act of kindness. Later on the nun was more directly attentive to me, thereby sweetening my lot – perhaps someone had told her about the 'von'. When I began to groan without even realising it owing to the intolerable pain in my back and face, she hurried to me with her benevolent little phial and sent me back to the limbo of my fathers. Some emotions are highly complex. She was transferring her own mental anaesthesia to the physiological one she was bestowing on me. She was neither old nor displeasing to look at. Just a little masculine and brusque.

So next morning the nun found me sitting up, my eyes open and my hands which had not even a scratch spread out on the coverlet. The expression on her face was heartfelt but undefinable; perhaps she had thought it more salutary for me to abandon this vale of tears rather than remain in it. But the imperceptible hesitation vanished when she realised (as she must have) that it was the Lord's will that I should not die; and, indeed, that I should have been put in her care in those crucial moments to be the object of her prayers and, moreover, to be saved by them. So she devoted herself to washing my hands and only left them when she had made them shine like those of a duchess.

Shortly afterwards Lore Kurt arrived, having been notified heaven knows how of my return to consciousness. As soon as I was pointed out to her as the man she was looking for, she made a gesture of despair and sat down beside me with tears in her eyes while producing presents that were perfectly useless, given my condition. Then she started to recount a whole string of painful details – very rapidly in view of the limitations of her French – while I looked at her through the gaps in my gauze headgear. As I could not answer her with my voice, we got hold of some paper and pursued our conversation in this way, I asking questions, she answering partly aloud and partly in writing, a scene that was repeated in the days following. But after one of Madame Kurt's visits the nun, who had watched everything, unexpectedly pounced on our sheets of paper still scattered over the bed and quickly read them; so she knew French. After this intervention which luckily did not provide her with any dangerous information, she seemed to relapse into an unswerving subjection to the decisions of heaven, and did not feel any kind of obligation to justify her indiscretion.

The ward had six beds, but as the days dragged by there remained only a soldier of the much-feared SS who, however, was in a coma for a long time and died without ever coming to, though his eyes were wide open as if deep in thought; and an old sea-captain of the river traffic. A large piece of shrapnel had carried off one of his feet, but he did not know this and thought the foot was there inside the bandages, and kept on asking for news of it, even from me. Shortly afterwards Captain Ceci came to visit me; he was a patient in the same hospital, had his arm in a sling and looked to me under great strain; and indeed he had suffered considerably in the early days through not knowing what had become of his young love – but fortunately she was safe.

Whereas Magaldi's 'Kitten' had been flung arms-first on to a sausage-slicing machine at the pork butcher's – where she happened to be at the time of the raid – and was horribly mutilated. I wrote a note to the nun in French begging that Ceci might be with me at the moment when my bandages were removed. And I read the sympathy and compassion in his eyes. I then looked in the mirror and did not recognise myself, but though I was resigned to remaining disfigured for the rest of my life, nature's unexpected resources, added to many operations and much cruel pain, finally enabled me to regain a fairly reasonable appearance.

At the beginning of March the crowd of fugitives swarming along the road beside the hospital were machine-gunned at low level and reduced to a furrow of blood. Though I could still hardly stand I saw myself without further ado accompanied to the door by the Emergency Service men; and in the indescribable tumult of the stretchers with their tragic burdens not even the nun could spare me more than a glance, for which I am still grateful to her after all these years. Berg itself was over a mile away; and with Captain

Ceci supporting me, and avoiding the hazards of the main road
with all the people and the heart-rending cries, we made our way
over the fields and the low walls and ditches dividing them, and
reached the village after four hours. Ceci was immediately abducted
by his beloved who took him off to her house; while Lore, after a
seemingly agitated scene with Herr Kurt, gave me Kate's little
room in the upper regions of the house – Kate having fled elsewhere: Kate whom I saw in that dawn light on our first morning.

The room overlooked the already archaic grass square, now
reduced to a sort of lunar surface with its arid craters, and here I
once again pondered the human condition in all its inexplicable
complexity. Having left for the war to fight beside the Germans, I
was now a prisoner in their country; and having here been made a
slave owing to my coolness towards Nazism, I had also been ill-
treated by the Anglo-Americans who pounded everyone indiscriminately in their hatred of Nazism; nor would this even protect
me from that final extermination to which Himmler's secret orders
had vowed us – or so persistent rumour had it; and certainly not
from other unforeseen occurrences, given the hostile attitudes of
Stephen's companions who haunted Lore's nights.

Lying on Kate's little bed I contemplated the ceiling, and its
fanciful corners fitting into the edges of the roofing. The room was
very pretty, and had I not known that girl's habits I would have
though it the sweet refuge of a child, as Ariadne is described in the
Epithalamion of Catullus 'in her mother's bosom, in her little bed
redolent of her chastity'. It was strange that my chastity should be
there instead, now no longer defended by intention but by my lack
of blood and the protests of bones, joints, tendons and muscles every
time the smallest demand was made on them. And Madame Lore,
on her side, interfered with my indolence no less than eight or ten
times a day, as if afraid that her talisman might fly off through the
window. When I looked at myself in the little mirror that had
formerly belonged to Kate, I asked myself how far a woman's
constancy can go when she has some purpose in mind. The shaving
inflicted by the dentist on the centre of my skull now looked like a
discouraging greyish area crossed by the dark slash of the wound;
my eyes were dull and swollen; my face puffy and divided between
Tiepolo-like yellows and greens (though he used them magisterially
for tufa or fabric). It was unbearable to look at my chin, lips and
jaw. But Lore Kurt, who now saw me as a soldier of the Reich on

account of these wounds, seemed to find in them a new stimulus to devotion. So the Cardinal of Este was wrong when he called Ariosto's stories 'nonsense', including the one about the spell cast by Alcina on Ruggiero which caused him to see that terrifying witch as a gorgeous woman.

Meanwhile, with only a fifth of its houses still habitable, the village had lost every trace of tranquillity. The Germans (who listened attentively to Radio London and knew that the Allies were pressing in great strength along the Rhine from Wesel to Coblenz and had already occupied Cologne) were always frenetically babbling together and articulating at least twice in every ten words 'Invasion, invasion . . .' They were living in constant fear of enemy parachute troops, as the Central Command persisted in ordering resistance to the bitter end. So on the one hand they put up anti-tank defences, following the instructions of the mayor, and on the other they called this individual a half-wit and a criminal. A desperate effort was made by the German armies on the Eastern Front to fall under the occupation of the Anglo-Americans rather than the Russians. But the treaties signed between these parties made a mockery of even that last hope. As they were almost on the frontier of the two presumed zones of influence – the Elbe – the inhabitants of Berg lived, so to speak, with a map, a watch and a compass in their hands. Lore's anxiety became a fever; perhaps she was now convinced that I would do everything for her that I could; however, she must have feared that in view of my condition I might be transferred elsewhere; or else in the frenzy of those days, and confronted by my listless spirit and helpless limbs, she was really moved by love. This is what Herr Kurt must have finally thought because he never came up to the attic; he acted secretly and prompted by the unexceptional motive of procuring me the attention I needed. Such authority as still existed in Berg served to provide me with an obligatory travel permit to the hospital of the main town of the district, Uelzen, a few hours' journey by train. Lieutenant Magaldi was detailed to accompany me. This move took Lore by surprise and there was nothing she could do to counter it.

The first time I saw Magaldi again he had seemed to me gloomy and disturbed. He had had to dig in the debris of the hut to recover Second-Lieutenant Gifuni – literally chopped into pieces by the myriads of planks that had been trajected from all around by the force of the explosion and gone hurtling through the air like whips.

But it was the ghastly amputation suffered by his little cashier of the cinema that really overwhelmed him. Having been detailed to accompany me, he was unable to refuse – not so much the Germans as me – and presented himself, grim and silent. I would willingly have released him if I could. We had hardly any baggage as all our belongings had been destroyed, including my story of Esther and Pilate's wife. But he had found a sheaf of my papers in the remains of a drawer, fragments of a diary I had begun at Bay, and these I took with me.

The Kurts' two geese were safe: they had been recovered from the bottom of a bomb crater, no more than slightly dazed. As I was leaving – this, too, was at the crack of dawn – I caught sight of them over in the distance in the shining eye of a tiny pool, alone and at peace.

The journey from Berg to Uelzen should have taken less than two hours, but this time lasted five. The train stopped continually under cover of the woods to escape enemy reconnaissance planes, and as soon as the sun rose I noticed how oddly its rays fell through the many bullet-holes in the train's roof – enemy action on previous journeys. I had plenty of time to study Magaldi, and I was forced to the conclusion that he had sustained a psychological shock of some intensity; he was incapable of overcoming his obsessive fear; and on his dark face his pallor looked almost blue and moved me to pity. Uelzen station, a macabre skeleton of twisted and foul-smelling ironwork, could hardly have consoled him.

The hospital was rather far away for my faltering powers, and when we got there we were greeted by the usual spectacle of crowds of people and feverish work certainly inadequate to their needs. A group of surgeons were in grim confabulation at one side; one of them, a small nervous man, came over to me of his own accord, looked briefly at the wound, consulted in undertones with another who had followed him, and with no further explanation handed me a paper referring me to a specialist. Those gentlemen did not concern themselves with people still standing on their own feet. So off we went again.

It was past midday when we arrived in front of the elegant residence of the person in question. The hot city seemed deserted: it was the moment of rest for lunch which even war does not refuse. We sat on some steps like beggars and ate our rations, Magaldi morosely chewing his bread. By now his silence was an overt reproach to me – who was dragging him through an unknown country where no one would even have looked for us had we disappeared. So I decided to try to get through that door alone, though I assessed pretty accurately how difficult this would be now that I was reduced to the level of a beggar. And it would surely have been shut in my face had I not pushed aside the terrified receptionist and crossed the threshold by force. Our raised voices brought into the hall a man with a severe and obviously ill-disposed expression. Suddenly Kolya's words flashed through my mind: 'You! Baron!' So I took two steps towards this man and said in French, without defiance but without humility either: 'I am the captain of cavalry Baron of Sansevero, Italian, and prisoner-of-war. I have been referred to Doctor Aesckloni.'

The doctor, for it was he, jumped as though pulled back by a violent tug at the reins; straightened himself, made that bow peculiar to Germans who just bend their heads with a jerk, and pointed to a door at the side. It was a washroom for visiting ladies. He picked up a pair of tweezers – also looking as if it served for women – and lightly pulled aside the edge of the wound in my jaw that I had kept uncovered for several days. And suddenly his eyes lit up; the interest of the doctor and the zeal of the surgeon had sprung to life. Nothing would have made this man forgo the exaltation of the scalpel, the only exaltation capable of arousing those dedicated to it. A complex and dangerous commitment that can become a vice like drugs.

A telephone call to the clinic, a few excited words of explanation to his family, a little girl crying because her birthday party had been spoilt, and ten minutes by car through the devastated streets empty in the sun. What followed lasted almost two hours. Aesckloni refused the famous gold sovereign that I hurriedly ripped out of my jacket. He assured me that my survival was due entirely to chance because, clinically speaking, I should have already been eliminated by septicemia; he consoled me with the assertion that there were no immediate dangers but that the operation would have to be completed later and, to my mute question, merely extended his arms with a shrug of the shoulders. Half of Uelzen was burnt out and all that could be done was to send me back to Berg. He got the necessary papers ready and made off. It was three in the afternoon. We had been on the move for ten hours; I had walked enough and endured a cruel operation. In front of the clinic there was an open space with trees from which one could see a part of the city that spread out into the country. We threw ourselves down on the grass and I immediately fell asleep.

In accompanying me to the hospital Magaldi had hoped that they would take me in and he would be able to go back home. Terror prevented him from understanding that we were equally unsafe wherever we were; and, like all frightened animals, he thought that the best refuge was the one most familiar to him. He must have been grappling with conflicting possibilities while I slept (as in Shakespeare's sonnets) and the temptation must have seized him to leave me there alone, if not (still following the poet) to pour a phial of poison in my ear. However, he was still beside me when I woke at sunset, but he had made up his mind.

'Captain,' he said to me point blank – his wide staring eyes were the first thing I saw as I opened mine – 'you certainly won't want to go back to that station!'

Now that the effect of the anaesthetic had worn off, my freshly bandaged wound was giving me acute pain. The sun was gently sinking behind a landscape of surviving villas surrounded by their gardens. Magaldi's extreme agitation showed that during my sleep he had had to force his will almost to breaking-point; there was no opposing his nervous charge; so I looked at him without saying anything.

'In the clinic I studied a map of the city,' he went on. 'The first train for Berg leaves tonight at ten – exactly when the raids start. You've already seen what the station's like; you know we'll never get away from there. But if we walk to the first little station after Uelzen in the direction of Berg, and wait for the train there, then we'll be all right. So let's get going!'

As it was a walk of ten or twelve kilometres he was asking me to make a superhuman effort; but I felt sorry for him, because if I put him in the position of abandoning me then he would have to bear the shame of it for the rest of his life: for man has a treacherous nature and it can betray him when he least thinks it will, at the moment of our crises. But if Peter denied his Master, all the more could Magaldi deny the cultivated man and Roman citizen that he was, especially when he was groping like a slave along an enemy road.

'Let's go wherever you want,' I said, heaving myself up.

We arrived at the little station he had in mind at nine that night –

I in a state of total extenuation. I collapsed on a bench as if dead. But after some vague interval of time I felt myself being roughly pushed while hoarse voices shouted imperious orders. I was blinded by a strong torch directed straight into my eyes. We finally found ourselves in the station-master's office and kept at bay by the machine-guns of two men whom we recognised as belonging to the dreaded SS.

Luckily the explanations were not long as the doctors' papers seemed to possess sovereign powers. Magaldi's disquieting looks had been noticed by someone who had forthwith supposed us to be Allied parachutists. The two disappointed SS men got ready to search us, and I would have readily given them my pathetic gold sovereign (by now a family heirloom), but Magaldi who perhaps had considerably more – though he had never said so – passed over his knapsack to the German's outstretched hand with the words:

'*Achtung! Loese!*' – meaning to convey that it was infested with lice.

So the men dropped his knapsack with disgust while the station-master quickly showed us the door. We were back in Berg by three in the morning, twenty-two hours after our departure, and I regained my attic where Lore whispered words to me which she must have flattered herself that I was in a position to understand. But I had saved my life by stating that I was a member of the cavalry and a baron, and I had safeguarded my poor possessions by appearing to be a verminous beggar, and this surely was enough for one day without adding in love at the end.

The alarming flow of refugees from the East had been diminishing for some time and now almost completely stopped – a portent of what was happening on the Western Front. The Allies had crossed the Rhine some time ago and were slowly penetrating into the heart of Germany and the country was awaiting its doom. The railway ceased functioning in early April. On the half-destroyed and isolated Berg there fell one of those perfect calms whose significance may easily be divined. The fresh green leaves made their voice heard in the crystalline air, and the stream that encircled our small stretch of ground added its own solitary one.

My operation at Uelzen not only brought back my fever, but owing to the enormous effort expended that day, drained away all the energies I had managed to build up in the hospital near Berg and afterwards. The effect of this was to deflect Madame Kurt's attentions, because as I hardly answered her when she came to visit me or showed myself as half-asleep with exhaustion if I heard her coming, she had to resign herself to walking about on tiptoe and then leaving me alone for hours on end. I was grateful to her for her devotion, yet did not feel the slightest possibility of responding to it while all my instinctive energies were concentrated on saving my life. Meanwhile I found incredible peace and calm in my mind, freed as it was from any duty towards others and even towards the limbs it inhabited. It was in my mind and imagination that I found my equipoise and my delight now that I was liberated from needs, commitments, aims and from matter itself; my solitary and unquiet spirit (as already in the distant past I had always liked to think of it) rediscovered its buoyancy and happiness in conditions which to others would have seemed provisional and uncertain in the extreme.

The destruction of the hut had dissolved our already somewhat loose community. With Gifuni's death his fellow-countryman *bersagliere* Penne had gone off elsewhere. Magaldi's panic went so far as to make him look ridiculous to the Germans who, when it came to courage, had plenty and to spare. He put his things in a wheelbarrow – of the kind used by the local people to transport anything from potatoes to babies – and took to the woods he knew so well.

Captain Ceci was the only one I still saw and together we wrote a report on the death of our comrade, adding a sketch of the place where he was buried so that he could be found should his relatives inquire. The grave was simple enough, just a mound of earth and an uncarved stone, and it lay outside Berg at the top of a gentle slope going down to the great river, the Elbe, winding along with its huge loops between humps of hills dense with trees; and it seemed almost possible to descry a river of calm air up in the heavens following the water down below – the two clarities vying with each other in brightness above and within an endless landscape of un-matched dignity and loveliness. If once I had chosen to die beneath the burning sunsets of the Roman sky, now there was another place where it would be sweet to end my days; a soil to which I could entrust myself without fear so that it would make me part of its gentle womb. But I was sure that I still had a long time to live; I asked myself why; and found I was convinced that the third-time-lucky would let me off for a while.

Soon I was again spending the day at the far end of the clearing, cheered by the gentle swaying of the trees and the tinkling of the stream, and enjoying the love-affair that the two rescued geese made no attempt to hide from my benevolent eye. With the advance of spring the river water often rose to cover the meadow; and that prudent gander displayed his excellent memory by letting me pull the odd blade of grass a few paces away from him while he preened himself like a king in that fresh greenish water. At the same time even Herr Kurt laid down his arms.

The old scruples that had tormented me long ago in Ferrara regarding Marsi in the days of Mavì, now came again but more strongly – because now the force of things was entirely in my favour and not, as in those days, largely against me. In the early days my sheer physical prostration had served to postpone things; at the same time I could reassure Madame Kurt by showing her how deeply I felt my obligation in honour to protect and defend her. She would also naturally have supposed that I had ties in Italy which were soon to be reforged; and she also believed me to be a convinced Catholic (a somewhat broad interpretation) and as a former pupil of monks at least bound by the ten commandments (which was true). But from her point of view some new episode was needed to give her reassurance – and indeed it is true that an action speaks louder than words.

We were out together one day, assuming that little Martin was with his father, when an attack at low range was made against Berg exactly like that previous one that had caused such havoc. The people fled without looking where they were going and we ourselves were swept along in the midst of the tumult and with the heavy thunder of the guns getting louder and closer every moment. Then suddenly we saw Herr Kurt running with all the others, but he was alone, and when Lore desperately signalled to him he answered back that he did not know where Martin was. So the child must have been in the house or in the meadow. Madame ran back to the village. The road was empty now and her solitary figure must have been only too visible from the air. The enemy planes coming against us were almost exactly over Berg as we entered it – for in defiance of reason and through an invincible instinct I had not been able to leave her alone at that moment. Within the village walls the roar of the engines was deafening, and as I ran blindly I expected flames and explosions to break out at every instant. But the excruciating noise diminished and the bombs struck further on, in the woods. Lore leant against the wall, gasping. I caressed her and I believe I kissed her, but lightly and as an encouragement. Afterwards she avoided any form of direct invitation on my part almost as if she had resigned herself to my decision, whereas I now felt attracted by her. So what had finally decided the outcome and saved Herr Kurt's marriage from shipwreck was precisely Herr Kurt's own weakness.

Warned by an instinct lurking somewhere in the depths of his torpor (and having avoided me in the attic, be it remembered, as if awaiting what was to come) he seemed still in some doubt as to the relationship when I started my convalescence in the meadow. For while I lay there watching the geese, he would sometimes join me, sketch his characteristic abortive smile, and though keeping himself apart, seem in some way to want to join in our heterogeneous company. But as he did not know a word of French and I only a very little German (not easy to study in those times of stress) no conversation was possible between us. With the result that that man's thoughts were as incommunicable to me as those of a strange exotic animal, and (I must admit) did not tempt my capacities to understand any more than those of the gander. But as I was incapable of depriving anyone of his rights without feeling that I myself was diminished by doing so, I raised my eyes to Herr Kurt with nothing but respect, like someone who knows he is touching a painful area. I had no idea what his relationship with Lore could be, what she had told him or was telling him, what she was forcing him to believe or submit to. In the early days my inclination for her had been clouded by the mere thought that she shared a bed with him; but now I was worrying about what went on in this poor man's mind: a man unlucky from birth, threatened with desertion by his wife, his property destroyed, and his very life in the balance.

The gander's rock-like fidelity was a solemn warning to us all, like the face of Nature itself. It gripped me and humiliated me, and Herr Kurt seemed to understand.

After the first ten days of April the skies were emptied of Allied reconnaissance planes which formerly had been ceaselessly patrolling them. The radio transmitted only censored news – though Goebbels and Hitler himself continued to dictate that Berlin must be defended to the bitter end in spite of the fact that the irrepressible Russian armies were already almost there. Every day the Western Front was gaining more and more territory this side of the Rhine. That Berg would come under fire was certain, as it lay on the main route to one of the important bridges over the Elbe. The calmness and orderliness of those people thrown back on their own resources and foresight was exemplary. They had heard how the Allies behaved in the places they took over. With or without authorisation the people of Berg removed the stupid anti-tank defences, put up by the Nazi mayor – they felt that creating a point of resistance would inevitably bring about the final destruction of what remained of their village. The shops distributed their supplies house by house. Everyone killed their animals, learnt how to cure them, and buried their potatoes against future hunger. They hid their silver, their precious objects, their furs, and I was begged by Lore to keep her jewels in my knapsack – I must admit that the jewels made me smile, for they were those unfashionable trinkets handed down from one generation to the next to which a sentimental and even a money value are attributed, both largely non-existent. Finally, they camouflaged their cars and tractors in the woods; while they stowed guns, tools and equipment of all kinds in chimney-stacks. or hayricks When a vast red halo rose on the horizon which was recognised as the burning of Luneburg, and when the roar of the cannon was heard, little Berg was fearlessly prepared for its ordeal, and I was ready for mine.

The village was attacked at midday. The wise decision of its inhabitants to surrender without giving battle was overruled when half an infantry company appeared unexpectedly towards ten o'clock in the morning and formed a thin line with a few machine-guns placed in ditches in the fields. What is more, they planted a small cannon just at the back of the Kurt house where a silent group of women and children had taken refuge because it was a little bigger than the other houses. As their chosen place had thus become an obvious target, I advised them to leave it. Herr Kurt – the only German civilian present – seemed willing to hand over the command of the operation to me as being more expert in military matters, and we moved while the first enemy cannon-fire decapitated the little church tower not far away from the sawmill.

The riverbank seemed to me a fairly safe refuge from these shots (from tank guns, I thought), though this meant crossing about a kilometre of open space directly behind the German emplacements. The American shells were diving into the deep rich soil with a dull thud, but often they did not explode or hurl splinters of stone into the air. So I thought it was a risk worth taking. Having issued brief instructions through Lore to my little band of women and children, I saw my plan executed in a way I would not have obtained from Italian recruits after a week of hard sweat. The little group took cover with me behind a mound of earth protected from the firing; then I made a dash to the next cover, and one by one the others did the same. As soon as our little platoon was again assembled we repeated our military operation to the next cover; meanwhile no voice was raised nor question asked. Herr Kurt was the least prepared for this exercise, but he went through with it, if awkwardly. I myself carried little Martin pickaback — a first instalment on my debt.

At one point during our run we passed close to a German machine-gun manned by three soldiers who were awaiting the attack so calmly that it could have been a routine military exercise. They exchanged a few words in undertones with the women, without showing any surprise at what they were doing or who was leading them, though they saw he was a foreigner. Once again the inscrutable orbital movement of things was leading an Italian officer to guide a group of German women and children into shelter from the cannon of the free world. A point in favour of Democritus who, as Dante said, 'Explains the world by Chance!' When we finally arrived at our goal, Berg looked like a distant stage whose doings we would be able to watch. It was only then that a girl of about thirteen revealed a splinter wound in her shoulder which was forthwith bandaged up with strips of clothing and without her uttering a word of complaint.

The cannonade on Berg lasted seven hours, or until sunset. We saw the shells striking the village, stones and tiles flying in all directions, rising columns of smoke and dust. The women and children watched intently but without visible agitation; they exchanged remarks about where the shells had fallen, anxious only to identify the places that had been struck. It was their own houses that were at stake and yet I heard no complaints or imprecations. When one of them thought that it was her house that had been ripped in two she consulted with the others, and if they nodded she said nothing but withdrew into herself. The small lonely German cannon persistently returned its fire from the Kurt house which was for us of prime importance – but it was not hit. As evening came the guns fell silent. We saw the mines gleaming under Berg's little bridges; then it was night. In the belief that the Allies had occupied the village, we made our way towards it. The German emplacements were empty; but shortly before we reached the house there leapt from the shadows a small tank marked with a swastika, and coming against it there appeared another one, bigger. The two of them exchanged numerous shells and machine-gun volleys that whistled past us. Leaping like a hare, and still with little Martin on my back, I threw myself into the Kurt cellar and the others followed. But as it turned out, the Americans had not entered the village. Instead, throughout the night while we lay listening, they continued sending over tearing volleys of grenades about every half an hour.

Once again I was surprised by the silence, reserve and acceptance of their fate with which the community faced this ordeal in their own lacerated village. The women did not pray as they would have done in Italy. And Lore, who from the moment of joining the group – and as its 'first lady' – had busied herself with comforting all the others, continued to do so and to treat them as her guests because they were in her cellar. Having recently been affectionate towards me, she was now deferential as I was the provisional leader of her people; and as I was sharing their fate I believed I was also sharing their thoughts, their very human, simple and moving thoughts. At a given moment we heard the crackling of flames: the nearby brewery was on fire, and we could hear the fierce neighing of the horses trapped inside it. Herr Kurt and I went out to look, for if the fire spread to the sawmill there would be little hope of saving his house. But this time he showed the same character as his people; he lifted his hand to measure the direction of the wind, and once he was satisfied that it was blowing in a favourable direction he did not even go out again to reassure himself. And indeed it was the buildings beyond the brewery that the fire burnt out as it moved away from us.

Shortly after dawn, when silence had fallen, I went out to see what was happening. A ridiculous and unexpected procession was moving off to offer surrender with a small white sheet; the people were dressed in black as if for a funeral, and the idiotic Nazi mayor was at their head. A quarter of an hour later the procession returned – still more comic if this was possible, because behind the mayor, their feet scrunching over the debris, there marched two American tank-men, the first I had seen, grotesquely encased in battle attire and their helmets covered in netting and brushwood. In addition, their guns were almost resting on the mayor's back – the caricature of an allegory portraying the immense pointlessness of war. And the climax of that labyrinth of absurdities occurred when Lore, having run to the roof to spread out a white cloth, appeared before me with a gleaming tray for the purpose of toasting heaven knows what: given that my liberation, and the end of the Nazi regime, and the fact that her life and that of her family was safe, all nevertheless represented the defeat of Germany and the beginning of untold sorrows. However, we all drank, and she not only drank but wept.

However, this joy-cum-sadness was short-lived because hardly had two hours passed than news came heralding fresh disasters. The two Americans who had been seen marching behind the mayor had soon been overtaken by a rapid little van in which they had disappeared. So that though Berg had been abandoned by the Germans it was not yet in the hands of those others. A swarm of Polish, Ukrainian, French and even Italian ex-prisoners – increasingly swollen by a nebulous band of civilians of all races as well as fugitives from a nearby prison – made an indiscriminate assault on everyone and everything. The uproar was infernal. Lore looked at me in despair; everyone sought their own hiding-places while we brought out Herr Kurt's fowling-piece. The rioters were certainly equipped with fury though not with actual firearms, so we were able to put up some resistance. Not that this was necessary in the event: because when I was sitting outside the door with the gun on my knees, a group of these people approached and made signs and shouts indicative of congratulation and praise; they thought I had captured the house and made off at once – out of respect (as they thought) for my participation in the looting. However, these pleasantries were interrupted by shells arriving from various directions. Americans and Germans were both now firing on our poor village which was viewed as a no-man's-land; and this put a brake on the sacking. But a final wandering band discovered a store of schnapps in a surviving cellar, and savage howls of delight accompanied those madmen as they ran over the neighbouring fields where they had gone to celebrate. Thus the revellers' last victims were our two romantic geese (and truly mourned they were). I found their severed heads torn off and left on the grass – together in death as, in their exemplary way, they had been in life.

As evening fell the shell-bursts diminished in intensity and then completely stopped. We all dined together for the first time, Herr Kurt, Lore, the child and I, as if we were alone in the world. The night was damp and airless. In the distance the sky was still glowing. The stream whispered quietly. Our words were few, our looks dark, our thoughts irrecoverable. Up in my attic again, I lay down and thought – then heard Lore coming quietly up the stairs. I did not move, and she sat down at the foot of the little bed which had formerly been Kate's, silent against the pale light of the window. I knew what was going on in her mind, all the vague, nostalgic, anxious imaginings; similar to my own, except that to mine were added all the things I personally had been through: the tormenting themes of an obligation to an image of the good outside all rules but nonetheless absolute – hence a devotion in freedom; and of a stirring of inevitable reasons which I did not doubt in my inner self and yet were inexplicable – hence a secret within truth. The silence was so perfect that we might have been on a desert island in the middle of the sea. From downstairs I thought I heard Martin's breathing in his sleep; and Herr Kurt's intent listening. Thus he on his side certainly heard our stillness, the sweetness and I think the goodbye. Finally Lore stood up, and in that movement I saw her eyes momentarily gleam in the darkness. We parted without having exchanged a word.

I fell asleep – submerged by great dark waves like the ones that had engulfed the men of Licudi in that storm. Then I heard echoing sounds and loud voices. These, together with the daylight, woke me up, and dashing to the window I saw a patrol in front of the house with arms at the ready. They were German soldiers who as soon as they saw me shouted in their usual raucous voices for me to come down.

On the stairs I met Lore who seized hold of my arm; she was followed by a terrified Herr Kurt. The agitated exchange with the sergeant in charge of the group was brief enough, but by Lore's feverish replies I realised I was in grave danger: she pointed out my wounds and then her child – who had arrived on the scene in pyjamas and his eyes heavy with sleep. I gathered that a detachment of the Wehrmacht had descended on Berg, no doubt at the request of its inhabitants, and had shot a number of the people guilty of yesterday's looting. The sergeant seemed to be thinking; but as he did not like the way Lore addressed a few halting words to me, he briskly turned to her husband with a direct question – so my life lay in Herr Kurt's hands. He shook his head and said something that made his wife's face light up.

Then the German signed to me to go in front of him to a truck in which there were already others, both soldiers and civilians. So although I had escaped reprisal, I saw myself forced to follow the retreat of an army in agony. Without even having time to fetch my haversack I was driven off, watching Lore and Herr Kurt and the child in a group in the doorway.

And as they disappeared from my sight – the symbol of a family that for a time had been my own, despite the doubts and disorders involved – so did that world of birds and flowers and grass. It had to make its exit from my life, like so many other apparent things. Only to return now, like a ghost in my memory.

TEARS

'But what good soul could have informed the sergeant of my existence in Kate's room?' I kept asking myself as the truck jolted over the cobbles and, in clouds of dust, transplanted me for the nth time into the unknown. But I was rendered speechless by the thought that if the looters, when they saw me with my gun in the doorway, had assumed I was one of them, then the same assumption made by some intimidated citizen could explain everything. But it seemed grotesque that the recent upheavals should have ended like this, cauterised by that inexplicable smile of mine which produced itself so readily and was really not called for, when – to use Demetrio's phrase – it once more fell to me to be 'heavily called upon'. A few more hours and the return of the Americans would have sorted out my long adventure in the becalmed river of time; whereas the demoniacal finale was dragging me right back into the middle of the furnace. The invincible Russian armies had been pressing on Berlin for months and were now fighting in the suburbs; and whatever the loss, the Germans were not to yield a single stone of the capital save at the price of blood. An upheaval of earthquake dimensions, where a human life counted no more than a speck of dust in a storm. My truck, and all the others in the convoy, were going straight into the lion's den.

Jolting along with me between cases of arms and kit of every kind were an old deaf Lithuanian and a Russian without a leg. The five German soldiers – who I took to be participants in Berg's summary justice – showed not the slightest animosity towards us; from a personal point of view their predicament was identical to ours, except that broadly speaking their destiny was more uncertain. For them, too, it was a matter of living through the final paroxysm, the Caudine Forks of a tight spot in which every hour counted; but if they possessed arms they were also under an obligation to use them. We only had to survive, whereas they could look forward to the concentration camp which swung from one side to the other like a pendulum with the rhythm of things. So we just had to show a certain submissiveness so as not to annoy them, so that they would not act cruelly simply out of resentment or so as to prevent us ever going home – given that in their opinion we were unjustly free whereas they might truly never see their homes again.

From the height of our truck – which, as it belonged to the army, was to some extent a solid rock in the turbid sea of humanity ebbing and flowing all around us – our stupefied eyes surveyed that immeasurable dissolution. Berg is about 130 kilometres from Berlin as the crow flies; but to cover the twenty kilometres that separated us from Wittenberg, our first port of call, it took the whole of that day, April 18, the day on which (as I learnt afterwards) the Russians established their strangle-hold over the capital. Those days, and especially the 20th, which was Hitler's birthday, were fatal ones for Germany, for in a good-wishes action bearing this time the stamp of British humour the Allies sent over thousands of aircraft to sow death on the already defeated country – twelve thousand on a single day, it was said. The formations came over in waves, alternating with the clouds in a wind-blown blue sky. The streets were flanked by the charred ghosts of houses, and the groans of the wounded were drowned in the thunder of the oncoming wave. The German people, its structures torn to shreds and its links with its leaders severed, was writhing beneath an apocalyptical scourge and sweating blood like a body under torture. It was a horrible punishment for the horrible crime that had incurred it. This was the melting-pot of the two barbarisms that now faced each other, and the mind could not really conceive of them or encompass them in any way whatsoever.

The soldiers roughly pushed off the many people who tried to climb on to our truck or even cling to it. It seemed absurd that three precious places coveted by their own people should be sacrificed to transport three useless prisoners. Only one person was permitted to join us – a woman of good standing who could stammer a few words in English. That night when we halted at the Wittenberg bridge – it was impossible to cross owing to the hordes of fugitives – it was through her that I established contact with the commander of our convoy: an elderly officer who came up and spoke to her. He threw me a rapid glance then asked me to give my word of honour that I would not try to escape. This was absurd, because he had no means of preventing me had I decided to do so, and the other two prisoners – the Lithuanian and the Russian – were only following him because he was carrying them in the direc-

tion of their country. But by asking me to give my 'word of honour'
he was trying at the eleventh hour to bring back a chivalrous usage
that was two centuries out of date, and in a Germany that had
thrown off every kind of rule, law or convention so as to replace
them all with the law of Brennus – which is anti-law. But on some
strange whim I decided at that moment to press on to the bitter
end, whatever the price. So I ceremoniously gave him my word of
honour for which he seemed grateful. We would spend that evening
together.

The speed with which things changed around us meant that we
had to be constantly re-examining facts and people, and as our
very life depended on these, the soundness or otherwise of an
immediate judgement was decisive for what would inevitably befall
us in the logic of events. Like a tightrope-walker who is slightly
shifting his balance every fraction of a second, or a mountain-
climber on a cliff-face who has to decide not only his route but the
exact amount of support his foothold will give him, so I sailed on
that ocean, putting my trust in Providence, yes, but also in my own
wits. A dangerous yet fascinating game. So I scrutinised at some
length the German woman and the captain with both of whom my
destiny had become involved and on whom it might in part depend.

The woman was elderly and certainly related to high-ranking
German officers – which had won her her place on the truck – and
though her face was authoritarian it was not hard. Her clothing,
though now torn into shreds, suggested that it had originally been
that of a woman who had dressed suitably for the day, had gone out
as was her custom, and through who knows what misadventures
had ended up alone on the main road. Her fatigue seemed almost
unbearable and yet she managed to say a few low words, and if her
dusty eyelids seemed in danger of becoming moist with tears, she
quickly pulled herself together. When I told her not my name, but
my rank and regiment, she must have derived from them some
hope of understanding, a glimmer of the world she had belonged to
but which was now sinking headlong together with the whole outfit
of the ideas belonging to it. As for the German captain, he was not
to be envied. When darkness fell he found that six of his nine
transport trucks had disappeared, and that he was also short of a
number of soldiers, including the one who had come to the Kurts'
to take me. Presumably men with homes and families on this side
of the Elbe had no desire to cross to the other side, so had vanished

into thin air leaving bag and baggage. The other soldiers had set up
their bivouac a little apart, in sight of the deaf Lithuanian and the
Russian. The latter, who was of powerful constitution, remained
calm and silent and seemed not to worry about his disablement –
and anyway I had noticed that he manipulated his crutch with
enormous flair.

After the storms and stresses of that hellish day the night seemed
calm. Once cries had been soothed, an appalling weariness enfolded
the multitudes in sleep. The darkness was reddened by distant fires
and now and again penetrated by shots which, however, hardly
made a hole in the silence. I sat opposite the German woman on a
case of biscuits. The captain stood between us. Made equal to each
other by a common danger, and perhaps destined for the same
lightning death, we were separated by rules and conventions that
were all the more paradoxical because, of the three of us, I was
certainly the freest.

The captain was silent. I guessed he was certainly over fifty. His
hair was almost white; a tall thin man with a distinguished bearing,
a lean face yet slightly softened by a reddish rather than a brownish
tinge, pale questioning eyes, delicate hands. He obviously belonged
to the reserve and perhaps had been called up only very late and for
territorial service. Up till now he had said no more to me than those
few German phrases asking me for my word of honour. But after
he had thought a while he suddenly came to a decision. Unexpectedly addressing me in accurate Italian, he said:

'I know the islands of Procida and Ischia. I've lived quite a time
in Positano.'

'Are you concerned with art?'

'Yes,' he replied. 'My name is Rolphe and I'm a painter.'

'In that case,' I ventured, 'I think we can complete our intro-
ductions.'

And I stood up and gave my name. He bent his neck forward
with a jerk exactly as Doctor Aesckloni had done, and held out his
hand which I shook by the fingers; then he turned to the woman
and introduced me to her in German, at the same time telling me
her name: Frau Haendel. When I sat down again the captain did
so too. With all the solemnity peculiar to their race the two of them
then settled down to give me an explanatory lecture.

'All this,' Rolphe began after a pause and with a sweep of the
arm that seemed to take in the whole immensity of the darkness,

'all this is meaningless compared with the real German people. I love Italy and I understand Italy, but – quite apart from individual people – there have been appalling mutual misunderstandings. I was in the '14 war; Germany was misjudged then as she will be again now – a mistake that was and will be the cause of infinite subsequent evils. This land is the body of Europe. At the moment it's being torn to pieces. But it's the suicide of Europe.'

'Does the Signora understand Italian?' I asked with a slight bow in her direction.

'A little I understand,' Frau Haendel answered, finding her words with difficulty. 'I often in Venice.'

'In a few days, perhaps tomorrow,' went on Captain Rolphe, not allowing himself to be diverted by my trivial interruption, 'the Anglo-Americans will reach the Elbe; then the Russians will arrive, and what will they be able to do but fight each other? We're expecting this encounter any moment now. If we had been understood by the rest of Europe, today the continent would be a mighty body, and not a heap of ruins from the Pyrenees to the Oder. Those who were with us, those who have been against us, and we ourselves, all ruins, nothing but ruins. How is it believable?'

'It's strictly unbelievable, Signor Rolphe,' I admitted, thereby demilitarising him at a stroke. 'But you know very well that in politics, and still more in war, only facts count.'

Rolphe threw me a dissatisfied look. It would have been useless to point out to him all the countless 'unbelievable' things that the Germans had poured down on us since 1940 – among which, for instance, that Captain Sansevero had been put to hard labour. But as his generalisations tended towards acquittal, it was important to bring him back to the particular.

'That's why,' I said, 'it is up to us to look at the facts. Do you think it serves any purpose to take that deaf Lithuanian and crippled Russian to the other side of the Elbe?'

'Those are my orders,' Rolphe answered without conviction. 'Justified by the excess of prisoners in the undefended areas.'

I had not mentioned myself who was standing before him as a living refutation of what he was saying. I had to suppose that he had another reason and it was not opportune to go against him: but this was not why I did not want to press him, but rather out of compassion perhaps touched with a slight contempt.

'Just the wheels-within-wheels of things!' I was able to say in conclusion, 'from which mankind to this day has never been able to free itself. That's what war has been; that's what the whole of history has been, which unfolds and develops and makes judgements solely within itself – or so it seems to me.'

Frau Haendel obviously failed to follow this over-complicated dialogue; but as Rolphe said nothing, she said nothing either and did not ask for a translation of my remarks. We wrapped ourselves up in our blankets. And with my head resting on the haversack of one of the deserters – the captain seemed to have passed both it and its contents on to me – I fell asleep.

But I doubt if the captain slept at all. He was already up and away before dawn in an effort to reassemble his convoy. An almost incessant rumbling could be heard from the pale sky and from not far away I recognised the tearing sound of American shells. The tumultuous tide of fugitives had unexpectedly disappeared. Having escaped from the Berlin area under attack by thousands of Flying Fortresses, they had then come up against the cannon, so one could guess that they were now swarming and stumbling through the woods and over the hills sloping down to the river. The bridge had now been cleared, and over it there streamed the detachments going back for the hopeless last-ditch defence of Berlin, following Hitler's orders. Though these troops were still fairly numerous, they were a rather haphazard collection and even included civilians, or boys of hardly more than sixteen who were already utterly exhausted, and yet were singing. It was the *Volkssturm* of the Nazis' final hour. Enemy fighters dived to machine-gun the bridge a number of times, but it was adequately defended and the flow of soldiers continued, slow but regular. Rolphe was standing meditatively on the bonnet of his staff car. Frau Haendel was anxiously watching. Our soldiers said nothing; but it was an untrustworthy silence because the moral collapse of the German comes suddenly; and it is here that lies his personal inferiority to the Englishman, whose so-called phlegm is no more than an unlimited tenacity.

That halt lasted five hours. In Rolphe's truck there was all the stuff I could have needed, and I packed the haversack that had become mine with all the deftness and common sense that my *Lager* experience had given me. Frau Haendel then helped me put a fresh dressing on my wounds which I had neglected for two days and they were hurting badly. She wanted to lend me the little mirror she carried in her bag. Her kindness was extraordinary in view of the discomfort and palpitating fears she was enduring. I promised I would visit her in Germany after the war to thank her, or would receive her as a welcome guest in Italy – formalities which served, I think, to prove to ourselves that we still stood for something. The thunder of the cannon had got much nearer when we left, and the sun was already high and burning. Up to this moment Rolphe had ostentatiously avoided looking in my direction. He had put me on parole and perhaps he wanted me to break it so as to despise me and be one up on me for the thoughts I had expressed. Whereas I wanted his misplaced verbiage to turn against himself with a woman of his own country and rank as witness and judge. While mulling over these inconsistent motivations and imprecise impulses of my mind, I watched the great silent whirlpools of the Elbe swirling below me. There were other prisoners in Rolphe's truck but all of them, like the Lithuanian and Russian, from the East. In looking at the Elbe, which at this point was about a mile wide, I was able to evaluate the insuperable barrier lying between me and freedom. This bridge was already mined and I had no idea where the others were; I assumed they had already been destroyed or were very far away; and in such circumstances a stretch of road more or less could be the price of life.

We avoided Wittenberg which was enveloped in an ashen-grey pall of smoke, and I lost not only my sense of direction but any desire to concern myself with it – so absorbed was I in the details of a catastrophe so atrocious as to leave one stunned to the point of insensitivity: devastated factories, gutted hangars, contorted metal-work smelling of decay and unburied bodies. Poor Frau Haendel was so appalled that she kept her handkerchief pressed to her nose and mouth. In an area that might have been Rathenow we were obliged to halt again. It was then that Rolphe threw me a quick glance and I in my turn looked back at him. Once again, as with the Greek guerrilla disguised as a workman in the doorway at the Krano Command, the obstinate Sansevero put into that look all he had staked in his game of dice with existence, a game always lost yet never lost: the truth that (whatever I myself had said to the contrary) there exists a world completely different from the one governed by 'the force of facts'.

At a sign from the commander the soldiers leapt down from the truck, followed by the prisoners. Rolphe was standing stiff as a ramrod in front of an officer clothed in a cloak from top to toe, in spite of the heat. This man was obviously a General, and he was giving orders. The soldiers forthwith disengaged their small field-shovels from their packs and formed into a squad. Rolphe came up to me.

'Captain,' he said, 'we have a fatigue here until nightfall and won't be moving off till tomorrow. I have your word of honour: you'll keep Frau Haendel company until we get back tonight.'

And off he went in the wake of the General. But I saw them stopping less than a hundred yards away; and I saw the soldiers begin digging, while a horrible stench drifted towards us. Frau Haendel blenched. I quickly concocted two masks from my supplies of gauze, one for her and one for me. Then I signed to her to keep calm as we would only be a short distance away, and I set off towards the group of men rhythmically digging, their faces covered with dirt and sweat; and the poor woman went and ensconced herself in the cab of the truck so as not to see. But Rolphe barred my way.

'You're an enemy officer and a prisoner,' he said. 'There's no reason of any kind why you should take part in this work.'

His voice was shaking with anger and a sense of shame that I should so much as see the atrocities that had taken place. I found the indiscriminate bombing of a defeated Germany a horrible act of barbarism – that was true; but not that every individual German should be confronted with the shame of having abused his power over others. I was certain that Rolphe, as he knew Italian so well, would at some point have been in charge of an Italian prison camp. It was a bit late in the day to snatch from my hands a spade I wanted to use in a work of mercy – that of burying the dead who, after all, were men – when in the past just such an implement had been thrust upon me as if I were a slave. So I pushed him aside and took my place beside the others. He could not produce an answer; his face was so white he looked as if he was going to faint; and he moved away. We pursued that labour of love and sorrow until darkness fell; and whenever any small decision was to be made, the Germans looked to me and followed me, though no word was spoken.

Again that evening I shared my rations with the captain and Frau Haendel. New orders had arrived, and Rolphe's detachment had been joined by others which were to be used as a single unit in the final defence of the capital. And in fact we were not far from Berlin, perhaps to the north of Potsdam, in woodland that seemed to cover a wide area. Scattered lights could be seen between the trees on all sides and there was the noise of running water. The sky glowed now here, now there, or suddenly became clear again. There was the dull roar of high planes going to do their work in unknown directions. As a perpetual background to the darkness was the distant throb of the cannon. Exhaustion numbed my limbs; or perhaps it was the tangible and crushing force of the unknown that was weighing us down.

Wrapped in a cheap blanket, Frau Haendel looked like a seated clay figure roughly hewn by a sculptor of the grotesque school. She had had to remove her own shoes and pull on a pair of military boots, perfectly new but unlaced owing to her swollen legs which protruded above them together with her torn stockings. Nevertheless she had imperviously retained her small hat, that object by which – according to Francis Carco who has gone deeply into the subject – a woman's extravagance may be judged. There was some lace around her neck, but though it was dirty and crumpled it was still adorned with an old-fashioned brooch. Behind her pince-nez (one glass of which was broken) her short-sighted eyes were peering vacantly at the biscuit she should have been dipping in her soup; she had placed her bowl on her knee without realising she was letting it spill, and neither Rolphe nor I wanted to tell her so because we did not want to add to her confusion. The old lady's white plump hands were trembling in the half-darkness; she seemed at that moment weaker than a babe in arms. And then she was tormented by her memories.

Rolphe was a little way off, absorbed and rigid. His uniform clinging to his lankness made him look like one of Callot's nervous etchings in which colour and joy are alike inconceivable. That morning he had had to make an enormous effort not to give in entirely, a thing he especially dreaded doing in front of me who stood before him with searching eyes and as the symbol of that judgement from which he needed to defend himself – together with all the rest of his country. His pig-headedness in wanting to keep me in his power had roots in deep-seated complexes of his own, because I do not believe he had clear ideas or precise motives stemming from the ghastly realities around us. Perhaps he remembered Hitler's angry injunction after the 1943 armistice: 'Every

German soldier is arbiter over the life of every Italian soldier!' – or perhaps he nursed some ancient bitterness compounded of desire and contempt and resulting from what he had gained or lost in those Italian trips of his. But he certainly wanted to convince me of the crime that was being perpetrated against Germany; yet at the same time it was intolerable to him that the witness should look right down into the wound: torture, perhaps; and perhaps also punishment. And yet I suspected that in the depths of his confusion he was simply suffering from fear; not physical fear but moral fear; and that in the tragic solitude of his German soul and in the annihilation of his country, his need of me was greater even than the old lady's. I belonged to the world that condemned them both and from which they would be excluded. I was perhaps his last contact with what he both loved and hated; with what he wanted to punish, and by which, deep down, he sought to be exculpated. But he must have understood that, together with the rest of his country, he had to resolve a problem within himself that concerned the human conscience in particular and the whole of history under the eyes of God. That was why I said nothing and he found my silence intolerable.

He put down his mess-tin from which he had eaten practically nothing and started to hold forth in the manner described a year or two later by Vercors in a small book that had its moment of fame: the endless soliloquy of the German at grips with his demons. England had her full share of the invective. And so did we.

'You call yourselves masters of life; yet in five hundred years you haven't even provided cemeteries for your southern regions! Is that why, here, everything has to become a cemetery?' There was anger in his eyes and at the same time supplication. 'The Russian prisoners? And what did Caesar do? The Jews? Haven't they shouted for two thousand years that they are the Chosen People? Why do they think it odd that another people should call itself Chosen, after them and instead of them and for much better reasons?'

I got up and put his bowl back in his hands.

'My dear Captain,' I said, encouraging him to pick up his spoon, 'this is a tragedy not only for you or Germany but for all men. We're all victims of the disaster. But I'd like to say to you what Nausicaa said to Ulysses: "You suffer these things because you're a man; so endure them like a man!" '

This classical quotation falling anachronistically into a wood full
of people who did not even know whether they would live through
the next day, had a calming effect on Rolphe who once more
started to gulp down his soup – but with a trembling hand and
spilling it on his jacket in his turn. I thought with tenderness of
Pannuzzo and his famous jacket drenched with grease – perhaps
due to some circumstance similar to this one. Where was poor dear
Pannuzzo, with his angelic goodness, on this cannibalistic night?
Frau Haendel made me repeat word for word Nausicaa's magic
phrase that had so soothed Rolphe. When she had finally grasped
its meaning she made an instinctive gesture as if looking for a
pencil. This admirable woman had not lost the typically German
habit of noting things down.

We stayed in that area for another two days, though gradually
moving to the western borders of the capital. The Russians were
already shelling Berlin and fighting in its eastern suburbs and were
soon to start an invasion also from the south. The detachments into
which Rolphe's column had been incorporated now looked like a
real army corps and was establishing positions round the forest of
Grünenwald. The prisoners still following the troops as auxiliaries
were submitted to the killing work of digging or reinforcing the
labyrinth of fortifications concealed in every fold of the ground;
but as Rolphe had omitted to hand in my name I took part in his
and his men's activities without anyone giving me orders, though I
agreed to do my share of their work only if I so wished. And it
sometimes happened that if he was absent the soldiers again took
their cue from me. Though I had been attached to the Germans
ever since my Athens period, there was no logical reason why I
should not be recognised as an officer of the Allied army; but so
much water had flowed under the bridges since then that only the
desperate peculiarity of the situation could have so bizarrely
restored me to my rank. As for Frau Haendel, who had a house in
the centre of the capital and was living under the delusion that she
would be able to get to it, she was kept almost hidden by Rolphe
owing to her important relations: so there was this sixty-year-old
lady in the firing-line, a pathetic symbol of that ultimate Germany
that was about to be wiped out.

On the evening of the twenty-second we were again called on to
perform the heart-rending task of freeing bodies from ruins caused
by the incessant bombardments; the last one had lasted a horrific

eighteen hours and had almost levelled the area to the ground. A
half-destroyed hangar served as assembly-point; and the orderly
spirit of that uncrushable people had not failed even on this occasion,
with the addition of some subtle and absurd talent for the macabre,
or perhaps it was insensitiveness on the part of the agent or the man
behind the scenes – similar to the insensitiveness that transfixes a
butterfly with a pin so as to classify it, or places a marriage-bed and
a bier side by side in a shop, the prices and measurements of both
duly displayed.

How and where in that cataclysm had the authorities requisitioned
so many coffins? From the massive magnificent carved ones en-
throned in the foreground of that extraordinary array, to the less
grandiose ones, the ordinary ones, the simple ones and the very poor
ones. And when the commercial range had been exhausted it was
supplemented by the private product made by the local carpenter,
with whatever means lay to hand and in any sort of wood: even
rough planks or packing cases. There followed blankets, tent
material, furniture-covering and finally sacks – all methodically
laid out on the bleak cement floor and with concern not to waste
space.

On the other side were the bodies: a ghastly jumble over which
the searchers lavished endless patience, like a surgeon dissecting a
wound with grim punctiliousness, or like a philosopher when he
lays bare evil in the clarity of his thought. The people intent on
identifying the bodies passed over that frightful area, whispering
and pointing. I could make out torn bits of flesh lying in the
abandoned shamelessness of death; young girls, old men, a tiny
baby; ghostly discolourments, horrendous fragments, frozen eyes.
And while on one side the industrious ant-like line was slowly
reducing the funereal pile, on the other new teams came in to refill
it; between the doleful wail of the sirens, the thundering explosions
coming from the sky, and the shattering ever-advancing shells; until
slowly that multitude of shadows faded away; the carved coffins,
the ordinary ones, the poor ones; then the packing cases and all the
make-shift wrappings; the vast mass of misery disappeared into the
mouth of death. It was during those very hours that within the city
itself the German lion and the Russian bear were clasping each other
in a ghastly embrace and tearing each other to pieces. Through the
tunnels of the underground railway, trains bristling with men and
arms came up behind the Soviet advance troops and destroyed

themselves so as to destroy everything and everyone else. Similarly
loads of explosives in the sewers were let off beneath ground already
trodden by the enemy and burst out in flaming gas and putrid slime.
Meanwhile the exasperated Kirghiz, Tartars, Kalmuks and
Siberians, under Rokosovsky, Koniev and Zhukov, were converging
towards the legendary Bunker of the Chancellory. There Hitler's
demon, or his genius, was about to be consumed in a crackle of
sulphur, leaving nothing behind but the echo of a final, epic
malediction.

That very night our corps set off again to penetrate the Grünenwald which was threatened by the endless fire obliterating the
capital. But in the few hours that the march lasted everything was
scattered and swallowed up by the human lava pressing in on us
from all sides. It became impossible to recognise the places or roads
of a nightmare journey during which we fought desperately backwards and forwards like a wave within an imprisoning and ever-
narrowing circle; finally it was like the tunny-nets when the fishermen bring them under the hull before the frenzied and bloody
massacre. Perhaps one contingent of the men met the Russian
advance-guard coming from the south, fought with them over an
obscure strip of land with the fury of a wild beast who knows he is
condemned, killed and then died. Rolphe's trucks did not reach that
far, they lost contact and got separated; dawn found us once more
alone, two trucks, five soldiers, Frau Haendel, Rolphe, myself and
the Russian prisoner. It was our last halt and, for me, the culmina-
tion of the tragedy.

This time, too, we were in a gloomy suburb; devastated factories,
burnt-out houses, clouds of fetid dust, and sudden silences into which,
like jets of flame, there burst cries, explosions and the dull roar of
falling buildings. Over in the direction of the city a funereal vapour
rose from the horizon and darkened the sky. The growl of the Russian
cannon never stopped – similar now to the hoarse incessant roar of
the sea crashing on the rocks in a storm. Ragged bands of men
came and encircled us as though scenting prey, then withdrew at
the sight of arms and let out menacing shouts. Defenceless soldiers
ran away from us, heedless of Rolphe's somewhat petulant orders.
The five who still remained seemed to be thinking. It was then that
that obsessive drone started again, grew louder, came nearer, and
seemed to shake the whole arc of the sky. And we, too, shuddered
as we saw squadron after squadron coming over, myriads of

bombers, flying low, gleaming in the light, the tight formation testifying to a sole invincible determination; and our condemnation.

'*Mein Gott!*' exclaimed Frau Haendel softly, while beads of sweat (I saw them) broke out on her forehead. Her eyes were blank; she was not thinking of herself but of her family whom she would never see again. I took her arm and she automatically followed me. The soldiers had already disappeared into the ditches. Rolphe remained standing.

'Rolphe,' I shouted, 'lie down!'

Almost simultaneously the ground rocked. A terrifying shower of stones and rubble leapt up in front of us, as if the earth had let loose a spectre from hell. The dust was blinding. Then stones, slag, splinters hailed down. The stench of TNT cut one's breath. Frau Haendel was stretched out beside me and her hand clutching mine pulled me down.

'Frau Haendel!' I called breathlessly, trying to turn her over for she was lying on her face. But when I touched her I felt the blood running between my fingers. I let her fall back and she stayed still.

Then through the smoky hell of that gehenna I made out various vanishing shadows – they were our five soldiers who now viewed the war as over. Rolphe was still at his post, but now on his knees. He did not seem to be wounded, but he contorted his face every now and again and the thick coat of dust overlaying it made it look like a grotesque mask.

It was then that a shot rang out just near me. And it was only then that Rolphe doubled up. A man was running away with a strange rolling motion of the body. It was the Russian limping off with the aid of a German rifle. He had got his own back on the imprudent captain who had signed his own death warrant by taking this enemy into his truck.

I tried to lift Rolphe's body up but the bullet had got him through the throat. So I was alone now. And the formidable quake of the bombardment as it sank deeper and deeper into the unhappy earth seemed like the breathing of a monster inimical to every living thing and prepared to stop only at annihilation.

Terrified shadows came and went; slow groans penetrated my stunned senses like painful needles. My faceless weeping woman, my little statue, had found her way here from the house of my soul destroyed at Licudi; the woman who had been stolen from her dead and stolen from me, the woman who beat her head and struck her breast with her cold clay arms: tears of horror and desolation still intact across the breadth of the centuries. And hearing her weep in my absolute defencelessness as I lay on the open ground, I put my hands over my eyes for a moment and then fell into a faint for many hours; or perhaps I fell asleep.

That was a very long day! I had walked for many hours, guiding myself by instinct towards the West and with every step getting nearer freedom. I did not feel my life was seriously imperilled; I had brushed with death so recently in Berg, and then again this very morning, so I did not think it would visit me again for a while. My mind was in a fog because I was not unable, but unwilling, to organise my thoughts and was continually distracting myself from myself by concentrating on the details of the road: the rubble, the rags, the gleaming splinters of metal. And I never looked around and about but closed my eyes and my nostrils and my skin to any stimulus likely to arouse perception. All I wanted was to press on. Later I would stop; later I would remember, and think.

I had been unable to find Rolphe's map in our shattered and overturned truck, and I could not find it on his person either. I had laid out his and Signora Haendel's bodies before leaving. Both were already cold. I laid them behind the truck and covered them with canvas on which I placed his military cap. There was nothing else I could do. I did not want to bury them because in that case they would never be found. I knew I was about a hundred kilometres from the Elbe and I wanted to reach its banks before the Russians. It was not impossible that the Russians would come into armed conflict with the armies who had previously been their allies, and if that happened, and I was behind their lines, as an Italian I would again be seen as an enemy and again receive the pounding from which I had just escaped. I was not thinking only of Italy at this stage but of establishing any kind of life outside that appalling graveyard of thoughts (worse even than the graveyard of flesh) by which I was surrounded. My jaw was hurting terribly as a result of those heavy days – the only sensation that I could not ignore; the rhythmic throbbing of the blood at that tender point beat more or less in time with my footsteps; and I noticed I was saying with every beat, giving it a kind of musical lilt, that line from Dante: 'I saw our madding little threshing floor.'

As evening fell I stopped out of sheer exhaustion. I was in a kind of wasteland that had once been a residential area. The houses had been destroyed with scientific precision, but this was some time ago because the ruins were old and cold. Each house had its large green wilderness around it; and each had had a direct hit so that the roof had fallen straight in on its shattered foundations – making a kind of instant funeral monument for those within. The trees had suffered less; or perhaps the greens of spring had covered over their wounds; at any rate only a few, those killed at a stroke, raised absolutely bare limbs into the air. I climbed through a window and made free of the wreckage; I laid down my blanket, and with my head pillowed on my haversack watched the stars appearing in a portion of the sky. And I tried to imagine the thoughts of a man who knew himself to be the only person alive in the world, the only survivor. From the East came the incessant growling of the Russian cannon. Perhaps I was in a fold of the countryside, because the noise seemed slightly muffled. Or had I travelled further than I thought? How far, I wondered . . . Rats creeping across the rubble looked at me with luminous eyes; but perhaps my eyes shone in the night too; they kept their distance; and finally everything fused into a single darkness.

During my days with Rolphe everything in the trucks had been at my disposal, so I had carefully foraged through the luggage and equipment knowing that my subsequent survival depended on them. My shoes were not new, like poor Frau Haendel's, but they were strong, and I had given them a coat of reddish aniline to disguise them. And in all other ways I carefully avoided any sign of belonging – not only to the German army but to any group or nation whatsoever. I had come across some anonymous civilian clothes earlier in a bombed house, and with Frau Haendel's help had sewn my identity card into them so as to have it available if it were really necessary. Naturally I rejected any idea of carrying arms. I tore away the outer part of my haversack and only had the lining, and here I concealed what food I could; I bound my blanket tight around my waist so that it would not be seen; and I put conspicuous bandages over my wounds to hide my face. The smallest possession could become an object to be coveted; the slightest mark of distinction could arouse a hostile emotion. As it was I was strong, provided for, and determined; but I looked like a castaway belonging to nowhere, a tramp at the end of his tether. This could help me to get through.

But there were many unknown elements, and these were serious. In coming from Wittenberg to Potsdam we had travelled in a south-easterly direction; but as the crow flies the Elbe was nearer if I went west; but I had no idea of what bridges lay ahead of me. So crossing the river would be the final problem, but meanwhile it would take at least five or six days' walking even to get there, without a map or road-signs. The food was enough, if I apportioned it carefully and made full use of my experience as a prisoner. But what about my wound? My jaw was hurting badly; and perhaps a fragment of bone, buried at the edge of the fracture, was working its way to the surface; this would mean an abscess, very painful near the trigeminal nerve, and probably producing a fever. That is what I was afraid of. So as I walked I spared myself every superfluous movement: walking yet saving one's strength with every step is an art not very well known. In the evening I made a thorough check on shoes and laces, because any flaw could bring me to a halt. Over this I profited from Binutti's instructions at Ferrara. At every crossroads and bifurcation I gave deep thought to the new direction to be taken. Sometimes some surviving little road-sign helped, but almost always I had to trust to my own intuition and the sun. When I stopped for the night I dossed down in such a way that I could keep an eye in all directions, and like a bandit kept an escape route always clear. I took off none of my clothes or belongings so as always to be ready for a getaway. Then I settled myself for sleep, though always on the alert mentally, and I think sleep came. All these precautions will make people smile today. But no one will ever know the number of people who disappeared or were murdered in that no-man's-land during those lawless weeks. The Anglo-Americans were already on the left bank of the Elbe, but by the Yalta agreement the Russians were given the honour of reaching the other bank, an area choked with ruins, abandoned by the final remains of the Wehrmacht, and teeming with disbanded troops, deserters, fugitives and robbers. Endless armed brigands roamed the countryside, ransacking villages and taking all remaining supplies; with savage fury they destroyed factories, broke up machinery and set fire to stocks. Total strangers would suddenly group themselves together for violence then separate again, like storm-clouds that gather and then part and fade away. Myriads of people, each with a soul, a past, an aim and an ambition of his own, would join forces for a while then disperse in as many directions as they had come from. A strange abyss where the circles of hell were all jumbled up together, and also perhaps those of heaven; a mass of memories, passions and greeds, irresistible in its fury and taking no account whatsoever of life.

Like a huntsman in a thicket with an eye alert for the slightest incident, I made my way by laps of about a quarter of a mile at a time. I decided against using the road, the haunt of restless hordes and sometimes of demented cars whence issued shouts or even shots; and nor did I go through the woods where a man-to-man encounter could be fatal and where fear could produce worse things than malice. So I kept to that neutral area that is neither too frequented nor too deserted, the area fairly near the road, where one could be seen, yes, but by an eye that sees more than one thing at a time and has to make a choice among the things that claim its attention. And as stillness is nature's best defence, I lay down at moments when I thought I could be seen as no sight was so common in those days as that of some utterly exhausted wanderer. If anyone spoke to me I showed my wounds, pretending I could not answer or could not hear.

I must admit that this game afforded me a certain amount of entertainment – first and foremost, strangely enough, because it had the real tang of a game although the stake was life itself. In that immense disarray I felt I was carrying intact within myself laws, rules and measure. With all my strength and will I was engaged in creating a strong if fragile system in which a delicate balance of perception, cunning, readiness and energy would get the better of the brute force all around me and of the impassible adversities of space and time. This masterpiece to which I was committed even involved my pride, the more so as none of the things I was trying to overcome resembled me, so that the value of their opposite was put to the test. The creature patiently formed by the monks at my school so as to extract (perhaps) a cardinal's purple, was now challenged to extract himself from a dehumanised jungle where all was revolt, blindness, things; he had to tame it with the quiet intensity of his mind. I thought of James Cook, master of the oceans, yet who fell beneath a savage's club. And here Caesar was of help to me, not swathed in his red emperor's mantle and declaiming on the stage of history, but plunging headlong from the mole of Alexandria, naked; but as a sword is naked.

At night endless camp-fires appeared among the trees lining the roads. Under the impulsion of darkness and in the need for sleep, all those varied and diverse people – dangerous to others yet frightened for themselves – instinctively slowed down the tension and by silent agreement laid aside the conflict of wills. To the first group others would immediately be added, until in the end there was a vast encampment, yet hardly a whisper rose from it. As fifteen million foreigners had been brought in convoy to Germany and endless refugees had poured in from the East, the majority of these dispersed wanderers spoke unknown languages; but most of them would have said nothing even if they could. Each one kept himself to himself, though he studied those beside whom he would have to spend the night. So as not to lie on the damp ground they preferred to throw a plank over the ditch at the edge of the road – hence their resting-place was sometimes over the trickle of a stream. Each slept closely flanked by two others, and each was disguised as I was disguised; and the man beside me, who was communicating to me part of his animal warmth, was perhaps another me, or was perhaps my very opposite: a man of learning, a fanatic, a simpleton, a murderer. Words were few; but the secrets they hid were fascinating. There the encounter of lives was pure and unsullied, stripped of all spurious attraction; and perhaps there for the first and only time did I merge perfectly with men.

Four more days and four more nights passed in this way; and on the morning of the fifth day – after two hours' walking – I stopped in a meadow very like the one in which the Kurt geese had lived their happy days of love and together found death; except that the water of the blue pools lying in the fresh green grass came up from the network of streams and canals below Genthin, beyond the Brandenburg lakes. My abscess had flared up during the night, and the sedatives I had salvaged from the German truck were quite inadequate to relieve the excruciating pain – a pain that was hit as if by a hammer-blow with every step I took, so that it invaded my mind and made thought impossible. In that meadow I had seen one of those groups of refugees from the East who had appeared beyond the Elbe back in February in their flight before the Russian advance troops. I recognised this particular group by its antiquated horse-carriage. It is impossible to say by what vicissitudes these people, who had nearly reached the Rhine, should have now turned back to be threatened yet again by the Soviet advance troops. There were five of them, survivors of an entire village that had been put on the trek for four months. When I went up to them they seemed incapable of reaction and hardly moved: a couple of old people, a younger man, still strong though his face was marked with terrible bruises, and two little girls of about eight and ten. The smaller of the two girls was lying on the grass and she just stared at me fixedly, her white bloodless little face bearing witness to the sufferings she had endured. The look she gave me was totally without hope, and heavy with that condemnation of things that can always be seen in the eyes of the dying.

I tried to comfort the oldest of the group in my rudimentary German, and he told me that their carriage had been robbed of its horse and its contents. That unfortunate refugee, perhaps from the Mark region of the Oder, must have seen in my attitude some promise of assistance, and he in his turn tried to help me. He had just come back along the road I was going to take but knew nothing about bridges, he said, for he and his little group had ferried across the Elbe at some point; there were great stretches of empty country in front of me and many streams and small rivers, he said. Then he proceeded to draw a map on the ground with twigs and straws – only slightly more sketchy than the ones used by the first navigators to conquer the world. Meanwhile the little girl never took her eyes off me; she had the huddled look of someone who has always lain on a very narrow bed; and her head was resting in the other child's lap. The throbbing in my jaw was getting worse and worse and the pain becoming almost unbearable.

From what I gathered, the Elbe was about thirty kilometres away, but across country. I did not know that during those days Berlin was being fought for street by street, nor that the Russians would join up with the Americans somewhat later and considerably more to the south. I imagined that they had passed beyond the capital and that their advance patrols were already near the river, and I thought I had a narrow but decisive margin of time at my disposal. Free of pain, I could if necessary do those thirty kilometres in a single forced march, and in that case I would have no further need of my supplies – which would be equally useless to me if I failed. Like that shipwrecked lieutenant of the Alpini, who had to make a choice between a final sprint or death, I had to come to a decision and quickly; and I thought I was acting according to reason. But now I know that it was the look in the child's eyes that decided me, for that look swept away the differences between our conditions and asserted a value that I would not be able to recognise later – but which was nevertheless the only true one.

I took the blanket from around my waist and spread it out on the ground, signing to the children that it was for them. Then I took out my packets of food, one after another, and put them down – with the same dumb-show towards the children. Finally my groping hands reached the medicaments, and I brought them out too. The elder child sprang to life in the belief that the other could now be helped; but I knew that the little one was at death's door and that not even a major operation could save her. But a gentle light came into her eyes too, as if she, like me, knew it was only a game, but a game it would be fun to play, with a pretending doctor and a pretending bed and pretending medicines of pebbles or bits of chalk; so at least she would not die without a smile.

The others looked at me without a word – like country people looking at a conjuror setting up his props, unable to guess at the surprises in store. But when I showed my wound to the old man, and gave him my penknife – after passing it a number of times through a flame – he understood. Perhaps he had had some experience in these things or else my abscess had reached the exactly right point; but at any rate he lanced it with a single stroke, and yet, in that harsh cut, I felt myself liberated. Then the two of us, God knows how, made another dressing, after which I fell into a deep sleep, the first really relaxed sleep I had had for some time, for I knew I was being watched over by others, and anyway had nothing more that needed to be guarded. At midday I awoke, ready for my undertaking. But I would have preferred not to wake up just then, because from the silence of the others and the way they were grouped I knew that the little girl had died; I saw her pathetically huddled up on my blanket, with my medicaments arranged around her by her sister as funeral offerings, and my packets of food next to her hands: exactly as the age-old inhabitants of Licudi had done things for their dead thousands of years before.

I made the sign of the cross (which I had not made for years), not only for myself but for the others; and they made it too. We bade each other goodbye with a gesture of the hand, each one of them to me, and I to each one of them individually. Then I went off towards the uncertainties of dusk, and in the quiet glimmer of the night I no longer thought of the Elbe, or the Russians, or Italy, but only of the little girl lying in the middle of that meadow, and I would have liked to go back and be with those poor lost people who were keeping watch over her.

I walked for many hours. It was a misty night, but perhaps high up above there was the moon casting a faint but even light through those low vapours and making all shapes look mysterious in the deep silence. As my refugee had warned me, I saw little but the outline of some distant cottage but no sign of life. I often heard the sound of running water and the floods were up in some of the fields I crossed. At first I had carefully chosen my way, knowing that if my shoes got soaking wet it would be a great nuisance; but now I could not pick and choose because everything depended on my being able to hold out those ten or twelve hours. So I forced my pace, intent only on not losing my sense of direction which was difficult in that ghostly gloom, and trying to drown my thoughts so as to concentrate on the continual questions that arose from the necessity of choice. Every strip of ground I covered was a small victory contributing to the total victory; at every doubtful point I paused for a moment; tested my muscles; stroked my wound which was hurting again, but from the sharp pain of the cut, so as to ease this away; concentrated on 'sensing' whether to go to the right or the left; then set off again. On some stretches I think I almost fell asleep and found myself on that interminable walk over the Krano mountains, and had a sensation of safety because of having that little shepherd to guide me; and into that dream there entered the other pilgrimage to the All-powerful Virgin of Licudi, which also had merged me with the common people. Then I shivered with cold, and when the darkness cleared a little I thought it was the dawn – until I realised it was only a thinning-out of the mist letting in more light. I now dimly made out a large stretch of deserted country-side in front of me, with, in the distance, a sort of thick homogeneous wall, as if a cloud were resting on the ground. I told myself it was a river, but when I got there down the slope I found I was in a marshy wood; yet water was flowing near, wide and dark; and through the rolling mist I discerned a dark low-lying shape. I realised I was on the bank of an obviously impassable waterway, and the shape was that of a barge at anchor.

Between the Oder and the Elbe there is a network of canals cutting across rivers, lakes and pools, and navigable for hundreds of kilometres; and that captain without a foot in the hospital at Berg had been wounded on the quays of Dessau. This barge, like those on the Rhine, served as a house for the river-men who plied the small coasting-trade; I would have to take the risk; but I had not even had time to shout when a huge dog leapt at me out of the blue and bit my thigh. I reeled back, tripped and fell. I now thought he would make for my throat, but I suddenly saw him rearing up on his hind legs, barking furiously, but unable to reach me because of a restraining hand on his collar. A man with a lantern had appeared from the boat, and now looked me over. '*Gefangen Offizier! Verwundet!*' I said, still lying on the ground. He had a think, then quietened the dog and went back to the boat, where I heard him talking in undertones with a woman. At last he came ashore again, helped me to get up and took me on board. Blood was pouring from my bite. A worried-looking young woman was in the cabin, but she put down her baby and helped me to bandage myself as well as possible, while the man looked on, frowning.

Owing to the behaviour of ex-prisoners throughout the country, not much could be expected from these Germans, torn as they were between hate and fear. These two had hidden themselves in a lonely place among impassable marshes, and it just happened that I had chanced on them.

'The Russians are coming!' I said, summing up in a phrase my position and intentions. And the woman immediately muttered some sentences to him, pointing to the baby. So they intended to cross the Elbe for the same reason as me. It was lucky for both of us; the man had a young wife and a boat, both very dangerous possessions in a region teeming with outlaws. He had found someone to help him, and someone in such poor condition that though he could perhaps use me he had no cause to fear me. So my misfortunes were still my best defence. I would get across because on the practical level I was worth almost nothing.

He weighed anchor almost immediately. He knew that waterway network like the back of his hand, and though keeping well away from the banks, he halted now and then in some inlet, so as to listen, or turned aside over shallower waters so that I heard the scraping of the keel on the river-bed. With dawn the mist grew thicker and it was impossible to make out the mysterious thread by which he got his orientations. I realised that a third person had been absolutely indispensable for him, for he depended on poles and grapnels for his progress much more than his modest engine. Once the sun was high he again got under cover in a thick growth of reeds and gave me to understand we would wait there till nightfall.

To say I was utterly drained would be an understatement. It was five days since I had eaten anything hot. My leg had been stiff since the dog's bite (he was now stretched out on the prow without seeming to remember anything about it) yet I had had to use it for hours on end in steering the boat. In those very hours Berlin had fallen and Hitler was dead, having called down a hundred thousand devils on the West and impervious behind his last ditch. But we were not aware that that dark shadow had withdrawn from the earth, hidden as we were in our marsh, our huntsman's paradise, the innocent retreat of frogs and dragon-flies. There was a chorus of croaking when finally we weighed anchor beneath a delicate crescent moon. And it was under the discreet eyes of the moon, in a landscape of uncertain light and romantic shadows, and in the silence of a deep peace undisturbed by men, that I crossed the Elbe that night.

'What is a wise man?' I found myself asking myself while enjoying the last rays of benevolent sunshine lingering on my bunk. The bunk was enclosed within a low alcove scooped out of the wall, and the setting sun cast its rays on a crowded array of brightly coloured holy pictures fixed to the back wall which was also adorned with all sorts of fanciful paper decorations; and the curtains around the alcove were a real feast of colour. Two memories crept almost imperceptibly into my mind: the way Téolo used piously to pull his curtains when he said his prayers, and the last rays of the setting sun on Marchese Lerici's penthouse window.

'What does "knowing" mean?' I asked next, as I looked obliquely through the small deep-set window from which I could see the heaped remains of the pillaging that had been going on for the last two weeks: a slow fire in the square burning at its own sweet will but now reduced to a single scab of dried filth. Every now and then someone came and stirred the mass of decay with a pitchfork, and a nauseous cloud of black smoke was let loose.

'A philosopher?' I asked myself, going on with my soliloquy. 'A down-at-heel old man who talks to you about good and evil and perhaps about God. But he doesn't even know what a child is really, if he's never had one, never brought one up, never loved one or lost one.'

'An intellectual?' Even my Rolphe looked on himself as that, and the others would have accepted his judgement. Yet he hadn't managed to find the key to anything and was as tangled up in his arguments as a fly in a spider's web; incapable of standing up to the spectacle of death, or of saving himself from what he so dreaded. And what does an intellectual's knowledge imply? Knowing the names of things but not knowing the things themselves? Of course he knows what it means to 'flee on foot'. But if he hasn't walked for six days, with fifteen hours at a stretch on the sixth, and hasn't felt at his back the people on whom his very life may depend, then he understands the concept behind those words but nothing at all of the reality. And how about hunger? – especially if he always insists on having his egg mayonnaise, like Omobono. And what about wounds – if the only blood he has shed is from his nose at school? Thus some did the living and others did the theorising. The two currents evolved separately and hardly ever merged. For obvious reasons a judge knew nothing about murder; and one half of the world contended with the other half, wanting to enclose within words the absolute force of facts.

Tecla came in, the boatman's wife, holding her baby in one arm and bringing me a bowl of soup with the other. Eight days had passed. The Russians and the Americans had not wanted to fight each other after all and, by all accounts, had met at Torgau with mutual congratulations and thereafter had withdrawn to their respective banks. Patrols passed swiftly from one side of the river to the other rejoicing in their victory – even though there were a few dead in the process. Perhaps the war really was over. In view of the fact that many people had reasons for crossing from one side to the other, Tecla's husband had found a couple of partners – not Germans, but strong this time – and an excellent machine-gun from the army, and in association with a Russian lieutenant on the opposite bank, was tacking back and forth across the Elbe. It was dangerous work, but he must have made a lot of money. In theory Tecla had been entrusted to me; but facts, incontrovertible facts, arranged it that I depended absolutely on her.

That heap of muck on the mud of the square! Sometimes there was such a mountain of fresh rejects that the fire reached as high as a first floor, and I had the unbreathable smoke all around me for a couple of days as it slowly decomposed and fell in and burnt down to a height only two feet from the ground. Then from the filthy mess there emerged a little iron bedstead which would not burn and had stayed there at the bottom for weeks – revealed by the low tide and then again submerged, to appear again thirty or forty hours later, each time blacker and more eroded, a symbolic relic of that enormous shipwreck. It was a child's bedstead over which who knew how many times a text-book mother had bent to kiss her good little son goodnight? Where was the little boy now, and the mother, and the school satchel? And whoever thought of saying good morning or good night to anybody now?

Situated a little to the north of the point where the Ohre joins the Elbe, and far from any centres of habitation, this strange human conglomeration where my march towards the West had ended up was managed in conformity with the strictest piratical traditions. A row of sheds outside a large walled factory housed a mass of about five hundred men of all races vowed to robbery and plunder; while a resolute band of two or three hundred women occupied the enclosure – a paradoxical gynaeceum whose one gate they guarded even more fiercely than the Amazons of old. It was Tecla who had obtained me my place within the walls, using a ferry-crossing or two as bargaining stakes, though I think it was my obvious weakness that really won the day. My cubby-hole had previously been occupied by a Serbian girl, and she it was who had left me all those decorations, the holy pictures and the little paper curtains. I was the only male element in the stronghold; and when she left the Serbian girl paid her respects with a hint of piety, as if I had become part of her little shrine; and all under Tecla's neutral but vigilant eye.

With the relaxation of the tension that had sustained me over the last period I barely had the strength even to lie down. The unknowable power (to which Demetrio denied the name of Chance) had measured out its doses of trials and aids with such judicious parsimony that it deserved a round of applause. When things in the *Lager* were at their worst, then the devout Téolo's parcels had arrived; when loading the coal was at its worst, Herr Kurt had come to my rescue with that merry saw; at the worse than worst moment, after Berg had been smashed to pieces, Lore's bowls of soup up in Kate's little room had given me just enough strength to survive the final saraband; and even at that I would not have got by without the deserters' belongings found in the truck; without the refugee-become-surgeon; and – the most recent incarnation of Providence –

without Tecla. I was certain now that she was setting me up for some further ordeal. No one in that place seemed to be interested in looking for contacts with regular organisations, whatever they might be, and Tecla's husband less than anyone, for he depended on that conglomeration of bandits – excellent clients for him; the worst possible neighbours for me.

According to the Latin learnt at my school, 'I pondered within myself' – and pondered the same thoughts, I believe, as an early nineteenth-century explorer, wounded in a savannah and looked after for a while by a Congolese tribe. My people here were nearly all Slavs or from the Balkans and they, too, lived by hunting, for every morning they set off over the countryside and every evening came back with what they had plundered. News reached the encampment immediately from any point on the horizon, and the flight of the vultures started. They had carts and sleighs at their disposal; they ganged up together for particular raids and then dispersed again; they tore one another to pieces for the division of the loot; they filled their lair for a while with mattresses, carpets, linen, poultry, which all immediately rotted in the general filth. After a few days a thick sediment of mud, frills, feathers, skins, broken china, bones and human excrement covered the floor of the huts. If one group decided to move off, then its successor cleaned things up with pitchforks and the whole lot ended up on the smouldering heap in the middle of the square, while the new inhabitants started to behave exactly like their predecessors.

Those people had a way of stealing an ox or a horse, and slaughtering it, though without the slightest possibility of conserving what they would not be able to eat yet not wanting to give it away. Sometimes Tecla brought me a piece of roast meat, but so burnt that it was impossible to eat, so I cut it up into tiny pieces with a penknife and swallowed it like pills. Once from my little window I saw six or seven people skinning a pig of over 200 pounds, eating a tenth part of it and throwing away the rest. As for the supplies of food for the regiment of women, this just happened according to nature: though the men were excluded in a draconian way from the enclosure, they nevertheless came with their offerings as if to a sanctuary. Of course they had a few women with them in the horde, but very few, for the women preferred to be together, even if they had come from a penitentiary, a rehabilitation camp, or forced labour. And there were women of every quality and condition:

women still decked in a remnant of fur; Ukrainian viragos who were stronger than a man; consumptives in the last stages lying inert on their bunks; mothers with children; disguised collaborators; the impure of every origin. They could be heard quarrelling, crying, swearing; yet mine was not the only niche decorated with pictures of saints; indeed, the female chaos was as moving as the male chaos was repulsive. Some of the women, still young, who had been through tragic experiences, affected arrogance and aggression and sang coarse songs; but prayers could be heard too; and many of them were just silent and kept themselves apart: so much so that I thought they must be like me.

Conversations with Tecla were necessarily of a basic character and consisted of signs rather than words. She was perhaps about twenty-five; a flat, unemotional type, though there was a rather animal-like intensity in her pale eyes. I did not understand her thoughts although I lived for the most part entirely by her help. The baby she was always carrying was pretty, and sometimes she let me hold him for a short while – and in so doing displayed un-limited trust. I enjoyed playing with that baby as he crawled around on my blanket; and when his charming little ways made me forget the train of my thoughts I managed to persuade myself that there was nothing better in the world that I could do.

Often other women came to put their heads round the opening to my cubby-hole, and they looked at me with a thousand different expressions, then went away gossiping and laughing. They seemed to enjoy looking on me as the protégé and perhaps even the mascot of their strange brigade. Sometimes Tecla brought someone in purposely to visit me – doing so with a hint of ceremonial, perhaps feeling that she should do the honours of who knows what ancestral cult. It is possible that such things have happened in other places and at other times, as matriarchy is as old as the world. My favourite among these visitors were two Jewesses of the cultured classes who knew a little English. They kept me informed of events.

The war in Europe was certainly finished; but it seemed as though nothing had taken its place, as though confusion and uncertainty were still reigning; the vast dust-cloud of collapse, deafness and blindness following on a measureless deflagration. Without it seeming so, the moralists of the Pentagon left things so that a further decreed punishment should be played out on Germany: the punishment of leaving her defenceless at the mercy of millions of foreigners who had formerly suffered slavery there. The occupying troops touched nothing of German possessions, contenting themselves with machine-gunning the radiators of agricultural tractors, cars and other machines, perhaps out of a simple dislike of their trade-marks. But they let everything be looted and destroyed by the foreigners. In this way, too, they had their pretext for rounding them up, when this was necessary; but for the time being the combing of the country areas was proceeding very slowly. Here and there they put up road-blocks to halt the wandering bands and take them in convoy to assembly centres; but they did not keep guard over them and any who wanted to could easily escape and go back to robbery. The troops carried out various manhunts: against the SS who, as they were branded under their armpits, could hardly evade identification; against Nazi criminals; and against individual enemies. The Germans of the defeated and disbanded armies were all just trying to get back to their homes, separately, usually through the woods. This was happening all over the Reich, and as many were armed their rancour against their victors made them dangerous. The two Jewesses advised me to wait in patience until the Allies decided to clean up our encampment. We only had to wait for them, without trying to seek them out. I held Tecla's baby in my arms, trying to hold him in exactly the same position and attitude as I had usually seen his mother adopt; and he played with my chin with his little hands. That contact was of an indescribable sweetness and was almost enough to compensate for my misfortunes and even my wounds.

'This morning,' one of the two women said, 'Leitz was sacked. The people had received orders to evacuate the village within two hours as it was requisitioned for troops in transit. So the Germans had their suitcases prepared, but these were all left in a row on their doorsteps because they were bundled on to the lorries without being allowed to take luggage. But our people from here got there before the troops arrived. Leitz is fairly big; our people couldn't carry off thirty or forty cottages, farms and houses full of stuff. Even the suitcases were a bit much. So they threw everything out of the windows: thousands of plates, glasses, lamps, furniture, pictures. And all the ripped-open mattresses shed their feathers as they fell so that it was like walking in a snowstorm. Hilda told me all about it; she was there.'

This woman had the pure type of Jewish beauty – a perfectly

oval face, an ivory complexion and heavy very black hair. The other, the one who had been at Leitz, had a pair of lively green eyes and a sardonic turn to her lips which, when she laughed, revealed teeth that seemed to want to bite. Her extraordinary overcoat, hanging in folds around her, emphasised her astonishing thinness, and her nerves were as taut as a hungry cat's; she was rocking backwards and forwards on her chair with an expression of savage bliss on her face.

I listened without saying much. I did not ask them about their previous lives nor how they had landed up on the same bank as myself; and I did not want to know what they had been before; just as we do not ask the dust of ruins what sand and what sea it came from, now that what it first went to build has been swept away in the flux of time. From below I could hear the looters quarrelling over the division of their booty; and the crackling of the fire which was very high again now. Again the little iron bedstead had been submerged: a strange root – but perhaps only of my thoughts.

Tecla came to fetch her baby. I was left alone with my two Jewesses who now fell silent. Once the brief animation of their story had died down, their faces seemed to me completely empty: inert remains, worn away to nothingness. For centuries the wailing wall in Jerusalem has been maintained, a grey blind wall, a final barrier where you could only stop, all thoughts drowned, all hope abandoned. Where all you could do was wail, then as now.

Standing in the very place where Magaldi and I had sat like beggars about three months before, I tried to take in what had happened to that quiet residential area in the suburbs of Uelzen where Doctor Aesckloni had lived.

Only half of his villa remained, though this included the door which was still in good condition, and closed. In the half that had been destroyed I could just make out the ladies' cloakroom where the surgeon had made his preliminary examination – it was recognisable by a few surviving tiles. The other houses scattered among the trees had undergone the same fate. A dust-laden silence weighed heavily over the place, and the summer sun beat down oppressively on that wilderness. In the distance I could still just hear the jeep that had brought me as far as the square, put me down, and then moved off again too soon.

The women had bade me farewell with cries and protests while I was helped down the steps by Tecla of whose animal warmth, so strong and close, I was very much aware; I had thanked her and kissed the baby – still in her arms as if he were part of her body. The pirates' encampment had been evacuated. Gigantic bulldozers manned by Negroes had razed everything to the ground – huts, furniture (such as it was), rubble. The spectral iron bedstead had gone down like a piece of straw and now lay buried deep in the earth.

The door of Aesckloni's house opened unexpectedly and a man came out. I called to him sharply. At that time it was difficult to establish who was in authority. He looked at me uncertainly for a moment but then gave way.

'Unfortunately Doctor Aesckloni is dead,' he said in English after he had read my papers. 'Unknown people attacked and set fire to the house. The doctor had his little girl with him and was hit in the forehead while protecting her. It could have happened because of the doctor's political background. There's been a lot of trouble.'

He had mastered the use of that invaluable word 'trouble' whose significance only the English understand, as it can refer to bloodshed and rebellion as much as to a broken tea-cup.

'And what about the clinic?' I asked.

'It's out of commission at the moment. I am Doctor Gann, Aesckloni's first assistant. I myself am working at a military hospital. That's where you should go, but I can't come with you. All our cars have been destroyed or requisitioned.'

'Does anyone still live in the house?'

'The widow,' Gann replied with deliberate impassivity. 'And a British officer who, it appears, is very demanding at night.'

Another month dragged by while I went from one hospital to another, from one camp to another. The July heat beat relentlessly down on the ruins marked with crosses in coal or chalk. The immense body of Germany lay with its face in the dust. Yet another month, and the atomic bomb was to wipe out Hiroshima. The High Command gave no consideration to the place accorded to charity in St Paul's first epistle to the Corinthians; and they intended to solve the measureless enigma of the war by listening to the lawyers' harangues at Nuremberg.

On the eve of repatriation at the beginning of August I nearly tripped over Captain Ceci in the assembly camp of Garmisch.

'Thanks be to God!' he said. 'I've been thinking so much about you!'

Ceci was fine, with a good colour on his dry skin and an almost new uniform resplendent with his epaulettes, the ribbons of his campaigns and the *croix de guerre*. Many things had happened at Berg which he would rather not have told me and I would rather not have heard. *Bersagliere* Penne had landed up in prison owing to obscure dealings between him, Kate and a couple of Americans who had appeared on the scene. Magaldi, who had graduated at Harvard, found himself promoted overnight to the position of right-hand-man of the American Command and with quite considerable power in his hands. That university freemasonry! He had shown himself merciless towards the Germans, Ceci said.

'And what about Herr Kurt?'

'They say he's in a concentration camp for Nazis. He would have got out of it if Magaldi hadn't denounced him. And then,' Ceci went on, very reluctantly now, 'his wife had to pay the price too. She had to follow him, dragging the boy after her. I didn't like it at all. I didn't like it for your sake. And finally,' he concluded, taking a smart leather wallet from an inner pocket and tipping a coin into his hand, 'and finally, here's your gold sovereign. I knew it was in your jacket so I salvaged it for you. I'm so delighted to be able to give it back to you at last!'

I had arrived at Garmisch from a camp at Harburg, together with three thousand other officers who had been assembled in the former barracks of the tank corps, one of the only buildings left standing in an urban conglomeration that had been razed to the ground for over four kilometres. The Allies intended making use of it later. There was also a large factory still standing, together with its fine surrounding wall. They said it had been built with British capital. When the British airmen, for once on foot, arrived at that nightmare scene they demonstrated their characteristic phlegm by saying in mild astonishment: 'We didn't realise we'd achieved results like this!' The Harburg camp was among the first to be evacuated because serious fighting broke out between the foreigners installed there and the German soldiers who had got back to their homes round about – there were not only many wounded but even a few dead. The German railways had of course been devastated as if by an earthquake, but with quiet determination and a tremendous effort the Germans got a part of them sufficiently operative to transport back to their frontiers those millions of invaders who were laying waste to the little of Germany that remained. So by means of a maze of railway tracks that wandered capriciously for hundreds of miles to cover a distance a fifth of that length as the crow flies, we slowly made our way towards our homeland. To many the endlessness of the journey was a crowning frustration and they were a prey to anxieties of every kind. But for me those days seemed like a safe shore that was leading me back to a life I would understand better; and I would have liked them to have lasted longer so as to savour them to the full and prepare myself better for what lay ahead.

I now realised that it was true, and I had already heard Paolo Grilli say it in his flat in Rome: mankind had persistently blamed the Evil One for what was really the preserve of human nature; only human nature was capable of defiling creation, of denying it and blaspheming against it instead of singing its praises. And it was pride – in virtue of a potency derived from the Creator himself – it was pride to usurp his powers, to overstep the limitations of the species, and replace the solemn rhythms of common living, of things, plants, animals, souls, with a violent game of lawless tyrannies and undisciplined impulses from which only perversity and unhappiness could spring. Animals were harassed and their species extinguished in the process; all growing things were exploited or uprooted; the earth itself was treated with contempt. Would not Eternity – compared with which the millennia were but infinitesimal fractions – would not Eternity wipe us out as some kind of vicious deviation from its changeless order? Then the rivers would invade the plains and give back their ancestral homes to the myriads of insects and reptiles and amphibians; the mountains would again be covered with woods to regulate the falling of the rain; and the circulation of the air, brought back to normal by the free interplay of the currents, would revivify the earth. Then the myriad of events that take place between birth and death, having recovered their balance in the equipoise of the whole, would pursue their course without even a suspicion of Evil.

And yet (as Descartes's syllogism reminded me), no awareness, no history. For both the inescapable price lay in our human drama. The fortune of a Vanderbilt was not enough to pay for my night

outside Berlin, and my wounds were a minimal diminishment for
all I had learnt and understood through their agency. When
Nerina died I felt I had exhausted my capacity for suffering, burnt
out my share of punishment here below; that was why I was still
alive when Arrichetta, too, had to leave me; that was why I
wandered about for years thinking that the world could offer me
no other kind of love. But so far I had only looked at myself; and
now I realised that what I had expected from dedication could
come from renouncement; that where affection had not succeeded
in binding me, suffering had succeeded; and that what had not
been identified or sanctified in one single name had countless
names. Denise, Demetrio, Albertina, just as much as Zagara and
Niko; Pannuzzo, Téolo, Theodora; and Spiropulos; and all the
others, all the others. I had felt a catch in my throat when I saw
the silent group of the Kurts standing on the doorstep of their (and
my) home and watched them fading into the distance, and also
when Frau Haendel's blood had trickled through my fingers; nor
could I forget Rolphe's ravaged face and his white hair rising over
that grotesque mask of dust. All these, together with the dead child
in the meadow, and Aesckloni who had died with his little daughter
in his arms, and Tecla, just recently, instinctive and warm like a
servant in an inn – all these had been my brothers and my sisters.
That account which had been closed at least ten times where
individuals were concerned, had now been boundlessly reopened to
include anyone, everyone, in a circle as large as mankind. And as
for Evil, I was going back to render my account to Uncle Gedeone.
I felt that even if I stood as a miserable beggar before a closed door,
the fact that I had said no to it was enough to conquer it entirely.
I knew that (as the ancient Poet saw it) the Divinity who rules the
world had assented to my infinitesimal but bold refusal. He had
sustained me in the interests of what he had reposed in me and
entrusted to me. And he was leading me back so that I could bear
witness to it.

On our way we met troop-trains of disarmed Germans coming
down from North Italy – so full that the men were crouching on
the engines. And they were finding their country torn to shreds by
the same acts of violence as they had used on the countries of others.
And when we had passed the Brenner, and civilians and workmen
mixed with us, we in our turn heard their stories; and when we saw
the gaping wounds in our lovely cities and knew how blood had

been spilt without law or pity, by all, against all, from the Fosse Ardeatine in Rome to the piazza Loreto in Milan, I was overcome with shame.

There were countless women gathered all along the railway lines. They were shouting the names of their men, showing their photographs, and asking, asking. Others were scrutinising our faces, one by one. Or else they were lost and silent, not seeing.

And tears, blessed tears, gushed forth without pause, passed on from one group to the next, the matchless rosary prayed in hope. And I answered them in my heart, as in my childhood, when I answered one praise in the litany by another.